Chasing Crazy

Chasing Crazy

KELLY SISKIND

New York   Boston

Copyright © 2016 by Kelly Siskind
Teaser excerpt copyright © 2016 by Kelly Siskind

Cover design by Brian Lemus
Cover copyright © 2016 by Hachette Book Group, Inc.

Forever Yours
Hachette Book Group
1290 Avenue of the Americas
New York, NY 10104
forever-romance.com
twitter.com/foreverromance

First published as an ebook and as a print on demand: January 2016

Forever Yours is an imprint of Grand Central Publishing.
The Forever Yours name and logo are trademarks of Hachette Book Group, Inc.

The publisher is not responsible for websites (or their content) that are not owned by the publisher.

The Hachette Speakers Bureau provides a wide range of authors for speaking events. To find out more, go to www.hachettespeakersbureau.com or call (866) 376-6591.

ISBN 978-1-4555-6520-7

Acknowledgments

Writing *Chasing Crazy* was a chance for me to re-experience my travels to New Zealand, a backpacking trip I took too many years ago. The country is spectacular and awe inspiring. I've used many known trails and landmarks and have added fictional locations, too. Any discrepancies are for story purposes.

You wouldn't have had the chance to read this novel if it weren't for my agent, Stacey Donaghy, aka the Rock Star. She's my biggest cheerleader, she works more hours than there are in a day, and she has the world's best laugh. Thank you a million times over for all you do. My editor, Megha Parekh, has made my transition to published author seamless. I love our phone calls and talking out plot with you. I'm thankful every day that you fell in love with Sam and Nina. You and the team at Forever Yours have been a joy to work with.

A writer is nothing without her community, and mine has

been there with me through the ups and the dramatic plummets. In its infancy, I entered this manuscript into Brenda Drake's Pitch Wars contest and worked with the amazing Brighton Walsh to polish it. Brenda does more for writers than any other person I know, and Brighton deserves an entire chapter to thank her properly. Mad love for you ladies.

My critique partners, old and new, are my lifeline. I gift you all the chocolate and gummy bears in the world as well as my love. Marian, your feedback on this novel helped make it that much better. Celeste, a girl always remembers her first. I love you long time. Kristin and Esher, I'd be lost without you. To my beta readers, Meggy, Lisa, and Sarah, your time and insight on this novel were invaluable. Not sure where I'd be without my friends—you keep me sane and grounded...and often drunk. To my dragonfly sisters, my Twitter and Facebook families, and the Den: The number of dirty and immature jokes you tolerate astounds me. I promise to keep upping my game if you promise to keep encouraging me. And to the ladies of the Life Raft, you have kept me afloat and laughing. Huge gratitude.

My family is my safety net. Mom and Dad, thank you for always encouraging me to jump, and I'm sorry about the sexy parts. Julie, a better sister there never was. Adam, many years of talking books led me here. To my husband, Steven, there are no words. You put up with my crazy. Wherever you are is my home. Thank you for believing in me.

Lastly, this dream of mine wouldn't exist without my readers. I loved writing Sam and Nina's story and hope you enjoy the ride. Always remember to chase your crazy.

Chasing Crazy

One

After much deliberation, I've determined there are three official have-to-pee stages.

Stage one: *Acknowledgment in the brain that liquid has been consumed and hours have passed since the bladder was relieved, but the matter isn't urgent.*

Stage one happens at the terminal when I break my cardinal flying rule: Always pee before boarding. Otherwise, I'll have to use that tiny bathroom, banging into the walls when turbulence hits while trying not to sit on the toilet seat barely protected by the paper cover. Then there's the awful sucking sound.

I always pee before boarding.

Unless, of course, I'm distracted by the ridiculously hot guy sitting opposite me at the boarding gate, his long legs stretched in front of him owning those dark jeans. He lounges on his faux-leather chair as he thumbs his iPhone, oblivious to the surrounding chaos. Two seats to my left some kid whines incessantly, distracting me from Hot Guy's excessive hotness.

The young boy slams his back into his seat. "But, *mu-uum*, you said I could use the DS after Lisa. She's had it for, like, ten minutes. This is *so* not fair."

His mom's exasperated voice drifts over, and I can't help but smile. I've been on enough trips with my five younger siblings to know that tone all too well. Exasperated Mom is almost as dangerous as I-had-a-bad-sleep Mom, but not quite as rough as I-burned-dinner-again Mom.

Mom. Tinged with sudden guilt, I pull my phone from my purse. Still no messages. When she sees the note I left, things could go one of two ways: effusive gushing over my independence and bold decision, or they could go south fast. I worry my lip and grip my phone, expecting the thing to come to life, filling the terminal with high-pitched crying and screaming. Maybe I should have written something longer, more poignant. Something Mom and Dad could really get behind. Instead, I wrote:

I dropped out of U of T. I'm going backpacking. When I get wherever I decide to go, I'll message you. Sorry. Don't forget to pick Mercedes up from ballet. There are a couple of casseroles in the freezer.

> *Love you both.*
> *P*

My thumbs hover above my phone. Should I tell Mom I'm going to the other side of the world? To New Zealand? If she freaks out, I'll likely trudge home and go back to university—the promising fresh start that pulled a *Titanic* first thing this morning. It took all of one minute for people to realize who I was and what I did in high school. The culprit? None other than Becca, formerly known as my best (and only) friend, who thought the share would push her up the social ladder. Like the mother of airborne viruses, my Public Speaking Incident replayed in triplicate on every cell across campus.

That's when I snapped.

Home. Pack. Note. Leave.

When I arrived at the airport an hour ago, still high from my decision to take off, the shiny green letters spelling out *New Zealand* on the departure board called to me. They shone like a beacon. A lifeline. A place as far as possible from Toronto and my past. Silently thanking Gran for the generous gift she left me in her will, I bought a ticket.

Mom can wait until I land.

I stuff my phone back into my purse and rearrange the bags on either side of me, fortifying my barrier against any potential friendly people thinking they should take a seat. My gaze returns to Hot Guy.

He's busy texting while I'm busy drooling (and, unfortunately, not peeing), as I soak in the brown curls that brush his forehead and skim his ears and a jaw Channing Tatum would covet. His thin white T-shirt settles on what appears to be a well-defined chest. *Well* de-fined. Hot Guy probably works out. I bet he goes to the gym and lifts weights and works out in his tank top or—*oh*…maybe topless, sweat dripping down the length of his neck and over his muscles.

I pluck the water from my bag and take a generous gulp.

Hot Guy laughs at his phone and looks up to catch me gawking. He smiles suggestively, curling his lip like he knows exactly what I'm picturing. My cheeks flame. With my pale skin, they're likely the same shade of scarlet as the overused carpet I'm now studying with the intensity of a hawk. I chug more water.

Several heartbeats later, I chance a second glance. Deep brown eyes are trained on me. I contemplate diving under my seat and praying Hot Guy goes away, but that would draw attention to me. The only thing worse than being stared at by Hot Guy is being stared at by the hundreds of people milling around the terminal.

At nineteen, I've endured two lifetimes' worth of humiliation. The pointing. The laughing. The endless jokes.

Not happening.

I finish my water and hunch into my seat, sinking as low as possible without landing on the floor. I stick my book in front of my nose. But I keep sneaking glances. This is how it's been lately. Like I'm a thirteen-year-old boy hitting puberty. I picture guys naked or in various states of undress—how they'd taste, how they'd feel, and how they'd touch me. (Apparently I'm a gay thirteen-year-old boy with the *bow-chicka wow-wow* porno instrumental as the soundtrack to my life.) I play it safe, though, and stick to unattainable guys. Too risky to be seen with *that* girl who did *that* thing; popular guys avoid me. So I fantasize. No danger. No unwanted incidents. In my mind I'm always fearless, never making a fool of myself. I rule my fantasies like a sex goddess.

In real life, not so much.

Unfortunately, these daydreams inhibit normal brain function. So when a static-filled voice announces the final boarding call for flight 744 to New Zealand, I stop picturing Hot Guy soaping himself in the shower, and I hurry to the gate instead of the bathroom.

* * *

Stage two of the have-to-pee stages: *A gentle pressure on the abdomen indicates the bladder is full. With a few key position shifts, the feeling subsides.*

Stage two occurs about half an hour into the flight, in the narrow seat where I can't build a barrier against the prying neighbor sandwiched to my right. Even though I'm angled toward the window with my book firmly in my face, the nice lady beside me is not deterred. "Sure will be a long flight," she says, a slight hum in her voice. "I haven't seen my daughter in, well, a long while. A long, long while. And you, dear? Off to visit family?"

I glance over to make sure she's talking to me and not the large, sweaty guy in the aisle seat. A hopeful face beams back, eyes crinkled behind her reading glasses. "No," I mumble and smile shyly.

"Vacation then?" she pushes.

I fight the urge to turn away and stick in my earbuds. That's what the old me would do. Too terrified to say or do the wrong thing and effectively embarrass myself in the myriad of ways it seems possible, I've lived the life of a self-proclaimed hermit. Not any more. *I'm* heading to New Zealand. *This* girl is fearless. *This* girl talks to the way-too-nice lady on the plane.

Empowered, I turn and say, "I'm going backpacking."

Three whole words of fearless.

The nice lady lifts her reading glasses and sets them atop her gray wooly curls. The lines in her dark skin sink deeper as she smiles knowingly. "Going to find yourself, are you?"

My harsh laugh blurts out. "Yeah, no. More like reinvent." I reach above me to stop the nozzle from blasting recycled air in my face, but the thing is broken. No matter which way I twist it, a thick stream hits my cheek. My personal TV is defunct, too, and my seat won't recline. *If* I could handle a confrontation, this girl would be getting a free meal.

Big, huge, fat *if*.

The nice lady bundles her hands on her lap and tilts her shoulders toward me. "Now, I may be overstepping, but my grand-daughter, my Jasmine, she's about your age. And let me tell you, Jasmine had it rough in high school. Did she ever." The lady shakes her head with a *tsk, tsk, tsk*. "But I will share with you the words of the great Martin Luther King, Jr. The words I'd repeat to my Jasmine: 'Change does not roll in on the wheels of inevitability, but comes through continuous struggle. And so we must straighten our backs and work for our freedom. A man can't ride you unless your back is bent.'" The lady squeezes my shoulder affectionately. She repositions the reading glasses on her head, tucks away her in-flight magazine, and closes her eyes.

When I'm able to stop picturing Hot Guy from the terminal riding me, I return to my perch at the window, the endless landscape of blue on blue stretching to infinity. The air above blows flyaway hairs across my face. Sighing, I brush them away.

As nice as the sentiment is, Dr. King didn't have the pleasure of growing up in the age of YouTube where the world's most mortifying moments are immortalized. Especially when a particular incident occurs your first week of high school, gets more than four million hits, and defines your existence. That, and King's parents didn't brand him with five ridiculous syllables. In ink. On a birth certificate. *Forever.*

I hunch lower in my seat, and a sharp pain stabs my bladder. I can't believe I downed that water bottle at the gate and didn't pee before boarding. *Frickin' Hot Guy.* I lean forward and look right. The nice lady's head jerks as she falls asleep, and the sweaty aisle guy is snoring. At the same moment, the drink trolley begins its creaky journey toward our row. I tuck my skirt under my knees and shift a few times until the pain passes. No need to make a scene crawling over bodies to get to the aisle and use the gross bathroom. Then I'd have to wait for the flight attendants to finish their leisurely stroll hawking drinks before I even make it back. For sure I can make it to our refueling in Alaska. For sure.

* * *

Stage three of the have-to-pee stages: *Your bladder is full. It is close to bursting. The pain builds to the point where the slightest move could cause urine to leak down your leg.*

Stage three began forty-five minutes ago, and it's still an hour before we refuel. The nice lady and the sweaty guy are totally comatose, and I'm squirming in my seat, wringing my book, desperate to find any position that is maybe, slightly, possibly a little bit less painful. But, *holy God,* I can't wait another second. I flip off my seat belt, stand, and shake out my skirt, all while pressing my knees together.

Breathe. Breathe. Breathe. Breathe.

I squeeze my eyes shut. Why did I let it go so long? Why didn't I get up and use the stupid bathroom at the start of the flight when stage two hit? Why do I always make the worst decisions known to mankind? With my body still clenched, I open my eyes and do my best to maneuver past the nice lady, but the effort is wasted. She jerks awake, and the sweaty guy on the end jams his knees into the seat in front of him.

"Sorry, sorry. I'm so sorry," I whisper as I squash my body between the lady's legs and her tray stowed in its upright position. It's then I realize I'm still hugging my book. Now that I'm halfway out of my row, no way am I going back to put it down. The sweaty guy scowls at me as he gets up to let me pass, his thinning hair standing on end from sleeping. "Sorry. I'm so sorry," I squeak again.

He merely grumbles.

With my first step down the aisle, I suck in a breath and pause until I'm sure I won't pee right here, right now, in front of the entire plane. Most folks are sleeping or watching their personal TVs, which, unlike mine, are working. Back in control, I set my sights on the four metal doors at the rear of the cabin. Twenty-five rows to go. I clutch my book tighter. Quick, short steps are the key. No jarring movements.

With twelve rows left, we hit a patch of turbulence.

The plane drops minutely. Not enough to alarm anyone—any normal person, that is, who didn't hold in their pee to the point of having a full-on freak attack. The potential scene unfolds in my mind: the fatal wrong step, urine pooling at my feet. I tense from toes to ears, one hand gripping my book, the other clamped on an aisle seat. Several seconds pass, but I get it together. This will *not* turn into one of those moments. This will not be another "incident."

The red *Occupied* sign flips to green. *Vacant.*

My bladder constricts in anticipation.

Another big, sweaty guy squeezes from the door and returns to his seat at the rear of the cabin. With my eyes on the prize, I pick up the pace. My steps get longer. Quicker. I don't break eye contact with that door. I don't look down. If I *had* looked down, I might have seen the large black boot sticking out in the aisle. If I *had* looked down, I might have stepped over it. But I didn't.

In one glorious move, my sandaled toe smacks into the black boot…and I tumble. Hard. Fast. Face first. The corner of the book in my hand slams into my full bladder, and my vision from earlier comes to life. Every. Horrifying. Detail. Like a pathetic five-year-old child, I wet myself. I manage to stop the Niagara Falls portion of the flow, but I pee myself nonetheless. *Frickin' perfect.*

Lying with my face smashed against the rough airplane carpet, I squeeze my eyes, willing this to be a horrible nightmare, when two hands grip my shoulders. They pick me up effortlessly and place me on my feet. Mortified is not a strong enough word to describe my current state of being. My underwear is sodden, the front of my skirt is damp, and there's a pretzel bit stuck to my eyebrow. Still, that doesn't hold a candle to the level of horror I experience when I turn to find Hot Guy in front of my face.

His eyebrows pull together. "You okay?"

An animal sound explodes through my lips, something between a caw and a yelp, as I spin away and dash for the still-green vacant sign. I slam the door and fight with the stupid bar thingy to get it locked, then I whirl around looking for those god-aw-ful paper toilet covers. The bathroom reeks of some sort of foul I can't describe. The guy before unleashed a whole lot of awful in here. I dance from foot to foot, knees knocking, as I get the cover down. Underwear off, skirt up, and the stream flows before my butt hits the seat.

It keeps flowing. And flowing. And flowing.

I stretch the neck of my fitted white T-shirt and stick my nose inside while the marathon continues. I pick the pretzel bit off my eyebrow and fling it on the floor. There must be something seri-ously wrong with me. Here I am, trying to start fresh. New me, new life. And I can't make it a minute without creating havoc. Maybe it's all the pot my folks smoke. No matter how many times they've denied it, I bet Mom smoked boatloads while pregnant with me. Boat. Loads.

When the trickle ends, I stand and stamp my foot on the flush button then step back to avoid being sucked into the atmosphere. Although nose-diving to earth might be preferable to facing Hot Guy Who Saw Me Pee when I leave the bathroom. I could lock myself in this tin can until we land. Unfortunately, it smells like a Taco Bell meal gone wrong.

With no other option, I prepare to exit the lavatory. I remove my underwear and cram it into the trash. Barely. I dampen some paper towels and blot the front of my skirt. Luckily, the blue and purple floral pattern is busy enough to hide the wet splotch stretched across the fabric. I shove two wads of paper under my armpits to soak up my stress sweat. After shaking out my red hair and retying it into a ponytail, I wash my hands a third time. Fi-nally, I shove the latch to *Vacant* and push the door.

I almost yank it shut.

Hot Guy Who Saw Me Pee is leaning against the side of a seat with his arms crossed. His are eyes locked on the bathroom door…and me. *Double shoot.*

He straightens and shoves his hands into his pockets. I try to hurry past him, but he steps in my way. Taller than me by a head, he dips down toward my ear. "You should watch where you're going when you're running inside an airplane, Ginger."

What the…? *Ginger?* Is Hot Guy making fun of my hair? To my face?

This weird, hyper-ticking thing starts in my jaw as I ball my hands into fists. He's too broad to bolt past, and the longer I stand here, the angrier I get. As if every kid who ever called me names has morphed into this one tall hot guy staring me down.

With my nails biting into my palm, my whisper-yell explodes before I can stop it. "*I* should watch where I'm going? Maybe you shouldn't sprawl across the entire aisle, Mister…*Man.*"

Wow. I just said that. I called Hot Guy *Mister Man.* I can't even get angry right.

Mister Man, Hot Guy…whatever, he looks more amused, a suggestive smile on his lips. He leans closer, his brown curls flopping on his forehead. "I was joking, all right? I'm sorry about the tripping thing. Seriously. You sure you're okay?"

Before I can answer, a girl pokes her head around his shoulder. "Excuse me. Mind if I get by?" She nods toward the bathroom.

Hot Guy slides his arm around my waist and draws me against his chest to let the girl pass. I suck a sharp breath. Hot Guy *definitely* works out. The hard contours of his pecs are unmistakable through his cotton shirt, the sharp ridges of his muscles firmly against my body. His palm flattens on my lower back, and he pulls me tighter. *Oh, God.* My fingers itch to touch him. Every chiseled inch. If he didn't see me wet myself, this would be way better than picturing warm suds dripping down his body. In a shower. My hands trailing between his legs.

Then I flash to the last time I was this close to a guy. Hypnosis couldn't repress that memory deep enough. Better for me and everyone involved if I stick with fantasies. Placing my hand on his chest, I push back from Hot Guy, a little disappointed to lose the contact.

Two long fingers find my chin and lift my gaze. "Look, Ginger, I'll let you by when you tell me you're okay. So are you hurt, or are you cool to make it back to your seat?"

There's a scar on his chin, long and jagged. I blink to stop staring. "First, don't call me Ginger. And second, yes. I'm fine. No thanks to your boot. Can I go back to my seat now?" I fiddle with my skirt, sure everyone nearby knows I'm flying commando.

Hot Guy studies me a beat, then raises his hands. "Watch your step on the way back." But he barely moves, so I'm forced to rub against him (pantyless) to get by.

Holy heck, that chest.

Two steps away, I see my book still on the floor from my fall.

The rest happens in slow motion, an instant replay of pure awful.

I bend down to grab my book, and the airplane jiggles as though it's bouncing from cloud to cloud. The floor tilts back. I reach to grab the nearest armrest, but a man's arm is planted there "resting." Next best option: launch myself forward to grab the back of the man's chair. This super-smooth move occurs as the plane rights itself. The laws of gravity kick in, and I pitch forward. I don't do this elegantly. No points for good form. I land on my elbows, and my skirt flies up to my hips.

Yes. My skirt. The skirt that covered my pantyless behind is hitched around my waist. *OhGodOhGodOhGod.* I flip on my back and tug the flimsy cotton down to my knees. I do it just in time to see Hot Guy close his mouth. His eyes darken ten shades before he slips into the bathroom I recently exited, where he'll *for sure* assume it was I who dropped the atomic stink bomb.

Reminder to self: Always pee before boarding an airplane.

Two

I'm one of the last to make it to the customs line. The train of bodies coiling through the man-made maze is shorter than I expected. Pleased, I step toward the entrance, but there, squatting on the ground and rifling through his backpack, is Hot Guy Who Saw My Privates. *Perfect.* No way am I waiting in line behind him. No frickin' way.

I bolt toward the bathroom at the back wall. Safely inside, I drop my bags and lean my (still pantyless) butt against the counter. The gray stall doors are all ajar, the whir of a running toilet looping. I used the first bathroom after disembarking, so I tap my foot and massage my hands, my pale skin insanely dry from the airplane. Sifting through my purse, I pull out a tube of moisturizer and apply a thick layer. Then I swivel toward the mirror and retie my ponytail.

Of all my five siblings, I'm the only one with red hair. Mom used to joke that I look a lot like my uncle Tony, Dad's auburn-haired brother (wink, wink, nudge, nudge), until I tried to dye my hair black at fourteen. It turned zombie green. Of course. The day of my class photos. Mom thought it was hilarious and made me go to school, green hair and all, to take the pictures.

Her favorite is framed in our hallway.

A sudden vision of our kitchen in flames as Mom attempts to cook sets my heart racing. I grab my phone from my purse. As soon as I power it up, I bite my lip, still unsure how my parents took my sudden departure.

Mom: Knock 'em dead, baby girl. Let us know where you are when you land. And you better message us every time you travel to a new town, or your father will turn your room into that ashram he's always wanted, complete with nude meditation sessions. Let this be your only warning.

I snort and reply: Warning taken. I've landed safe and sound . . . in New Zealand. I'll message when I leave Auckland. XOX

Relieved my parents took my Houdini act in stride, I gather my bags and leave the bathroom. Another plane should have landed by now, a few hundred passengers safely in the customs line between me and Hot Guy Who Saw My Privates. But luck, as usual, is not on my side. One lonely couple stands behind Hot Guy, his brown curls bobbing along to whatever's playing on his iPod. Eager to leave the airport and tired of standing in public washrooms, I weave through the roped line and position myself behind the couple. The man and woman keep shifting their feet and checking their watches.

With only two agents staffing booths, the line crawls forward at a snail's pace, agitating the couple further. When Hot Guy rounds the last corner, I turn and hunch behind the fuming man.

"If we miss our flight…" the man murmurs, his grip tightening on his luggage. The woman fidgets with her wedding ring.

Once at the front, Hot Guy removes his earbuds and turns to put his iPod away. I crouch lower behind the angry man, but Hot Guy pauses as he zips his backpack. *Oh, God.* I hold my breath while he stares at me, sure it will render me invisible. Or I'll pass out. As he tilts his head and parts his lips, the agent at the front of the line taps him on the shoulder. She motions to a new line about to open. I exhale before spots cloud my vision.

The rushing couple joins him in line, all of them waiting for the new agent to finish readying his booth. Brown eyes framed with thick lashes keep glancing back at me, at least once looking down at my skirt. *Frickin' Hot Guy.* As the light on the customs booth blinks on, the agent sends me to the same line. The rushing couple is talking to Hot Guy, waving their tickets and checking their watches. He smiles and steps back, allowing them to pass.

Those brown eyes are back on me, drifting toward the area below my waist.

With each step, cement practically hardens around my feet. When I get to the line, I stop about two feet behind him and dump my backpack on the floor. I search through my purse for the imaginary *thing* I have no intention of finding.

"I don't bite," a low voice rumbles.

Huffing into the depths of my purse, I peek up. With his head cocked to the side and a grin splitting his face, Hot Guy looks less *GQ* and more approachable. Almost boyish in his cuteness. My lower belly tightens as I envision him shirtless, lying in the grass, sunlight playing over his skin…until he says, "I really like your skirt."

No, he did not. "You—"

The customs agent calls, "Next," and Hot Guy spins around before I unleash my sure-to-be-lame comeback, but not before he winks at me.

This guy has some nerve.

Squishing my lips into the face Mom likes to call my angry-old-lady face, I yank my passport from my purse and bruise the papers as I flip to my photo. The five syllables of my name leap from the page. I'm already dreading the *look* I'll get when the mustached customs agent scans my passport. My name manages to inspire a range of facial expressions you'd find in a Jim Carrey movie.

First day of class with a new teacher usually goes something like:

Spectacled eyes scroll the attendance sheet several seconds longer than usual. Repeated blinking occurs before the teacher looks up. "Pi-nin-fa-ri-na?" Each syllable drops like a bomb, and all heads turn to the Indian kids in the room. With no choice but to answer, I squeak quietly, my fingers grazing the air to claim those five syllables.

Ensue pointing and giggling. *Frickin' Pininfarina.*

Dad's obsession with cars was a blessing for my five younger siblings. Bestowed with the names Mercedes, Aston, Bentley, Royce, and Cayenne, my brothers and sisters embody cool. That DNA link missed my chain. My rise to shame began in the delivery room, the moment Dad, probably stoned, looked upon my wrinkled, goop-smeared face and branded me, "Pininfarina."

Like I care that Pininfarina designed the Ferrari and the Maserati. Like. I. Care.

Pocketing his passport, Hot Guy sneaks another look at me before heading to the baggage claim. I trudge forward to face the agent's ridicule.

* * *

When I spot my blue backpack rolling down the baggage carrousel, I say a silent prayer of thanks. "Excuse me. Sorry. Excuse me." I tap shoulders and bob my head as I try to breach the ring of bodies around the conveyer belt, my purse and backpack maiming at least one kid along the way. If I'd been thinking straight when I left, I would've packed lighter. Once through, I have to wait until my bag travels the full circle to avoid Hot Guy at the opposite end.

A big black suitcase mummified in duct tape is leaning on my bag by the time it reaches me. Grabbing one of the shoulder straps, I yank my pack, but my feet slip on the shiny floor and my purse drops to my forearm. Still holding the strap, I stumble along and give it a solid pull. I almost land on my (pantyless) behind but manage to right myself, then I drag my pack to the nearest pillar.

Planting my hands on my hips, I study my bag, losing focus as I stare at the blue nylon and black stitching. With each passing second, I grip my hips tighter to calm my shaking arms. The lights seem brighter, the people around me moving faster, and I become acutely aware of how alone I am. I've traveled plenty with my family, but never in my life have I done something this insane. But this is me, clearly nuts. So unless I want to fly another thousand hours back home and return to a university where people know what a mess I am, to take classes I don't even care about—my "general" BA is nothing but a lame attempt at future goals—I better start dealing.

I inhale until my lungs hurt and release my breath in a steady stream. Okay. I'm here. In New Zealand. NEW. ZEALAND. I made it in one piece, minus a tiny piece of clothing. I have my luggage. Now what?

"Hey," I hear from behind me. "Need a hand with your bag?"

That low voice hits me in my belly. *Hot Guy.*

A large yellow pack lands beside mine, a Canadian flag loosely stitched on the top. *Crap.* I don't have a flag on my bag. That's like rule number one as a traveling Canadian. I trace the red maple leaf longingly, half of it barely stuck to the pack.

Warm breath hits my ear. "I can rip it off for you, if you want."

Rip it off?

I whip around, half expecting the lights to dim and Pitbull to blare from the speakers as Hot Guy rolls his hips and tears his pants à la *Magic Mike*. With much difficulty, I detach my stare from the bulge in his jeans.

His lip does that sexy, curling thing as he stifles a laugh. "The flag, I mean. You can have it." His eyes wander to my skirt.

"No, no. It's just…I should've sewn one on before I left. I was rushing. I didn't think of it." In case Hot Guy has laser vision, I clasp my hands strategically over the pantyless portion of my lower half. Not that my goods haven't been displayed.

He rubs the back of his neck and shrugs. "Whatever, I'm not even Canadian. The flag's all yours."

"But I saw you at the terminal in Toronto."

Ignoring me, Hot Guy bends down and rips the poorly attached flag off his bag. He holds it out to me, smirking, waiting, until I grab its corner. "That wasn't so hard, was it? I'm Sam." He extends a large, strong hand toward me.

One-syllable Sam. Perfect.

His smile broadens, his hand hovering midair, as he waits for me to respond like a well-adjusted human being. Such a person would clasp his hand and offer their name in return.

My five syllables are lodged in my throat.

Heat burns my cheeks, my saliva solidifies, and I proceed do the most absurd thing imaginable. Clutching the rough fabric of my newly acquired Canadian flag, I inch around the pillar my bag is perched against.

"You know I can still see you, right?" he says from the other side.

I hug my arms closer to my sides, wishing I had Harry Potter's invisibility cloak. I'm in New Zealand, standing on the other side of the world, and the one guy I can't escape has already been privy to my propensity for large-scale embarrassment. This supposed fresh start is tanking fast.

"Ginger it is, then," he calls.

I smack my head into the plaster behind me. My disappearing act isn't working, and unless this post is a magical gateway to Narnia, I can't avoid One-syllable Sam. But "Pininfarina" will not pass these lips. I tried to ditch the name in school, begging and pleading with tearstained cheeks, but my folks laid down the law with their usual "Celebrate your individuality!" Having enrolled me in private school, they owned the faculty and made sure my five syllables stuck. But I'm on my own. In New Zealand.

The world-class super-freak I am, I inch back around the pillar, still fingering my Canadian flag. I glance up at Sam, who's resting against the pole, his hands stuffed into his pockets. He raises his eyebrows expectantly.

"Just, *please* don't call me Ginger. My name is…Nina." I squish the flag in my hand and cross my arms. *Take that, Pininfarina.*

He nods, his curls brushing his forehead. "Nina, hmmm?" He rolls the name around his tongue. "Nina it is. But seriously, you should own the Ginger. Ever see reruns of *Gilligan's Island*? You know, Ginger—the hot redhead on the show? Those curves, the lips, the catlike green eyes." He frees a hand and motions to my face. "You've even got that mole of hers. Embrace the Ginger."

Back up a mega-second. Did he compare me to a sexy redhead? With catlike green eyes? I shift my skirt and hunch my shoulders. "Me? What? No. My red's way brighter, not that nice auburn, and I could never wear those tiny bikinis. And those lips of hers? Not in a million years."

I look down at his big black boots, at the leather worn on the toes, the scuff marks on the heels. They step closer.

"Own the Ginger," he rumbles in my ear. He scoops up both our packs and starts toward the door.

"Hey, whoa, wait," I call as I scramble to get my bag and purse over my shoulder. "Sam, come on. Stop!" The last word is so loud people turn and stare.

All my limbs lock.

He glances back and frowns as I play an impromptu round of freeze tag. He makes his way closer, favoring his right leg with a distinct limp. He stops in front of me and folds his arms. "I didn't mean to freak you out. Just thought you needed a hand."

When it appears as though we've been forgotten by the roaming crowd, I speak as quietly as possible. "*Please* drop my bag. I can carry it, okay?"

"Sorry, what?" He tips his head down.

"My bag," I whisper-yell. "Please. I don't need you to carry it for me."

He exhales for about ten minutes. "Look. You've already got two other bags, and this one's heavy and awkward. You barely got it off the carousel. I witnessed both falls on the plane, and I know what's *not* under that skirt of yours. I'm not about to watch a repeat performance, so I'm carrying the bag for you, Canada." He eyes my skirt and swallows.

It's one thing to know what he saw, but to hear him say it out loud? I scan the airport for the nearest exit.

"At least let me get it outside for you," he says. Still limping, he leaves as I play another round of freeze tag.

When I catch up with him outside, he's got both bags on the ground by the taxi line. "I assume you're looking for a hostel, too?" he asks.

The idea of sitting in a cramped car, pantyless, next to a guy I don't even know, is not high on my list of things I'd like to experience in New Zealand. My reinvention doesn't involve hanging out with people who've witnessed the extent of my defectiveness. "No," I say quickly.

"No?" He squints at my backpack.

"Well…*yes*, but a family friend lives here and is picking me up." *Liar, liar, pants on fire.* I grab my backpack by the top and drag it back a few steps. "Thanks for carrying my pack, though. Safe travels." I wave and proceed to do my best meerkat impression as I scan the road for the family friend who doesn't exist, the one who *won't* be picking me up.

He glances at the taxi pulling up and back at me. "Sure. You too. Maybe we'll run into each other on the road." The veins on his forearms flex as he hoists his pack into the trunk. I bet those arms could do a lot of push-ups. With me beneath them.

He nods at my flushed face, then shuts the door behind him.

My breath whooshes out. "That's one mess behind me."

As his cab pulls away, I drag my pack to the stand. A breeze blows past my shoulders. I extricate my jean jacket from my pack and put it on. Since no active planning was involved with this trip, it's a good thing the weather's similar to home. But instead of cold and snow in my future, New Zealand will only get warmer. And *I* will act normal. I am now Nina—non–disaster magnet, ordinary, average girl.

Three

SAM

For the first half of the cab ride, I stare out the window, but all I keep seeing is red hair, pink lips, and those green eyes. That first fall she took was almost funny. It was all I could do not to snort in her face. But the second one? Jesus. A blind man could see the curves going on below her skirt, and *my* eyes are twenty-twenty. It was a dick move, but I couldn't resist grabbing her when that chick passed us in the aisle. And the way she dragged her eyes up my body? Sexy as hell.

Then…*that fall.*

If it didn't smell like shit in the airplane bathroom, I would've jacked off then and there.

She lied at the taxi stand—"family friend," my ass. She kept touching her skirt, blushing like crazy, likely freaking about her lack of underwear. It would've been adorable if her eyes didn't keep doing that thing where they zoned out while locked on my body. It's been too long since a girl has looked at me like that. Actually, I'm not sure a girl has ever looked at me quite like that. I wanted to pin her to the wall and bang her six ways from Sunday. Too bad she didn't get in the cab. Nina would've been exactly what I need, my first step to finding the old Sam. But there'll be plenty of other girls on this trip.

The taxi pulls up to a white house on a quiet street, the orange sign above the wraparound porch reading *Lambert's Lodge.* It's the first place listed in my guidebook, and the driver said it's pretty cool. Two girls are huddled on a bench drinking wine. They watch me as I pass.

Plenty of other girls.

Squeezing through the entrance, I drop my pack beside one leaning against the wall. I crack my neck and poke around. Some travelers are in a lounge area on the left—two on computers, others hanging on an orange couch. A chick's at the bookshelves, dragging her finger along the spines. Clanging echoes from the kitchen behind them, laughter drifting through the door on the heels of a familiar song, something by Jack Johnson. The next doorway reveals the check-in counter.

After a rundown of do's and don'ts, I'm given a bunk in the guys' dorm. It's a small space with orange walls, apparently a theme, with piles of clothes on most of the beds. I dump my stuff on the only one where the sheets are still tucked, and I leave, wallet in hand, in search of a grocery store.

Halfway down the block, the map the guy at the desk gave me slips through my fingers. I turn to pick it up as a taxi door slams. A girl staggers under the weight of her bags and trips on the first step of the hostel. The porch light shines on a red ponytail.

Ginger. Fucking A.

I almost run to help her with her bags, but judging by her freak-out earlier, she'll either fall on her face or take off. Better to go shopping and get back quickly. Turning, I try to pick up the pace, but it isn't easy these days. With each step, my limp feels more pronounced, the flesh of my legs rough against my jeans. The accident was a year ago, and I'm not as far along as the doctors had hoped. But I'm alive. And I'm *living*.

Mom would've wanted that.

Another day in Florida, and I was liable to punch someone. If one more person looked at me with those sad-ass eyes, I would've grabbed their hair and rammed their face into concrete. Halfway across the world, no one knows me. I can be anyone. But all I really want to be is the fun, cocky bastard who ruled the football field and turned girls on.

Blinking through the fluorescent lights of the grocery store, I scan the rows of shelves. The food looks pretty much the same as the stuff at home except for different brands here and there. I grab pizza sauce, cheese, a couple of bagels, and my stomach rumbles. If Nina's anything like me, she ate a few pretzels on the flight and one bite of that disgusting thing posing as chicken. She's probably hungry by now. I buy enough for both of us and hurry back to the hostel, cursing my leg the whole way.

It's dark by the time I get back. A chorus of laughter and a strange, high-pitched hyena sound drift down the hall.

I cross through the lounge into the kitchen to find three girls and a couple of guys on either side of a wooden table. The hyena cackle comes from one of the guys, an Italian-looking dude with dark hair and olive skin, who's thumping his fist on the table. A bottle of tequila anchors the center of the group, and copies of the same guidebook as mine are strewn about. Coffeehouse tunes strum from a radio in the corner.

"I can't believe this is the first I'm hearing of this," the hyena guy says in a British accent. "That's a legendary shag, mate."

The blond guy beside him pretends to shine his knuckles on his shirt. "What can I say? This smile gets 'em every time."

As I pass the table to dump my stuff beside the stove, one of the girls calls a loud "Hey," followed by a string of giggles.

I turn, cross my arms, and rest my hip against the orange countertop. The tan girl in the middle fiddles with the blond braid over her shoulder and gives me a flirty smile. Her head is inclined toward a dark-haired girl to her right who's whispering in her ear. On her other side is another blonde. This one's long hair is dyed pink at the ends like the celebrities in those stupid magazines.

The girl in the center tilts forward, the tops of her breasts spilling over her neckline. "I'm Reese," she says as she lifts her chin.

With her big tits, slim waist, and pouty lips, Reese looks the part of a cheerleader. She could be mine in a heartbeat. I'd splay her naked over my mattress and claim her in the darkness where she can't see my legs. Her gaze dances over my body, measuring, taking stock, but it's nothing like the way Nina's lips parted as she undressed me with her eyes.

I nod to the table. "I'm Sam. Drinking game?" I flick my head to the newly filled shot glasses.

"You assume correct, mate," says the dark hyena guy. "I'm Bruno, and Never Have I Ever is a smashing way to get acquainted." He wiggles his eyebrows at the girls before calling to me, "Fancy joining us?"

Could be fun. An easy to way to work this Reese chick, or Nina if she shows up. "Sure, I'll just make something to eat first."

Bruno tugs Reese's braid and winks at her, while the girls at her sides vie for her attention.

I flip around, turn on the oven, and build the staple meal that got me through two years of college: tray, bagel, sauce, cheese, and blister the shit out of it until it smells awesome.

I flinch at the sound of Bruno's mad cackle. The words *cherry* and *condom* explode from his mouth between each bout of hysteria. "Sam, you've got to get over here. You're missing the best bits."

"Yeah, yeah, yeah." I stack a couple of plates—orange, of course—rip off some paper towels, and load up the pizza bagels—enough for Nina and me, if she shows up. When I turn, I freeze.

Those eyes.

Standing in the doorway, Nina sucks on her bottom lip, her eyelids heavy as she soaks me in. It makes me feel like a legend. Like I'm whole again. In a simple tee and jeans—and probably a pair of underwear—this chick oozes sex. Her breasts strain against the thin white cotton of her shirt. Not as big as Reese's, but perky as hell. I almost drop the goddamn plates.

Maybe it's not having been touched by a girl for more than a year now, but I want to own her. *No.* Not own her. I want to fuck her. I want it raw and fun with no strings attached. Travel sex, pure and simple. Once and done. I can't have a repeat of Lacey and Florida. What's left of my ego wouldn't recover. I'm just not sure that's Nina's style. All shy and cute at the baggage claim, she doesn't seem the type. Not like Reese. Then she gives me *that* look.

When Nina shakes her head, blinks, and looks down, I tense. Like I'm a junkie needing another fix. I want those eyes back.

Knowing I need to play it cool so she doesn't bolt, I sit next to the blond dude and put a plate beside me at the head of the table. I drop Nina's two pizza halves on top of hers. When I glance up, her nose twitches and she licks her lips, her attention now on the food.

"Nina, great to see you. Come on over and have a seat." I pat the empty place beside me.

She approaches slowly and sits straight-backed, her hands folded neatly on her lap. The table falls silent.

"Nina, is it?" Bruno asks.

She nods, but keeps looking down at the bagels.

"I'm Bruno, and this here's Callum." He motions to the blond dude beside me, whose blue eyes are glazed from the tequila. "Callum's my mate from Bristol, and he shagged our science teacher."

Fresh hooting and hollering breaks out across the table, but I'm not sure if they're laughing at Callum's confession or that fucked-up sound coming from Bruno. Chewing, I tip my head back and laugh around each bite. Nina does one of those stiff laughs people use to fit in.

"These three lovely ladies all hail from California," Bruno continues, the self-proclaimed master of ceremonies. "Brianne at the end enjoys long walks on the beach, and she has a preference for cherry condoms."

Ahhh, the *cherry* and the *condom*.

Brianne sits across from me and rolls her pink-tipped blond hair around her finger. She elbows Reese beside her. "I can't *believe* you asked that. Just wait until it's my turn." She smiles at me, then at Nina, fluttering her pink nails.

Reese leans forward, taking in Nina's pale skin, the freckles, and that sexy birthmark. After a beat, Reese smiles. "I'm Reese." She drops her name like a stamp of approval, and Nina smiles back too eagerly.

Girls are evil. I've seen this a million times. The judging, the sizing up. Turning on each other like rabid dogs. Bitches in heat. Nina's desperation is written all over her face, her eyes wide and hopeful. At least with guys we're honest about our shit. I don't like you, go fuck yourself. You don't like me, tell it to my face. None of this quiet, emotional crap that plays on insecurities. It reminds me of my little cousin, a whip-smart girl who hooked up with the wrong guy—the head cheerleader's ex. She had to move towns and switch schools because of the bullying.

It kicks my protective instincts into high gear.

I scoot closer to Nina, but she doesn't notice. Her attention is on Reese.

I can't figure this girl out. At first glance, you'd for sure think she was prom queen at her school. After the scene on the airplane and her hiding around that pillar, I'm guessing that's not the case. Not with the way she's grinning at Reese.

Bruno tugs the blond braid swooping over Reese's shoulder. "*I* do the introductions, luv." His hand continues down until his fingers glide over hers. "This is the naughty Reese who once kissed a girl to see if Katy Perry was correct."

She draws her hand away and rolls her eyes.

"Lastly," Bruno announces as he spins his shot glass on the table, "is the dark, the daring, the one and only…Leigh. Leigh is infamous for streaking through the boys' locker room after a match of American football." He flicks his hands toward the girl at the end.

Dropping her head to her hands, Leigh groans. She uses her straight black hair to cover her face.

Nina's brow is puckered like she has no idea what's going on, her grin fading as she studies the girls. As far as I'm concerned, they're an easy read. Brianne whispers in Reese's ear, eager for her attention; Leigh fixes Reese's braid, happy to have her hands anywhere near that girl; and Reese, the queen bee, sits perched between them, basking in her glory. As long as Reese likes Nina, the others will follow.

I tear another piece of the pizza bagel while Nina moves restlessly. She gathers her hair, laying the strands over her right shoulder. Then she bites her lip, flips her hair back, and smooths it behind her ears. She adjusts her white T-shirt.

I swallow my bite and whisper in her ear. "They're playing Never Have I Ever. And stop fidgeting. They'll smell your fear."

She shoves her hands under her thighs and glares at me. "Never Have I *what*?"

As much as I'd like to suck that frown off her face, I want to see that *other* look. The one where she fucks me with her eyes. "Never Have I Ever. Someone says something like, never have I ever slept with a teacher, but if you have, as was the case with Callum, you do a shot. It's their little 'get to know you' game. With enough booze, it's fun."

Her frown deepens. Maybe Ginger has some secret past she doesn't want revealed. With a breath, her brow softens. Her gaze lands back on the bagel. She scrapes her teeth over her bottom lip, looking from me to the food I made her.

I nod to her plate. "You're not one of those vegan, no-gluten chicks, are you?"

"God, no." She shakes her head. "It's just…did you happen to have leftovers, or did you make this for me?"

Man, she's cute when she's nervous, those freckles bright against her pale skin. She probably thinks I've been stalking her. I could tell her I made too much, ease her mind, but there's no point lying. Ever since the accident, I do my best to say things as they are. Treat each day like it's my last. I know all too well how short life can be. "I made it for you," I say.

She scans the kitchen, for what I have no idea. A group of three is at the large map of New Zealand tacked on the wall, and a guy's at the orange counter snacking on toast and peanut butter.

She chews on her cheek. "How'd you know I was here? And how'd you know I'd be hungry?"

Bruno and Callum have the girls laughing, telling stories about school pranks, and I pop the last bite of bagel into my mouth. That's when that look of hers returns. Her eyes glaze, her lips plump, and she arches her back. She looks ready to devour me. Like she's starved for sex. Either she's longing for something she's never had, or she's a nymphomaniac on the loose.

I'm hoping for the latter.

She's still staring at my neck, burning a trail down my skin, and without warning, my dick strains against my jeans. What the hell is wrong with me? Sure, it's been a while, but I've jacked off plenty. So why does it feel like I'm the Hoover Dam about to explode? Thank God I'm sitting at the table.

Her gaze snaps down to her plate, and I adjust myself. I wipe my hands on a piece of paper towel until the blood pumping south returns to my brain. I plant my elbows on the table. "It's simple, really. As soon as I got here, I dumped my stuff so I could buy some food. You arrived as I was walking down the street. Figured you'd do that girl thing, you know? Shower, unpack, moisturize…put on a change of clothes." I lean to the side and glance below the table. At her jeans and the underwear she's probably wearing. "Must feel nice."

She scowls and crosses her legs.

"Anyway, I assumed you'd want to eat when you were done. Hence the gourmet meal you haven't touched."

With an audible sigh she says, "Thanks," and removes her hands from below her thighs.

As she picks up the bagel, I add, "Must be pretty handy having a family friend as a taxi driver."

"Shoot," she mutters and tucks her elbows to her sides. "I mean, what did you expect? Strange guy, strange city, unusual state of undress." She gestures to her crossed legs with her head. "Do you blame me for lying?"

Unusual state of undress. Now my mind's back on her fall, and that smooth ass propped up in the air. Fucking hell. Blood rushes straight back to my dick, and I almost groan. "No, Nina. I do not." I lick my lips, knowing her attention is focused there. "You should eat already."

Closing her eyes, she takes a bite, and I know how good it

tastes. The tomato sauce, the cheese, and the burnt taste of the bread's charred edges. Especially after a day of no food.

A delicious "*Mmmmm*," passes her lips as she slouches in her seat.

"Kind of makes you fancy being a piece of bread," says a glassy-eyed Callum beside me.

So absorbed in Ginger, I practically blocked out the group. Bruno, the class clown, has the girls in stitches, while Callum rests on his elbows to watch Nina eat.

I grip my empty plate. "Yeah, whatever. Looks like another round's about to start. You don't want to miss the action."

"Right," he says absentmindedly, his gaze still fixed on Nina's fingers as she deposits a piece of cheese into her mouth. He smiles at her then, the type of smile chicks probably dig, flashing his dimples under a layer of stubble.

Her attention moves from me to Callum, and I want to punch the guy in his throat. She's not giving him those sex eyes, but she's chewing more slowly and tilting her head. I'm not the jealous type, never been my style. Not even with Lacey. But as the seconds tick by, it's getting increasingly difficult not to pluck Nina from the table and strap her to my bed.

I really need to get laid.

Four

NINA

It's hard to tear my eyes from Sam, but Callum has this amazing smile. I chew slowly, uneasy with the attention, unsure if Callum's messing with me. But seeing Bruno with Reese as he plays with her braid and touches her hand, I realize these guys are flirting. An essential part of any travel experience: Hook up with random people you'll never see again. Bruno could star in an episode of *The Bachelor*. He fawns over Reese across from him. Brianne's giggles escalate as she flings her pink nails at his arm, and Leigh's eyes darken to the color of her jet-black hair. She shoots daggers at him.

My bet's on Reese for the rose.

I envy these girls. I'd love to be carefree enough to flirt and sleep with a stranger for fun. No strings, no expectations. There is Sam who, after much consideration, I've decided is less stalk-eresque and just plain nice. When I first saw him standing at the stove, I almost fled. I ran through several scenarios that might have led to us staying at the same hostel.

Scenario one: I am the missing character from a Percy Jackson novel about to find out I'm the bastard kid of a powerful god who's hell-bent on punishing me.

Scenario two: Maybe it was Mom. Maybe she got my note, planted Sam on the plane, had him trip me and follow me so he could help me embarrass myself. (Not that I need the assistance.) Mom's vain attempts to console me growing up always ended with, "Don't run from who you are, Pininfarina. If you accept yourself, others will, too."

Yeah, right. But Sam isn't her modus operandi—it involves actual planning.

Scenario three: Sam had me followed. He found out I can't resist melted cheese, and he slipped something into my food to take advantage of me later.

Even though I rejected each hypothesis, I could never consider sleeping with Sam. Aside from the fact that he knows I have a tendency to malfunction, he's way too hot to consider. He stays where he belongs, in fantasyland.

Now *Callum*…he could work. He's skinnier than Sam, fit but lean, and not as off-the-charts gorgeous. His cheeks crease when he smiles, his thick blond hair styled but messy. He's easy on the eyes. And so far, he thinks I'm normal.

But to be so daring, I'd have to address my androphobia. My fear of men.

The endless hours I spent locked in my room during my formative high school years were often used to research and self-diagnose all the phobias that resulted from my inability to function normally. My androphobia was acquired at the only party I ever attended close to graduation. Having had enough of hanging out with my siblings and tired of rewinding the sexy parts in movies, I took control of my life. Or so I thought. After a few drinks, things were looking good. I was on a bed. Clothes off. A cute guy above me drunk enough not to care about my past. Then Pininfarina Gabri, catastrophe magnet, made her unwanted appearance.

I may or may not have lost my virginity. The jury's still out after *that* disaster.

I'll stick with flirting and fantasies.

As I return Callum's smile, Sam's plate clatters against the table. He bends his lips to my ear, his nose brushing my hair. I almost drop my bagel. "You've got some sauce on your chin," he whispers.

Callum turns to chat with the group as I take a paper towel from Sam to wipe the offending smear.

So much for flirting.

Bruno hops from the table and returns with two more shot glasses. He deposits them in front of Sam and me. Having stuffed a bite of bagel into my mouth, I can't protest. I chew as fast as possible, but by the time I swallow, all seven glasses are brimming with tequila.

"Ladies and gents," Bruno announces, "it's time for another round. Nina, why don't you start? We need to get to know you better."

No longer hungry, I put the last piece of bagel down and push my plate away.

I've never run with the "in" crowd. Never been accepted. Unless you count Becca (the iceberg to my *Titanic*), who ditched me in twelfth grade when she lost her braces, a bunch of weight, and joined the upper ranks. Here I am—*invited*, sitting with cute guys and the Trifecta of Cool.

Any minute, I could ruin this.

Desperate for some help, I glance at Sam, but his eyes are downcast as he runs his finger around his glass. He puts his finger to his lips and sucks off the alcohol.

Now I'm envisioning those lips, that tongue, my bare breasts, and *oh, my God.*

It is seriously not normal to be that sexy.

"Nina, luv?" I jump at my name and face the group. "We're dying to know what you've never done." Coming from Bruno, the words sound dirty.

The Trifecta of Cool waits, fingers tapping the table, cheeks flushed from the alcohol. How did I get sucked into this?

Sam nudges my bouncing knee with his. "Just say the first thing that pops into your head."

Unfortunately, the first thing that comes to my mind is: Maybe I can climb out the window. I run my tongue over my teeth, the taste of pizza still lingering. "Never have I ever…" *What? What? What?* Please, *God*, don't say something lame, but I'd rather die than discuss sex and condoms. My sights lock on the half-empty bottle by Bruno's hand. "Never have I ever…polished off a bottle of tequila?"

The girls cock their heads, frowning. No one moves.

Callum's ticking watch is deafening.

Then Sam slams his shot.

Bruno and Callum nod, impressed with Sam's penchant for alcohol poisoning, and Reese claps while laughing. She smiles at me, and I could swear I'm flying. When Sam squeezes my knee, the flying hits light speed. Smirking, he places his elbows back on the table, but my knee still tingles from his touch.

Going next, Brianne at my right faces Reese and says, "Never have I ever been buck naked with a guy, getting hot and heavy on his couch, when his parents came home early from vacation."

"Bitch!" Reese cries in mock-horror as a chorus of "*Ohhh*" rises from the group.

"Drink! Drink! Drink!" Callum pounds his fist with each word.

Reese lifts her shot to her lips. "To Todd's mom and dad." She jerks her head back and slams the empty glass down.

Without the fanfare, Leigh at the end shoots her tequila.

Bruno points at her, that ridiculous sound bursting through his lips. "You too? Such naughty girls, you Americans."

The kids by the map are laughing, too, no doubt unhinged by Bruno's cackle.

Leigh shrugs. "Todd has a thing for couches, and his parents travel a bunch."

"*The same guy?*" I slap my hand over my mouth the second I close it.

"Aren't you the innocent?" Sam says under his breath.

"Whatever," I mutter, staring dead ahead. I doubt that would be his word of choice if he saw the pornographic film flipping behind my eyes.

Instead of the dirty looks I expected between the girls, Leigh tips toward Reese, her black hair fanning over Reese's shoulder. "Reese and I have the same taste."

Bruno smiles wickedly at both girls. "Well, now, isn't that lovely."

Apparently, the purpose of Never Have I Ever is to force people to admit to random sexcapades. And apparently the people who play this game wear their shame like a badge of honor. Unlike yours truly. Thank God they don't know about the sex I may or may not have had in high school. And they don't know about the Public Speaking Incident that tanked my reputation. *Unless*…I study the group more closely, but none of them are looking at me wide-eyed, trying to stifle a laugh, because they've seen the famed YouTube video. Viral is an understatement when describing that footage. There *is*, however, one person who's witnessed me in action.

Glancing back at Sam, I cringe. He's still staring at me. Unlike most people who look away when caught red-handed, he barely blinks. Heat crawls up my neck.

He squints and dips lower. "Are you really this wholesome, or is it just an act?"

"Blunt much?" I hiss, thankful the group is busy dissecting Leigh and Reese's joint history of hookups.

He chuckles. "New life motto: If I think it, I speak it. But seriously, you're gorgeous, hot as hell, but you blush five shades of red when sex is mentioned, and you're smiling at Reese like she's the admissions officer at Harvard." He leans even closer. "What gives?"

Wow. Just wow. Part of me wants to slide off my seat and crab-walk out the door, but *gorgeous* and *hot as hell* ring in my ears, blocking out all natural instinct. I fist my hands. "You need to jam a filter between the thinking and speaking part of your brain.

And just so you know, I can say the word *sex*." But it falls in a whisper, and my cheeks flame.

"Damn, that's cute." A wide grin splits his face. "I tossed the filter a year ago. Come on, Canada, say sex again."

Frickin' Hot Guy.

Bruno draws us back into the game—Leigh, then him, then Callum all playing. I haven't sipped my tequila, but the girls are buzzing, and Callum can barely focus. Sam's downed another shot, admitting to a blow job from a stripper. If he thought I blushed before, that doesn't rival the shade of fuchsia my face colors.

When the turn falls to Sam, he taps his thumb on the table. "Never have I ever…" His thumb stops, a mischievous glint hitting his honeyed eyes…eyes that are intent upon me. "Tripped on an airplane…" He pauses.

No. He. Will. Not. No frickin' way. I glare at him, probably using my angry-old-lady face, willing him not to be the world's worst human being.

"And fallen on my face," he finishes and winks at me.

Leigh frowns, her thin black brows angled at a clean forty-five degrees. Everything about Leigh is lines and angles. Blunt bangs, straight hair, sharp cheeks, and a cut chin. She'd be right at home in a protractor case. Her eyes dart from Sam to me. "What happened on that plane, you two?"

"Nothing," I say quickly. "Nope. Nothing happened. Absolutely no *stuff* in the happening department. Just a long flight. And I might have tripped over Sam's massive boot in the aisle."

She narrows her pointed gaze. "Uh huh." Her eyes keep doing that darting thing. "Drink up then, Nina."

With a huff, I sling the shot back, fire burning the length of my throat, and a five-minute hack attack follows. I don't do hard alcohol. I wipe my mouth with my wrist and scowl at Sam. "Happy?"

"Deliriously," he says. "Making you blush should be a sport."

That's exactly what I do when he winks again.

Tired with the game, Bruno pours a final round of shots, and we raise our glasses. He toasts to the trip ahead: new friends, adventures, and drinking games. This time, when the burn hits my belly, I only cough once.

A lively discussion on travel plans flows around the table. Sam has the same *Lonely Planet* guidebook as everyone else. He gets his copy, and we lean over the book as the group discusses the best route to follow and which hostels are the coolest. Bruno, Callum, and the girls all have passes on Kiwi Experience, daily buses that travel the country from town to town. The passes allow you to hop on and off, staying with one group or hooking up with other travelers. When Reese asks if I want to join them, I practically leap from my seat.

She reaches across the table to touch Sam's arm. "What about you? You should come, too."

It's amazing how easy it is for her to do that, just reach over and glide her fingers down his skin. That taut, tanned skin. What I wouldn't give to not overthink everything until I'm a quaking mess of nerves. Sam's eyes slide up Reese's arm, lingering on her full breasts. His nostrils flare, and my belly falls the way it does on Christmas morning when I unwrap yet another Grateful Dead T-shirt, tie-dyed and dizzying.

I shouldn't care. It's not like I'd go after him and risk the embarrassment that would surely follow. *Overthinking queen.* And he'd never be interested anyway. Not after that plane ride.

I'm still frowning when Sam slides his arm back, Reese's fingers slipping onto the table. He pushes the curls off his forehead. "I bought a car off a guy, organized it before I left. The thing's an old beater but should get me through my trip. I'll sell it when I leave." He looks at me, pauses, then turns to the group. "Maybe I'll head north. To Pahia?" When Bruno nods, Sam bends toward me and lowers his voice. "You're buying a pass, right? You're going north?"

My stomach drops again, but this time it's one of those about-to-plummet-down-a-roller-coaster drops.

I pick at my cuticles, still dry from the airplane. Normally, guys run the other way from me (unless their judgment is impaired by alcohol), but Sam's not budging. Not only is he not running, but I've caught him watching me at least twice over the last half hour, the light center of his eyes darkening with each glance. Each time, my ears burned and my chest tightened. His jaw ticked until he looked away, his gaze always landing on Reese.

He nudges my knee, and I look up. Sam's seen me at my worst, but he didn't call me out when given the chance, and he *did* make me a pizza bagel. There is that thing where he seems intent on embarrassing me to watch my skin flame, but I'd hate to lose him as the star of my fantasies.

"Yeah, I'll get a pass," I say before I change my mind.

His shoulders soften, and he clears his throat. "Good." He presses his knee to mine again. *Harder.* The pressure travels up my thigh and heat explodes between my legs, my underwear damp in seconds. We sit still, eyes locked, the air between us snapping with electricity. Seconds? Minutes? Hours? Time comes to a halt.

After another forever, he jerks away and turns his back to me.

Either that just happened, or it was one of my daydreams. Considering he was fully clothed, the daydream thing is off the table, but now I'm picturing a naked Sam's tongue easing the burn between my thighs. *Focus, Pininfarina.* I cross my legs and grip my chair. I'm sure he didn't notice anyway. Not with the way he keeps looking at Reese. Even if he did, I have androphobia.

Bruno slaps the table. "Smashing, it's settled then. We'll spend a few days in Auckland before heading north. Reese and Leigh can fight over who gets to sit with me on the bus."

Both girls roll their eyes.

Sam stands abruptly and gathers our plates, his limp more pronounced on his way to the sink. It doesn't seem to inhibit him as much as slow him down—a slight drag of his left leg. Probably a sports injury. With his wide shoulders and strong arms, he looks the part of the school jock.

Reese bends forward to catch my eye. "You'll sit with me on the bus, Nina. My girls can hang, and the boys will do just fine on their own."

"So cold." Bruno plunges a fake dagger through his heart.

I bite my lip and smile. "Thanks, Reese. Sounds cool."

Leigh stands abruptly, her face pinched in distaste. She says a curt "Catch you later," and takes off.

Sam grunts at the table and limps out after her. He doesn't acknowledge me or look my way. He just leaves, his fists balled at his sides. We're not exactly friends, and I obviously imagined what I thought passed between us, but I was getting used to his presence—a bit of familiarity in this foreign place. And he totally blew me off. Reese tugs my wrist to go wash up, and my unease vanishes. I'm no longer traveling alone. I'm not the outcast. I'm backpacking with the Trifecta of Cool and hot guys. I even get to sit with Reese on the bus. The reinvention of Pininfarina Gabri has begun.

Five

NINA

Pahia is beautiful. After acclimatizing in Auckland, we arrive to warmer winds, palm trees fanned over turquoise water, and boats moored offshore. It's only been three days since the Airplane Incident, but it feels like a lifetime ago. I barely recognize myself. Every time Reese cocks her head and looks at me with pouty lips to proclaim yet again, "I'd kill for that hair," I glow a little a brighter. Brianne agrees with everything she says, so the statement is usually followed with a dramatic, "*God*, I know."

Leigh's frown deepens with each compliment. Like she knows I'm a fake.

I am. I admit it. Absolutely no shame. After years of babysitting and taking tai chi with people who likely witnessed the invention of the wheel (Dad's genius idea to get me "involved"), I'm ready to interact with people my own age. If that means laughing at Reese's jokes or pretending I was popular back home with a laundry list of ex-boyfriends, that's what it means.

The beauty of reinvention.

We're going on a day trip with the boys today, north to Cape Reinga and Ninety Mile Beach. I roll over in my bunk and blink to calm the ache taking over my head. Another night of drinking, another morning of a vise tightening around my temples. I don't know how these people do it. None of them are sore and groggy in the morning. When the pain eases, I reach below the bedframe for my purse.

With a thud, Leigh jumps down from the bunk above me, practically landing on my head. I jerk back and smash my skull into the wall. Just what my hangover needs.

"Oops, sorry," she says.

Nothing about her looks apologetic. Her lips curve in a smirk, her dark eyes squint. Her prominent cheekbones sharpen. Distaste is the word I'd use. Or loathing. Or disgust. Over the years, I've catalogued twenty-seven adjectives to describe the emotion behind that look.

The good Canadian I am, I deal with her animosity by being really, really super nice. "No, no. Sorry. It was my fault. I was in the way." I rub my head and grin until my mouth hurts.

She makes a choking sound, rolls her eyes, and struts to the bathroom in her loose tee and boxers. Her swinging arms could power a light bulb.

This huffy girl is hindering my reinvention. The sweeter Reese is to me, the edgier Leigh gets. Words are swapped for grunts, answers for shrugs. My retaliation: Act like Father Christmas threw up a pile of good cheer on my face. Clearly, my lack of social interaction is inhibiting my ability to defend myself.

I yank my purse from under the bed and fish out my cell. I texted Mom last night that I made friends and was traveling to Pahia. No mention of surly Leigh or One-syllable Sam, who's taken to ignoring me.

Whatever chemistry I thought I felt between us that first night was one-sided. He avoids my eyes and sits at the opposite ends of tables. He barely acknowledges me. For me, having him around has been...challenging. Instead of getting used to his presence, the more I see him, the more I envision his hands on my skin, my skirt around my waist, his thick erection straining for me. (*Bow-chicka wow-wow.*) Once, Callum had to grab me before I walked into a pole.

I power on my phone, and two messages from Mom appear.

The first one reads: Pininfarina Gabri. Real live friends? With moving lips? And pumping hearts? Whatever will I tell Skippy the Bear? Or would you like to break the news upon your return?

I laugh and duck my head, worried people are watching me, but the dozen girls are going through their morning routines. All except for Brianne, who's snoring on the bunk across the room. I wrap my arms around my knees, the sheets bundled over my bent legs.

I type: Don't you dare! He needs to be let down gently.

Her next message is less amusing: Be good, baby girl. And FYI, I'm dangerously close to mastering the art of the chocolate soufflé.

Oh, God. The possible news report flashes in my mind: *Tragedy strikes in the ritzy Bridal Path neighborhood of*

Toronto. In the early hours of the morning, five children and their parents were discovered with carbon monoxide poisoning...

The year I was born, Mom had an epiphany and decided to write a baking cookbook. Why? I have no idea. She says it unleashes her "inner light" and gets her in touch with her "true self." If I had to rate Mom's cooking skills from one to ten, one being nonexistent and ten being perfect, she would earn a whopping 0.2, mainly for effort. In the nineteen years since she started this project, she has mastered just as many recipes. One per year. With the amount of charred food I've ingested in that time, I probably have early-onset cancer.

I type quickly: Stop. At once. All cooking halts until I return. If you do not comply, I will never again perform my Age of Aquarius dance number.

"EEEEE!" Reese's high-pitched screech sets my teeth chattering as she lands on the bed beside me. The entire bunk sways.

I manage to hit send before she grabs my shoulders. "Hurry, girl—I need a new pair of shades, and you're coming with. We have half an hour to speed shop, so get your ass in gear."

Arms limp at my sides, I lean back to avoid being hit by the bubble gum expanding from her mouth. With the way my head is feeling, the simulated strawberry smell turns my stomach. "What's wrong with those?" I ask, nodding to the sunglasses on her head.

"These? So last year." She jumps up, plucks them off her head, and tosses them on my bed. Her thick blond braid bumps against her shoulder. "They're yours if you want 'em. Now get up.

Where's your pack?" She chews her gum with her mouth half open.

The second I gesture to the blue nylon bag against the wall, she dives into its depths. Like a deep-sea fisherman, she tugs out my bathing suit, dangling it for all to see. She scrunches her face and turns toward me. "Really, Nina? *This* is what you packed? Were you, like, a competitive swimmer or something?"

My one-piece Speedo hangs midair, a neon billboard that screams: YOU ARE SO NOT COOL. "That? No. It's not mine. Don't be ridiculous. My little sister's a total freak. I packed in a rush. Must've grabbed it accidentally. I mean, who'd wear that, right?"

I twitch my nose to make sure it hasn't grown.

Leigh, now fully dressed in cutoff jeans and a black tank, her knobby shoulders as jagged as the rest of her, appears at Reese's side and folds her arms. "Looks like my mom's suit. But way more…matronly. Are there granny pants in there, too?" She reaches for my pack, but Reese slaps her hand.

A blast of a snore explodes from Brianne. The room quiets briefly, then everyone goes back to business. Reese rolls her eyes.

Still holding the offending suit by two fingers, Reese grabs Leigh's tank top and peeks down the front. "This green would look great on Nina. Go on, Leigh, change. Put on the blue bikini with the white stripes." She flips back to me, smacks her gum, and smiles. "The green's better on you. Come, let's dress you up."

So this is how Barbie feels. Or Chucky before he knifes unsuspecting kids.

She drops my Speedo on the floor, tugs my wrist, and pulls me past a fuming Leigh, who would sooner ingest live bugs than lend me her clothing.

"Now!" Reese calls to Leigh over her shoulder. "And wake Brianne. I swear that girl could sleep through a hurricane."

Leigh, of course, does her bidding.

* * *

This is a bad idea. Like cheese-in-a-can bad. Leigh has smaller boobs than me, so the triangles of her bikini top are holding on for dear life. I never dress this skimpy. Ever. Skimpy clothes mean people stare, which negates my intended life goal: to blend in.

Reese shushes my nervous protests and shoots me a look, daring me to defy her orders. "You're wearing it, Nina. It looks hot. The guys'll fucking love it."

I've already done my usual thing where each compliment received is followed by three things I hate about myself. I excel at self-deprecation.

Reese: "The green rocks with your eyes."

Me: "What? No. It makes my skin look paler. My freckles darker. And my eyes are more muddy-green, like rainstorm-green."

Reese: "It totally flaunts your curves."

Me: "Curves? *God, no.* My boobs look too big. The bottom's so small my hips look gigantic. And my bum's spilling out the sides. It gives me double bum."

Reese waves at my face to shut me up.

I cover my barely-there bikini with the (now washed) floral skirt I wore on the airplane and my light blue tank top. I pop some Tylenol and hurry out to join Reese's mission: Sunglasses. Now.

Twenty minutes later, Brianne buzzes through the store sifting through glasses as Reese studies herself in the full-length mirror. Hands planted on her hips, Reese sucks in her cheeks and tilts her face from side to side. "Nina? What do you think? The last pair was better, right?" She adjusts the frames on her face.

Brianne hurries to her side with a new pair dangling from her fingers. "Okay. These are *it*. Seriously. You're gonna love 'em." She waves the shades around.

Reese ignores her and turns to face me. "Nina? The last pair? Better, right?"

"Oh, sorry. Way better. Definitely the last ones." *Which ones?* It's been a blur of black sunglasses, a parade of varying frames. I nod my head repeatedly. "Yeah, definitely the other pair." I'm not what you'd call a shopper. My patience usually lasts ten minutes before I'm practically narcoleptic, nodding off on my feet. Reese, however, could go all day. I pinch my arm to get my head back in the act-like-I'm-not-a-freak game.

A throaty sound comes from Leigh, who's browsing clothes at the back of the shop.

Still not convinced she's found *that* pair, Reese takes the frames from Brianne's hand. Reese puckers her lips and does her modeling thing.

Brianne squeals and claps. "Oh, my God, yes! Those are *so* them. You look stunning."

"Nina?" Reese says. She lifts the shades just enough to peek under them. Her eyes lock on my reflection in the mirror. "They *are* pretty cool, right?"

Pretty cool…if you're okay looking like a fly-eyed alien. When I say, "Totally, those are it," she drops them back on her nose and goes to the cashier.

Leigh appears beside me but barely looks my way. "She'll tire of you eventually. She always does. And it's never pretty." She grabs a scarf and calls, "Reese, babe, check this out. It'd be perfect with your red dress." She struts to the counter.

A sticky feeling settles in my gut. Friendships never get this far for me, if I'd even call Reese a friend. Travel buddy, maybe? Girl my age who likes to play Barbie? But I'm Nina, not Pininfarina, and I'm not ready for Reese to rip off my arms and legs and toss me in her toy cemetery. I've been incident-free for three whole days. Surely that means something.

I stroll through the tiny shop so packed with merchandise it would take an extended episode of *What Not to Wear* to riffle through its contents. As I squeeze between a rack of hats and beach sarongs, a high shelf behind the cash catches my eyes.

Sunscreen. Shoot. Along with deodorant and tampons, something else I forgot to pack in my rush to leave. With the amount of skin showing beneath my clothes, I'll likely burn in five seconds.

As Reese finishes paying, I grab a tube of cherry lip balm, smile at the saleslady, and point to the highest numbered bottle they have. I pay and meet the girls outside.

"Sorry, guys. Do you mind waiting?" I ask, holding up the sunscreen. "I'll just be a sec."

Leigh clucks her tongue against her teeth while Brianne looks to Reese to see how she's supposed to react. Reese says, "Sure, whatever. If I had that porcelain skin, I'd load on the sunscreen, too."

Brianne: "*God*, I know. It's awesome, right?"

Me: "*Seriously?* I look like Casper on a good day. Like I've never seen sunlight. You can practically see my bones." Self-deprecation champion.

Reese huffs and turns to Brianne. "Tell the bus to wait for us."

Brianne runs off obediently while I lather up my arms and legs. When I'm done, Reese juts her chin toward the sunscreen. "I'll do your back."

Another gravelly sound comes from Leigh. She's leaning against the store, her knee bent with one foot against the wall in an equilateral triangle. Angle girl.

"Take off your top," Reese says.

My shirt? Off? Here? "Sorry?"

Two cars drive by at five miles per hour, a few girls from our hostel are across the street looking through a shop window, but I'd swear there are thousands of eyes on me. This in no way fits into my plan to blend in.

"We don't have all day," Reese says, annoyance creeping into her voice.

I laugh nervously and grab the hem of my top as my eyes flit every which way. I slip the cotton over my head, gooseflesh sending my hairs on end, and I clutch the thin fabric.

I am now half-naked. On the street. In public. Wearing Leigh's barely-there bikini. The words *stripped*, *exposed*, and *laid bare* hardly capture my shame. *Shorn* is closer. I turn away from Reese and jump when a cold glob of sunscreen hits my back. The second her hands feather over my skin, Leigh says, "Shit!"

Reese and I spin around. I hunch forward to stop the sunscreen from sliding onto my skirt, and I hold my top in front of my boobs to prevent them from popping out.

Cheese-in-a-can bad.

Leigh is glaring at a huge rip running up the side of her black tank. "I must've been leaning on a fucking nail." She flicks her head to the wall behind her. "I need your tank top, Reese—the black halter one. Come back to the hostel with me."

Reese huffs out a breath and shakes her head. After rubbing in maybe half the sunscreen on my back, she says, "Meet us at the bus."

I stay bent as she marches off, a few globs still dripping downward.

A guy walks by my folded body, his eyebrows cocked in amusement as he laughs to himself. *Perfect.* I squish my tank top between my legs and reach both hands behind my back to spread the remaining sunscreen. I twist and arch and contort, my shoulder nearing dislocation, until the bulk of it is rubbed in. Exhausted, I hunch forward to stretch out my back, only to see familiar black boots. I guess things *could* get worse.

"Something interesting down there?" Sam asks.

This guy is the magnet to my awkwardness, always close enough to witness my humiliation. "No. No. Just, you know, checking out the sidewalk. I think they use different cement in New Zealand." Could I be a bigger dork?

"Hmm. Didn't notice." He moves next to me and plants his elbows on his knees. He studies the concrete. "Yeah. Now that you mention it, it's a little more blue-gray. I could get some chairs so we can watch it for the morning. See if it changes color with the sun?" Straight-faced, he shifts his gaze to my pink cheeks.

"Sorry, it's just…" Why am I always apologizing? It's like I have Polite Tourette's. "It's a long story. There was a clothing emergency, followed by a sunscreen emergency. It's all under control now." I give him unenthusiastic thumbs-up while still hunching forward.

He straightens, no doubt expecting me to do the same…in my nonexistent swimsuit.

His long shadow casts over me. "Did you throw your back out?"

My head falls between my legs as I curse Reese's mom. She probably refused to let her daughter play with dolls. If I stay here a second longer, my kind-of-dork status will reach full-blown-dork status, and Sam isn't moving. Knees knocked together, I roll up. "Back's just fine, thanks," I say, keeping my focus on the pavement.

He clears his throat. "I thought you'd never be caught dead in something like that." His voice is suddenly rough.

"Sorry, what?" *Forever sorry.* I roll my eyes at myself.

I tilt my head back to peek at his face. His gaze drags down my body, that jaw of his clenched tight. He has a full jaw—heavy, masculine—the scar on his chin deep, skin puckered along its length. I'd guess it needed stitches.

He lifts his gaze to meet mine and steps toward me. "*Gilligan's Island*? At the baggage claim? You said you'd never wear one of Ginger's bikinis, and this one's Kardashian skimpy." He blinks once, slowly, his long lashes fanning his cheeks.

Lost in his warm brown eyes, I practically forget what I'm

wearing. I finger the top in my hand. "Kardashian? I didn't peg you for the reality TV type."

He laughs. *I made Sam laugh.* Wow. Look at me, having a normal conversation with Hot Guy while standing half-naked. I'm a small-talk ninja warrior.

"Me?" he says, shaking his head. "No. My little sister. She leaves those magazines all over the house, and that Kardashian chick wears bikinis bigger than this."

He nods to my chest, and I bite my lip. I put my hand on my hip and shift my weight, for once enjoying what people call banter. With my family I'm witty and sarcastic, always quick on the draw, but stick me with my own peers, and I revert to the speech level of a first grader. Apparently, that's not the case with Sam. "So you read those girly magazines?" I ask.

He draws his head back, shocked. "No. My sister. They're my sister's. Like I said."

"Okay, but which Kardashian?"

"Kim, the one with Kanye."

"So you *do* read the magazines."

A grin splits his face, stretching his scar. He shakes his head. "No. No way. I do *not* read that trash." He pushes his curls back from his forehead, the ones that always bounce forward.

"Liar."

He smiles. *I made Sam smile.*

"I will not admit to reading that girl smut." He folds his arms and widens his stance, a mock frown on his face.

"Would you take a lie detector test?"

"Bring it on, Canada."

This is banter, a friendly exchange, and possibly…*flirting?* I am flirting with One-syllable Sam. Sam, whose chestnut eyes dip down my body, practically searing my flesh.

Skin. Heat. Oh, God. Things take a turn for the worse.

I envision the sex goddess version of me releasing the string around my neck, letting the little green triangles drop to my feet. Sex-goddess me arches into Sam as he cups my breasts and bites my neck…

"Hey, careful," he says in my ear.

It's then I realize I've fallen against his chest while lost in my fantasy. *That chest.* "Shoot, sorry."

"Don't be." His words are barely audible.

His hands slip around my back, burning into my skin, and he tugs me closer. If he weren't holding me so tight, I would literally melt. Into a puddle. Or burst into flames. Then, *then*, his lips graze my ear. Forget flames, I am now a firework about to be lit. The one that bursts into stars. I whimper and press into him. When his tongue and teeth join the party along my sensitive flesh, I jerk and my head hits his chin.

Mortified, I try to jump back, but he's gripping my hips, and my hands brush his jeans. *Jeans?* "Aren't you coming to the beach? Shouldn't you be in shorts?"

He shoves me back and removes his hands. His smile disappears, the seduction on his face replaced with shadow. "Nah. I'm hanging here today. Catch you later."

He spins around and walks away, each stride purposeful even with his limp, his shoulders hitched up to his neck.

In a daze, I slip on my tank top and hurry to the bus. But my limbs are stiff, my body wound tight. Sam held me close and nibbled on my ear. *Nibbled. My ear.* And I wasn't a freak for half a minute. I stopped caring how I looked and had fun talking to him, except for the whole head-butting thing. If I were Reese or Brianne or Leigh, I'd have called after him to wait. No hesitation. We could spend the day together, the two of us roaming the town, getting to know each other. I've learned he has a younger sister (and he likes to make me blush), but that's the extent of my Sam trivia. Unfortunately, I *did* spaz out and I *do* have androphobia. So I let him walk away.

Six

NINA

The bus ride to Ninety Mile Beach is hilarious. Bruno takes the guide's two-way radio and launches a series of games, each more ridiculous than the last, culminating with Callum making the whole bus shout, "Hy-*ee*-na" whenever Bruno laughs. Then Bruno cackles louder. We laugh harder. And the bus bounces on its wheels. Once we get to the beach, we dig in the sand for live mussels and bodyboard down sand dunes, the sun never once blinking behind a cloud.

We all have a blast. All except for Leigh, who got World War Mad when I boarded the bus and Reese kicked her out of her seat. I sank into the warm, sticky vinyl reluctantly, happy to be sitting next to Reese, but terrified of Leigh's wrath.

By the time we stop for lunch, I'm ravenous. It's not easy work climbing sand dunes, each step forward more like two steps back. The girls are still in their bikini tops and shorts, and so, unfortunately, am I. I had tried to put my tank top on earlier, but Reese stared me down until I tucked it behind me on the seat. Brianne and Reese have on doll-size shorts rolled at the waist, barely covering anything. Leigh's cutoff jeans aren't much longer. I may be half-naked with triangles stretching over my breasts, but at least my skirt hits mid-thigh.

I fall into step behind them as we enter the waterfront bar, and a warm breeze blows through the room. I expected it to be more tropical this far north, but not this unseasonably warm.

"Table!" Bruno waves from across the bar, his yellow-and-pink neon shorts as loud as the rest of him.

As I step forward, a hand slides along my back. "This is dialed-down Bruno. You should see him when he's known you awhile. He's a right prat."

Callum's hand stays on my back as we move toward the table, and I can't help wishing it were Sam's hand. My skin still tingles from that touch earlier. But Callum is sweet. He's been attentive all day, helping me climb the sand dunes and staying close. I've been halfway normal, too. I smile and talk and don't head butt anyone, but the whole thing plays like a video game.

Smile. Don't smile. Laugh at that joke. Don't slouch. Laugh again. Twirl hair like Brianne. Giggle like Reese. Smile. Stop. Giggle. Giggle. Twirl hair some more.

I'm not sure I'm winning, but at least I'm playing.

And I might be maturing. I've been around Callum all morning, a person of the male persuasion, and haven't once pictured him naked. Or *me* naked. Or *us* naked. I do keep flashing to Sam's thick shoulders and hard chest. His tongue sliding over my ear. (*Bow-chicka wow-wow.*) The shirtless Callum to my right doesn't conjure such fantasies, but maybe that's a good thing. Maybe that's what I need to tame my pornographic mind—a hookup with a nice guy who doesn't cloud my thoughts with indecent performances. He's wearing blue board shorts printed with white waves, his flip-flops smacking against his feet. He exudes an easy confidence. If I keep my catastrophic self on lockdown, maybe I can conquer my androphobia. Big, fat *maybe*.

When we sit, Callum drapes his arm around my chair. "Hungry?"

"Starving." *Spin hair around finger.* I read the chalkboard behind the bar, a self-serve setup that suits the relaxed vibe of weathered wooden tables, plastic white chairs, and Bob Marley melodies. I zero in on my single favorite food group: soup. I love soup. All soup. If it can be boiled, blended, and sucked through a straw, I freaking love it.

Bruno slaps the table. "Drinks first, food to follow. The usual?" He points at each of us.

Everyone nods except for me. I bite my lip. "Um, iced tea?"

Reese dismisses me with a wave. She likes to wave a lot. "Ignore her, Bruno. Make it a Long Island."

He winks at her and heads to the bar.

Callum's fingers glide over my shoulder, tracing slow circles. "Not much of a drinker, yeah?"

Giggle. Don't giggle. Pout lips like Reese. "No. I'm just not used to drinking so much. Like every day."

Excessive drinking appears to be another intrinsic part of any travel experience.

Lunch—drinks. Afternoon—drinks. Dinner—you guessed it, *drinks.*

I'm not sure if it's the thrill of suddenly being legal, as eighteen is the drinking age in New Zealand, or if these people are early-stage mutants who need alcohol the way vampires need blood, but they're all bright and chipper each morning, while I rock a headache. Each time I try to order iced tea, Reese does her waving thing and forces another cocktail down my throat. Definitely alcohol-fueled mutants.

Callum's arm falls from my chair, and the next thing I know, his hand is resting on my thigh. He gives it a gentle squeeze. "You'll get used to the drinking soon enough. We just need to train your liver. Back home, there's a pub on every corner. We practically nurse on pints."

Although his lips are moving and sounds are coming out, not a word registers. Not while his thumb glides back and forth along the thin fabric of my skirt. My body tenses. My mind blanks. I try to recall the flirty moves I practiced today, but this is like the big exam. All answers slip from my mind. Instead of leaning into him or touching him back, my knee jumps, and his hand slams into the rough-bottomed table.

"Fuck." He cradles his knuckles and massages the chafed skin.

I just flunked Flirting 101.

Thankfully, Reese shoves back her chair, sashays over, and grabs my wrist. "Come to the bathroom. We'll order food on the way."

"Sorry," I call to Callum as Reese, my savior, drags me to the counter.

* * *

Before we leave the bathroom, Reese takes her time in front of the mirror, pushing up her boobs and glossing her lips. When she says, "I almost hooked up with Sam last night," my shoulder smacks into the hand dryer.

"Sam? What? Really?" I stammer as I rub my skin to dull the pain.

"Yeah, I mean, the guy's gorgeous, right?"

"Mm, yeah, gorgeous." I sigh. "Well, hot enough," I add when she pauses, her lip gloss hovering above her bottom lip.

"So anyway," she continues as she smacks her lips together, "he was seconds from kissing me." She gestures to her face with the lip gloss wand. "His eyes got that *sex* look, you know? Hooded. Stupid hot. Anyway, he leans down, and I grab him by his belt loops." She screws the pink lip gloss back together and deposits it in her clutch purse.

The way Sam watches Reese constantly, I'm not surprised he put the moves on her. I just don't know why he sexed up my ear only to walk off. Still, it's for the best. An actual kiss might have resulted in me punching him in the gut. "And?" I ask, breathless, wanting to live vicariously through her.

Safer for everyone involved.

She shrugs. "And the loser took off. Left me high and dry. I think there's something wrong with him. Fucked-up maybe. Like he's got a tiny dick, or, I don't know, it doesn't work? Anyway, Bruno's been dropping mega-hints. Like constantly. I'm thinking I'll let him seal the deal. Sam might be hot, but there's something seriously off. Don't you think?"

"For sure," I say, strangely relieved they didn't kiss.

She reties the end of her braid. "And Bruno has these great full lips."

My mind is still on Sam, his tall frame leaning over me.

She stamps her foot. "Nina? Are you listening? Doesn't Bruno have amazing lips?"

"Sorry." *Look pensive.* "Yeah, totally. Good lips." This is pretty much my tactic during any and all conversations with Reese. Agree with whatever she says, or ask questions to keep her talking. Say as little as possible.

"And his abs are ripped," she says. "He'd probably be an awesome lay."

Close mouth. Stop eyes from bugging out. "Definitely," I manage.

She spins around. "You don't have a thing for Bruno, do you?"

"Sorry? What?" The minuscule bathroom with its two stalls and tiny sink closes in around me. I replay our one-way conversation and try to figure out where I veered off course.

"A thing for Bruno," she repeats. "You just said he'd be an awesome lay. So, are you into him or not?"

She crosses her arms as I review all standard replies, but I have a sinking feeling this is one of those multiple choice questions I can't possibly get right.

Choice A: "Yes, I'm into Bruno."

Reese: "You total bitch, slut. Keep your skank hands to yourself."

Choice B: "No way, he's not my type."

Reese: "So you're saying I have shit taste? That you're, like, better than me?"

Choice C: "I'm not sure. I mean, he's cute, but…I don't know."

Reese: "Don't fucking lie, Nina. Don't play all innocent then go after him."

I bite my lip, the taste from my cherry lip balm suddenly bitter. She squints harder as the seconds pass.

Backed into a corner, I choose Choice D: all of the above.

"I mean, he's hot enough. For sure. But I don't go for dark hair. And, well…I like taller guys? Wider shoulders? Strong jaw? Bruno's a bit short. I mean, not *too* short. Just, you know, not *that* tall." She narrows her gaze as I ramble on. "Bruno's dark eyes are sexy. Just, like I said, not my thing. My ex (*lie*) has soft brown eyes, lighter in the center with heavy, thick lashes…" *Lie. Lie. Lie.*

She taps her flip-flop. "So you think Sam's hot?"

Shoot. Tall. Wide shoulders. Strong jaw. Gold-flecked brown eyes. I just described One-syllable Sam. "God, no. Like you said, he's super weird." I inch toward the door. "I'm gonna go pick up our food and meet you at the table." I squeeze by her folded arms, trying to ignore the way her lip curls in irritation.

As I wait at the bar for my soup and the girls' three salads, I breathe in and out to the count of three, but it doesn't ease the twisting in my stomach. No matter how hard I try, it seems I can't shed the stench of loser sunk into my pores. Destined to be a moth, never a butterfly. This is no *Cinderella* story. A wave rushes below the extended deck, the push and pull of the water joining the rhythm of the reggae piping through the speakers. The sound lulls my nerves. Some.

"Soup and salads," the waitress calls.

Soup. My comfort food.

My fascination with soup began the year Mom tried to master banana bread. Because the loaves contained fruit, she thought it was okay to make it for dinner. Every night. Thanks to Mom's 0.2 ranking on the I-Can-Cook-O-Meter, each loaf was denser than the next. Like don't-swim-for-five-hours-after-ingestion-or-you-will-sink-like-a-rock dense. Since she refused to order takeout, I took over feeding our family. I made soup and got darn good at it.

I hurry to the table with Leigh's and Reese's salads. Reese smiles with half her face, and Leigh doesn't glance my way.

Callum puts his burger down and swallows. "Need a hand, luv?"

"No, no. I've got it."

He shrugs, swigs his beer, and I return to the bar for my soup and Brianne's pile of lettuce.

"The soup's hot," the waitress warns as I grip the tray with both hands.

The smell of ginger and roasted carrots curls in the rising steam. I take a small step and close my eyes to inhale the yummy scent. Buzzing pricks my ears. My eyes fly open, and I grip the tray tighter as a wasp lands on the edge of the salad.

"I'm hungry," Brianne whines. She twists her pink-tipped hair around her finger.

"Be right there," I say too quietly. But I don't move.

"Seriously, Nina. Hurry up," Reese calls over the music.

My gaze stays locked on the evil insect. I try to speak louder. "Yeah." *Wasp.* "Sure." *Wasp.* "I'll be right there." *Wasp.*

I inch forward, and my soup sloshes in its bowl. The wasp flies off, and it lands on my skirt. *My skirt.* It sits there doing its wasp thing, taunting, terrorizing, letting me know it could possibly, probably, surely sting me at any second, provoked or not.

Frickin' wasp. I want so badly to drop the tray and run from the almighty wasp, but I'm three days incident-free. I'm Nina, not Pininfarina. No scene will be created. I can handle an itty, bitty, teeny, tiny wasp.

Swallowing heavily, I take measured steps. The wasp flies away then lands back on my skirt. Bruno's cackle drifts over, and Reese barks at me again to pick up the goddamn pace. All I keep thinking is *waspwaspwaspwasp.*

The rest is predictable, if you're acquainted with the inevitable horror that is me. The evil-genius wasp takes flight. It circles me once, lazily. Then it flies. UP. MY. SKIRT. An earsplitting yelp escapes my lips. The entire bar stills. I stumble the last steps toward our table and trip over my own feet.

Hot soup. Wasp. Tray. Floor. And...*oh, God.*

Desperate not to spill the food all over the bar, I try to keep the tray level. I do. By some miracle, I do. There's that, at least.

But the rest...

The tray lands upright with me hurtling on top of it at Callum's feet. My left breast, covered in Leigh's nonexistent bikini, lands in the scalding soup. My next scream is louder. Piercing. Instinct takes over. Not logic.

I spring to my feet, knocking Callum and his plastic white chair on the floor. Dying to ease the blistering sensation on my boob, I pull at the bikini top to separate it from my skin. I do this while reaching for any form of liquid. It's hard to say at which precise moment my boob pops out of my bikini top. It could be when I knock Reese's drink on her lap, or when I pour Brianne's cocktail over my aching chest like a girl-gone-wild exhibitionist, or maybe it's when Leigh holds up her phone to capture the moment, a grin the size of Canada stretching her face. Whatever the timing, it happens.

Laughter assaults my ears. Tears prick my eyes.

Someone at my left shouts, "Holy shit, it's *that* girl," and I know right away they've seen the Public Speaking Video. Like I needed this moment to suck more.

I cover my exposed self as quickly as possible, but my alcohol-soaked breast will undoubtedly hit the YouTube circuit in a matter of minutes. The words "fucking freak" hit me in the chest, Reese's voice thick with loathing.

I run to the washroom a sobbing mess as the evil-genius wasp buzzes off, giddy with delight, thrilled it could create mad havoc without so much as a sting.

Seven

SAM

Nothing is going as planned. I should be having a blast, banging chicks and slinging shots. Living it up. Instead, I'm limping around Pahia like a wounded dog, obsessing over the one girl I should forget. *Fucking Nina.* I didn't take this trip to meet a girl like her.

That first night at the hostel, I knew I could have Reese in a second, but Nina was different. Maybe it was the challenge of it. Maybe it was that ass of hers she displayed on the plane, or that hot, glazed look she gets. Whatever the reason, I couldn't let it go. When our eyes met while sitting at the table, colliding for one brief moment, I knew I was done for. Can't say why it was then, at that moment, and not on the plane or by the cab. But right then, my vision went sideways.

I spent most of the night wide awake, stewing. I thought a lot about my folks. They had one of those relationships that had my sister and me groaning in disgust for most of our childhood. They'd touch and kiss and flirt like newlyweds, provoking the usual, "Oh, my God, I'm going blind," from my little sister, Abby, and, "Ugh, get a room," from a horrified me. They'd ignore our dramatic efforts to curb their PDA, and we'd pretend we didn't secretly think it was awesome.

As I got older, I paid more attention to my friends' parents. If they hadn't divorced already, most couples were careful around each other at best. Practiced. None of the soft touches or intimate moments my folks shared. Until the accident.

All it took was one drunk driver to ruin my legs and take Mom from us forever. I miss her. So much it hurts. My throat still closes at the briefest memory, the pressure in my chest suffocating. She came to every football game, sent me care packages at college to make sure I was eating right, and gave me shit to keep my ass in line. Drove me nuts at times with her nagging, but I knew she loved Abby and me.

Yeah, I miss her so much it's painful, but Dad is destroyed. Obliterated. The man I looked up to who ran his own business, organized poker nights with his buddies, golfed, mountain biked, fished, and loved and disciplined his kids with equal measure, can barely get himself dressed these days. It was one thing to lose my mom, but to watch my father drown in grief? Love isn't worth that. Nothing's worth living like a corpse.

When my eyes met Nina's that night in the hostel, Dad's words rang in my ears. It was a few months after the accident. I was opening curtains and turning on lights at three in the afternoon. Dad rolled over in bed and faced me, fresh tears threatening to fall. "The first day I met her," he said, his voice hoarse and scratchy. "The first day, I knew. One look and she stole my breath."

She stole my breath. *Fucking Nina.* The world stopped on its axis when her green eyes locked on mine. This wasn't part of my traveling plan. For a guy who grew up laughing, pulling pranks, and generally fucking around, I am seriously uncomfortable with the amount of feelings boiling inside me these days. I've gone from tough to sensitive, carefree to agitated, walking a constant tightrope of emotion. This trip is about escape, about rediscovering the old me. Getting laid on the fly is a big part of that.

Then I had to meet Nina.

Every movement she makes turns me on, but something deeper snapped between us that first night. *Not* what I'm after. I want easy, light, and fun. Preferably in the dark. Lacey's rejection when she saw my burned legs was enough, thanks.

For three days, I ignored Nina as best I could. I worked on Reese. I focused on Reese. I didn't look at those damn green eyes. Reese is easy, predictable. No strings, no fallout. A quick lay. I tried. Fuck, did I try. But when I leaned down to kiss her, I couldn't do it. Nina's lust-filled gaze loomed large in my mind, and all I saw in Reese's mascara-drenched eyes was vanity, like I was a conquest. A story to be retold. Instead of getting laid, I limped off.

Maybe the accident messed up more than my legs.

That skimpy-ass bikini was the last straw, and when Nina fell against me, it sent me over the edge. I needed to touch her, taste her. See nothing but desire on a woman's face. The old Sam would be able to fuck around with her for a week or two and move on. Somewhere under all this emotional bull-shit, I'm still that guy, scarred legs or not. So now I'm here, waiting for the girl who stole my breath, because I pussied out instead of letting her see me in shorts at the beach next to Callum and Bruno.

The green Kiwi Experience bus pulls up to the hostel, gravel crunching under its weight. I stand from the bench I've been lounging on and shield my eyes from the billowing dust. The door hisses open. Reese stumbles out, Bruno behind her. He tugs her hips until she falls against his chest. *He can have her.* Callum follows next, then Brianne and Leigh. I step forward, craning my neck, but there's no red ponytail.

Bruno waves at me as he moves to Reese's side and drapes his arm over her shoulder. "Sam, you missed a helluva day, mate."

"Fun?" I ask, still glancing past his shoulders. Another girl exits the bus…but still no Nina.

They stop in front of me. Reese presses into Bruno's side, her free hand resting on his stomach. "Seriously, Sam," she says. "It was the lunch to end all lunches. Fucking hilarious."

Callum, Brianne, and Leigh have joined us, the three girls sharing excited looks like they found dirty celebrity photos. Leigh, in particular, looks ready to burst, her lips pulled tight to keep from smiling.

I frown at the lot of them. "Lunch is lunch. I thought you were hitting the sand dunes and Ninety Mile Beach?" The bus doors are still open, but no one else hops off. Knowing Nina, she probably dumped her stuff on the floor and is busy picking it up.

"*Oh, my God,* you didn't hear?" Brianne asks, her high-pitched, nasal voice making me wince.

Again with the shared looks, the girls giggling outright. Callum shakes his head, his shoulders bouncing with a light laugh. When Reese whispers in Bruno's ear, that mad sound explodes from his mouth.

My jaw ticks with irritation. "No, Brianne, I didn't hear. The magic grapevine between Cape Reinga and Pahia must've broken down. Maybe one of you'd like to share what the hell is so funny." My impatience is fueled by the sudden churning in my gut. More secretive glances pass through the group.

They seem hesitant to speak up, until Leigh tosses me her phone. "You have to see it to believe it."

I catch the phone as the bus door closes. That churning settles into something heavier—solid foreboding. "Where's Nina?" I ask, but the only answer I get is a snort from Leigh. "Where. Is. Nina?" I ask again.

This time a hysterical laugh comes from Reese. Brianne and Leigh lose it, too, all three of them walking in circles to catch their breath. "Look," Reese says with her hand on her mouth to stifle her giggles. "You just have to watch the video. I could try to explain it, but… *God*, you'd never believe me. Honestly. You can't script this stuff. It's epic. I mean, Nina's a little odd. Strange, I guess? But seriously, watch the video."

I grip Leigh's phone, almost crushing the thing. This can't be good. With a deep inhale, I press play on the screen.

It's worse than I imagined. I barely register Nina's exposed breast. All I see is the way her chin trembles and her eyes well up. There was a time when I would've laughed along with this group of insensitive bastards. Instead, I want to wrap Nina in my arms and shield her.

My head flies up. "Where is she?" At my tone, the humor dissolves from their faces.

Reese shrugs. "She left."

Straightening to my full height, I step up to Queen Bee and lean into her space. "Be specific."

Bruno frowns and tugs Reese back. Callum puts his hand on my chest. "Cool it, mate. Nina ran to the loo right after. The waitress came by to tell us she got a lift to the hostel. She took off."

I clench my jaw so tight my teeth hurt. "Let me get this straight. Not one of you went to check on her when she bailed, and you let her hitch a ride on her own. Is that what I'm to understand?"

Callum presses harder on my chest. "Back off, Sam. Nina's a big girl. She can take care of herself."

Leigh's still grinning, Reese is smug as hell as she pops a stick of pink gum in her mouth, Brianne twirls her hair, and the guys are all up in my face. "Assholes," I mutter. I toss Leigh's phone on the ground and head for the hostel, ignoring their "Oh, my God" and "What a dick" as I force my leg to move faster.

I practically rip the door from its hinges as I barge inside. I slam my hand on the bell at the front desk.

A young guy saunters out front and yawns into his elbow. "What can I do for ya?"

I grip the counter. "Redhead. Green eyes. Probably a ponytail—Nina something. Have you seen her?"

"Oh, yeah, sure. Kinda hard to forget that one, aye?" He wiggles his eyebrows.

Fucking horndog. "Is she in her dorm?"

"Dorm? Nah. She caught a lift, like, I don't know, twenty

minutes ago? Was hangin' here with her backpack, lookin' for someone goin' south to Rotorua. A couple was drivin' as far as Waipu. Coastal town about an hour and a half south. Your girl hitched a ride. I stayed with her 'til she left, you know, hopin' she might stick around." Again with the eyebrows. "But no luck. She seemed like a nervous wreck."

"Thanks," I call, already on my way to the dorm.

I shove my crap in my pack, head to my car, and peel out as fast as this relic of a ride will allow.

* * *

On the drive to Waipu, I alternate between cursing Reese, Brianne, and Leigh for humiliating Nina further with that video, wishing I hadn't been such a pussy and *had* gone to the beach, and wondering why the fuck I'm driving in New Zealand, chasing after some random chick.

If it were just because I'm hard up and can't get enough of Nina's seductive looks, I'd be checking myself into Crazy Town. But I feel secure in saying it's all my grandfather's fault. Dad lectures me regularly to take care of my sister and look out for girls in general, but Pops has a special way with words:

"Women are a gift. You abuse that gift, and your balls are mine."

"If a girl's in trouble and you don't help, I will skin you, boy."

And my personal favorite: *"Look out for the ladies, or I will tear you a new asshole."*

Lessons from the great Larry Cannon.

My sister, Abby, is on the flighty side, her feet going one way, her head in the clouds drifting somewhere else, and I always look out for her. Nina's level of accident-prone is Abby to the tenth power. If Pops knew I let her travel on her own, he'd be up my ass so fast I wouldn't be able to sit for a month.

I value my ass.

When I pass the sign into Waipu, I scan the one-horse town, hoping Nina's ride took at least one scenic stop along the way and didn't drive as surprisingly fast as this tin can allowed. The thing shook and rattled whenever the needle hit eighty, but it didn't overheat.

The main street is quiet, dotted with wooden storefronts and the odd person carrying a shopping bag. A boy rides by on his bike, his dog beside him with its tongue lolling while it keeps time. When I pass a girl bent over ninety degrees under the weight of her bags, I blow out a breath, relieved. Nina's blue pack is hitched on her back, her smaller one hooked over the front of her shoulders and cradled against her chest. Her chest that is probably sore as hell.

I pull over to the side, releasing my seat belt and shoving the door in one swift motion. My first few steps are awkward, my foot dragging the way it does, but I recover quickly and stop in front of her prone shape. "You must really have a thing for sidewalks," I say.

I hear, "Shoot," and some mumbling, but she doesn't stand up. "Yeah, well, you know me," she says to my feet. "Love the asphalt." She tilts her head to peer up at me. "What are you doing here, Sam?"

Being this close, I can tell she's holding her front pack away from her chest, which is probably why she's doubled over and walking like the Creature from the Black Lagoon. I move behind her and bend toward her ear. "I'll answer your question when I get these packs off your shoulders. Deal?" I can practically hear her thinking as she scrunches her face in that adorable way of hers.

Finally, she groans. "Deal."

She shimmies the front pack over her arms and lets it fall to the ground. I reach around her shoulders to find the clasp at her chest and unclick it while she undoes her waist strap. The dick I am, I let my thumbs graze her neckline to touch her smooth skin again. A soft puff escapes her lips.

Grabbing the pack from behind, I ease if off and drop it at my feet. "Better?" I ask.

She arches her back and rolls her shoulders. "Much, thanks." She swings her torso from side to side like she's doing an exercise video. When she's done, she cocks her head. "I get why you ended up at the first hostel. A strange coincidence, but I get it. But this?" She motions to me and to my car. "This is creepy. Did you follow me?"

I run my hand along my neck, glancing away, then back at her. "Truth?"

"Truth."

"Yeah, so, my grandfather has this thing about women. I won't get into it. He's a little chauvinistic to say the least. But if he knew I let a girl like you travel on her own, he'd string me up by my balls."

Her eyes widen then fall heavy as her gaze dips down my body, landing squarely below my waist. "Sounds painful," she murmurs. Her tongue darts out to wet her lips.

My dick lengthens automatically.

I'm a teenager all over again when I'm around this girl, those eyes, and that damn look. I grab her smaller pack and hold it just so, making sure I block my growing hard-on. "Seriously painful," I say. "No one messes with my pops." *God, I want to jump her.* The taste I stole earlier has only heightened my attraction. "Anyway, when I heard you left and where you were headed…" I exhale, wishing I didn't sound like such a douchey stalker. "I decided to look for you."

With her view now blocked by my strategic placement of her bag, she looks up at my face, crosses her arms, and grips her elbows. "Okay, that's maybe a little less weird. *Maybe.* But what did you mean, just now—a girl like me?"

To avoid embarrassing her further by reliving the boob-flashing thing, I tread lightly. "Look, I heard what happened at lunch today, and we both know about the plane incident." Remembering the vision of her tight ass, I glance down at her skirt. She blushes all the way to her neck, and I step closer. "I'm going out on a limb here and guessing this stuff, these accidents? They're not exactly new for you. This is kind of who you are?"

Still flushed, she bites her lip, shrugs, and knocks her knees together. "You could say that."

"Don't sweat it. Shit happens. To all of us. Some more than others, maybe." I nudge her shoulder, and her lip curves up. Slightly. My protective instincts from earlier come back, this time in the form of wanting to erase her frown lines. "It just seems like the safest thing for you, and for all of New Zealand, is to not let you travel on your own. I mean, what if you sank the country? Or worse, blinded the millions of sheep with your flagrant display of body parts? How could I live with myself?"

She rolls her eyes and fights the smile tugging at her lips. "That's quite the sales pitch. But…what are you suggesting?"

"Travel with me." I wasn't planning this. Any of it. I just needed to get to her and make sure she was okay. With the words out, I know it's what I want. I need to see those bedroom eyes again. Touch her bare back. *Again.* We can travel together for a couple of weeks, hopefully get down and dirty and then I'll take off.

"Sorry?" She swallows heavily. "*With* you?"

"Yeah, with me. You and me in my sweet ride, touring the country." She squints at my recently purchased rusted red station wagon. "Don't look at her like that," I say, motioning to the car. "I bet she's been through a lot in her life."

She hums to herself and chews her lip, but she doesn't speak. Getting her to travel with me might not be so easy. But I can't walk away. I chased her across New Zealand, for Christ's sake. I'm addicted to her sexy-as-hell glances.

I dip my head to meet her eyes. "So, Nina? What do you say? We can try to sell off your Kiwi bus pass. I mean, I know we've hung out a bit, but I don't think you get how truly awesome I am. I'm a blast to travel with. Like if there was a show called *Traveling New Zealand with the World's Coolest Travel Partner*, I'd star in every episode."

She leans back, sizing me up. "Then why does it feel like I'll be starring in the made-for-TV movie: *The Disappearance of Nina Gabri*?"

Verbal chess matches are usually reserved for my buddies, but she has me thinking on my feet. I nod thoughtfully. "Oh, okay. I get you. It's the weird I-chased-you-across-the-country thing.

That's fine. On second thought, I don't think you should consider getting in that car with me. And you definitely shouldn't think about how much fun we'd have driving around in my fine automobile."

"Reverse psychology? Really? I have five younger siblings, Sam. I am the reigning queen of reverse psychology. What's your next tactic?"

"Wow." I scratch my head. "That's it. That's all I've got. Usually I smile, and the girls hack off their own limbs to fit in the trunk."

I smirk, she smirks, and my dick nudges my jeans.

I have to get her in that car.

She frowns again, scanning the street as if she wants to get away. Jesus, I've creeped her out. For sure she thinks I'm a psycho dude who'll take advantage of her first chance I get. When she reaches for her bag again, something aches in my chest. Like I need to be near her to make it stop. I say the first thing that comes to mind to keep her from leaving. "I have a girlfriend."

"Girlfriend?"

Girlfriend? Why the hell did I say that? "Yeah, I have a girlfriend…Lacey. So, you know, you don't have to worry about me looking to get into your pants." *Classy, dude. Classy.* I cringe.

My chest is still tight, and the idea of her walking off is worse than knowing I'll have to travel with this pinup girl and not be able to touch her. Not since I have a "girlfriend."

She drags her teeth over her lip again, apparently weighing the pros and cons of traveling on her own versus being abducted, raped, and killed by me. The odds are not in my favor.

She lifts her chin, frowning. "But earlier in Pahia…on the sidewalk…"

Right. *Pahia*. Me molesting her on the street. As her voice trails off and her cheeks flush, I jump in to save her. "Sorry about that. Don't know what came over me. Things are strained with Lacey and me, which isn't an excuse, but, yeah, she's my girlfriend. And anyway, I blame the bikini."

That gets her smiling, and she tilts her head. "Do you have a picture?"

"Picture of what?"

"This girlfriend of yours."

Fuck. "Sure," I say quickly. I fish my phone from my back pocket and thumb through my photos. It's not hard to find one of Lacey. Half the images are of us. I settle on one of her long blond hair spilling over my shoulder as she kisses my cheek.

We'd just opened our acceptance letters, both of us getting into Florida State University. It doesn't hurt to look at our happy faces. Never did, really. Not even after she dumped my ass. I knew Lacey and I were convenient: the football jock and the cheerleader, prom king and queen. I loved her—at least I think I did—but I knew it wasn't a deep love like my folks had. It was fun, light. A love based on who we thought we should be and who I was at the time. Come to think of it, the courses I was taking and the direction my life was headed, that stuff belonged to another dude, too. It's like I woke up in that hospital a different guy.

Looking at us now on the screen is no different than seeing those smiling couples in store-bought picture frames. Strangers. No part of me would ever hook back up with Lacey. When it got hard, when it mattered, she walked out of my life.

I tilt the screen toward Nina, and she nods to herself as if I've confirmed something she'd been thinking. "She's beautiful. That's a great shot." Her voice is soft, and she looks away.

I die a little inside at her expression: flat. Withdrawn. Her disappointment plain to see. She wears her emotions openly, even when trying too hard with girls like Reese. She has no mask, no façade. Was she hoping I was single? Or is it just lust that blankets her face from time to time? There's no doubt she has *me* twisted in knots. She turns me on to the point it's hard to walk; I have this need to be near her, to make sure she's okay, but the last thing I want, now or probably ever, is to get in deep with a girl. Even thinking the word *need* has me picturing my father staring out the window, catatonic.

Either way, this lie of mine is planted and will grow between us every second it exists. I'm pretty sure I didn't say it for her benefit, though. To make her feel safe. I flash to Lacey cringing at the sight of my legs.

I said it to protect myself.

Eight

NINA

I slide into the front seat and close the door as Sam puts my bags in the trunk. In a daze, I grab the seat belt and give it a yank, but it barely moves. I tug the thing several times with no luck and finally slouch, still clutching the fabric. I'm in One-syllable Sam's car. Traveling with him. In New Zealand. *Him*—the guy who saw my privates. The one who kissed my ear. The same one who followed me from Pahia like a total stalker. And who has a gorgeous girlfriend.

The whole girlfriend thing has thrown me for a loop. I mean, what boyfriend makes moves on Reese and me only to claim his relationship is "strained"? There's something about Sam, though. An underlying sadness. The chivalrous way he chased me down to make sure I'm okay. His excessive hotness. *Definitely* the hotness. Now I'm in the guy's car.

I wish I could trade my mother in for one of those stern models whose voice of reason would ring in my head, warning me of my inevitable fate in a frozen meat locker. If I texted Mom that some random guy talked me into his car, she'd urge me to trust my inner goddess. "If it feels right," she'd say, "go with your instinct." If I lived by Mom's code, my inner goddess would be having a panic attack, knowing this is the Guinness record of bad decisions.

Sam opens his door and slides into the driver's seat as I yank the seat belt again. It moves but jams midchest. *Shit.* "Sugar," I hiss.

He freezes, his arm reaching to shut his door, and he snorts dramatically. He pulls the door shut and faces me. "Before we hit the road, we need to clarify what just came out of your mouth."

"Sorry, what?" He has my mind so muddled, I can't even remember speaking. I tug on the belt some more, but it doesn't budge.

He shifts toward me, one hand resting on his armrest, the other on the steering wheel. "I'm pretty sure the word 'sugar' just passed those lips of yours in some sort of adorable curse. Is that a fair assumption?"

Frickin' perfect. I'm so used to not swearing, I don't even notice when I word-vomit stuff like "sugar." My dork status just tipped the dork scale.

He cocks his head and studies me. "Explain yourself, Canada. Don't make me regret these travel arrangements."

That smirk on his face is infectious, and I find myself smiling with him. To explain what I said would mean I have to talk about my family, which is something I rarely do. Growing up, I never invited friends (my one former friend) over to witness the oddities in my house. If my clumsy self didn't send people running for the hills, Dad's tendency to hoard, Mom's always smoking oven, and their need to dance around to hippie music semi-clothed would surely do the trick.

I tighten my hands around the still-stuck seat belt, squeezing like it's a security blanket. I shrug with a tight laugh. "I told you I have five younger siblings, right?" He nods. "Well, I try not to swear in front of them. You know, to keep it clean. Old habits die hard."

His eyes roam my face. "Cool. I get that. And it's fucking adorable. Shit. *Shit.* Sorry. Do we have to make the car a swear-free zone?"

"No. God, it's not like that. I don't have a problem with swearing, I'm just so used to *not* doing it." I release one hand from the seat belt and wave it in the air. "Let the obscenities fly."

Scrunching his face, he throws his hands rapper-style. "Fuck, bitch, that's some motherfucking kick-ass skirt." Then he winks.

A yelp bursts from my mouth. I laugh, tipping forward into the seat belt, holding onto the thing for dear life.

He leans toward me, looking sheepish. "Was that too much?"

I hold my thumb and finger an inch apart. "A tad," I say, the remaining giggles still heating my face.

"Anyway," he says, "I think it's cool you look out for your siblings. I'm sure your folks appreciate it."

I snort. My free-loving, pot-smoking parents couldn't care less if I swear like a gangster. That's probably why I play the role of housemother. When I'm home, I'm the cook and cleaner, the chauffeur to all after-school programs. I'm the responsible one.

At home, I've got it together. In the real world, not so much. It's one of the reasons taking off on this trip felt so good. Like I'm finally acting my age.

I release the seat belt, and it slithers into its home. I smooth the creases on my skirt. "My parents are…on the eccentric side. The not-swearing is my thing, not theirs." I don't know why I'm discussing my family. After the sexiness that happened earlier, I should be embarrassed and awkward around Sam, but something about him puts me at ease. And it's nice to talk about them, instead of trying to avoid the subject as usual.

He shrugs. "Aren't all parents weird? I think everyone goes through one of those my-parents-embarrass-the-shit-out-of-me phases. I know I did." His voice drops an octave, his gaze turning out the window.

He seems weighted all of a sudden, heavy, our light conversation taking a different turn. The need to erase whatever is troubling him overtakes me. I don't know much about Sam, but it's clear he has a sense of humor. It's likely the best way to get his attention away from whatever is weighing on him. "Sure, all parents are, like, *parents*, but do you know any who accidentally used their stash of weed instead of oregano when making spaghetti sauce for their kids?"

His head snaps to me, a wide grin softening his face. "You're shitting me, right?"

"*Messing* with you? I would never. That's the night I choreographed my infamous 'Age of Aquarius' number. I won a Tony the following year at our annual family award ceremony—lip-synching is a thing in my house. Still think I went through a typical my-parents-embarrass-the-*you-know*-out-of-me phase?" I can't believe I admitted that. Sure, watching my siblings and me swaying like seaweed to the sixties song is hilarious for my family. But to an outsider? I must have a death wish in the form of social suicide. But Sam grins so wide, I can't regret one single word. *I made Sam smile.*

He smacks his forehead with the heel of his hand. "Canada, that's the best story ever. This is gonna be one hell of a trip. I need one messed-up family story every hour on the hour. That's instead of paying for gas. Let me help you with your seat belt."

He leans over me and grabs the buckle, that chest of his brushing the tender flesh of my recently scorched breast. I flinch and sink against the seat, the Hot Soup Incident suddenly all I can think about. The whole ride from Pahia, I was on the verge of tears. How stupid of me to think this trip would magically change me from a walking disaster to a normal nineteen-year-old. I don't do normal. I doubt I ever will.

"Sorry," he says, pulling back. He looks at my chest, then at my face.

Right. He *heard* about the incident. I bite my bottom lip to stop it from trembling. All I want to do now is get out of this car and travel solo. I shouldn't have caved at the sight of him. I should have stood my ground and walked off. On my own. Does saying he *heard* about the incident mean he *saw* the incident? It's probably crisscrossed the world on networks and data bytes invading every electrical device operable. How can I sit here next to him if he saw that video?

He releases the buckle and wraps his large hand over mine, my fingers fisted at my side. "You okay, Nina?"

I turn my head away and watch an empty garbage bag blow

down the street, surging up and down with the wind. "Did you see it?" I ask quietly.

"See what?"

The warmth builds between his hand and mine, making me light-headed. "The video of, you know—*me*. At lunch." The bag spirals now, stuck in an air current.

"Yeah, I saw it." His voice is a whisper, his hand leaving mine and coming to rest on the dip between my neck and shoulder. I've never had a guy touch me like this, with affection. He glides his thumb over my skin. Each stroke makes me ache to lean into his arms and bury my face in his shirt. This isn't the same as my over-the-top fantasies. There's no porno sound track. This is me wanting to find relief from my embarrassment in his soothing arms.

"Screw them," Sam says, his voice suddenly closer, a slight edge to his words. "They're not worth your time. You're traveling with me now. The world's coolest traveling partner." The edge to his tone is gone, replaced with tenderness.

My lips tremble more. Where was this guy when I could barely go out in public for fear of being recognized? And still, here in New Zealand, some idiot can spot me, exposed breast and all, reminding me I'll never escape the stigma of who I am. I keep my focus on the plastic bag so small in the distance I can barely make out its shape.

"I promise to do my best to keep you out of trouble," he continues, "but if it finds you, and odds are from your track record it will, I swear I won't memorialize it with my cell phone. I might laugh *with* you, but I won't laugh at you."

Now I really want to press my face into his shirt, and my porno music is back on. Full volume. It doesn't seem humanly possible to be that sexy and caring and know exactly what to say. If he didn't have a girlfriend, I might actually try to conquer my androphobia.

When I turn to thank him for talking me off the ledge, my breath hitches. So focused on that plastic bag, I didn't realize how close his face was. *Is.* Holy heck, do I want to kiss his lips, jaw, neck. All of him. At once. My eyes drag up his features and finally *crash* into his. My brain practically detaches from the whiplash. My motor skills cease. The intensity of his darkening stare has heat pooling between my thighs at an alarming rate. This is like the fireworks earlier, but on steroids.

And this guy has a *girlfriend*.

That's all it takes to break my trance, but there's no subtlety in the breaking. As I swivel away, I simultaneously elbow him in the ribs and smack my head into the window. He's no smoother. He jerks into the steering wheel, a piercing honk ringing for several seconds.

"Okay then," he says as he fumbles with his keys. "It's off on the open road. Just the two of us. Together. In New Zealand." He inhales deeply and looks at me as he turns on the ignition. "I was serious about the stories, Canada. One epic family tale for every hour in this car, or you can hitch your own way."

I rub my head, smirking. "Fine." But I'm still flushed from whatever just happened between us.

* * *

The four-hour ride to Rotorua is exactly as Sam promised it would be: fun. Fun enough to put the Hot Soup Incident out of my head. I've had years to perfect that particular skill. I am the founder and CEO of Repressed Memories, Inc., the Public Speaking Incident being the catalyst to form said company.

With all such incidents buried in my subconscious, I'm able to enjoy my time with Sam. Comfortable silences weave seamlessly with our sarcastic jousting, each of us trying to crack the other up. He's winning. The clincher was his Bruno impression. He nailed the guy's mad laugh.

So far, this is way better than sitting on a bus next to Reese, worrying over every gesture and chosen word. With Sam, things are easy. Easy, except when I envision my hands sliding down his chest to gain access to his fly. Easy, except for the quiet moments I catch myself staring at his profile as I overanalyze that intense look we shared. And I do mean *shared*. The way he slammed against the horn and got all flustered, I'd say he felt it, too.

One-syllable Sam, who has a girlfriend.

As requested, each hour is punctuated with a drum roll from him and a confession from me—one of my ridiculous childhood stories retold for his amusement. If I'm honest, mine, too. Usually, I'm so mortified by the eccentricities of my family I tiptoe around the subject. When Sam laughs, though, it doesn't feel like it's at my expense. The sound is deep, warm, and heartfelt, and it curls around me. It's fun laughing with someone about how nuts, yet awesome, my folks are. So I keep talking.

Come to think of it, we've spent the whole drive joking about my family and me, barely touching on all things Sam. Aside from the fact that he's from Florida and has a younger sister my age who is, and I quote, "A little out there, but not as accident-prone as you, Canada," he's steered our conversation away from himself at every chance.

It's dark when we roll into Rotorua, just after nine. Sam pulls up to the hostel we chose from his guidebook, and we shove our doors open. The metal creaks, my joints mimicking the sound as I unfold my body into an upright position. Sam reaches his arms above his head on the other side of the car, stretching from side to side. I get to the trunk first. His left leg drags more noticeably after sitting so long.

When he gets to the back, I lean on the car. "What's with the limp? If you don't mind me asking. I heard you say something to Callum about a football injury."

A few streetlights illuminate his face while he jams his foot into the pavement, each kick grinding against loose gravel. He does that thing I've noticed where he rubs the scar on his chin before he directs the conversation away from himself. Reading the signs, I shrug. "Sorry, forget I asked." I turn at the sound of laughter drifting through the hostel window.

"That's bullshit," he says, and I swivel back. "What I said to Callum," he continues. "It wasn't a sports thing. It was a car accident." He studies his feet, his injured foot still scrubbing the asphalt.

My heart squeezes at his confession. "I'm sorry, Sam. It must've been pretty bad to mess up your leg like that."

"Yeah, pretty bad," he says, still focused on the pavement. The veins twitch on his forearms as he fists his hands, the dusky light casting shadows. His jaw ticks mercilessly.

It doesn't take a genius to realize he doesn't want to talk about this. He lied to Callum about it, which means it was more than a little fender bender, something too personal or painful to relive. I touch his arm as another chorus of laughter floats from the hostel. "Seriously. I'm sorry I brought it up. I'll run inside to make sure they have room before we unload the bags."

Two steps away, he says, "It was just over a year ago."

I stop in my tracks, pulled by the sadness in his voice. Sam's laugh is infectious, one of those belly laughs that can't possibly be faked. But this? His tone alone could strike the smile from a clown. Unsure what to expect, I turn hesitantly. His eyes are still downcast, his brow pulled tight in a frown, but he must want to talk or he wouldn't have said anything. Instead of walking to the car, I sit on the curb with my knees tucked to my chest. He frowns harder.

He drags his hands down his face and settles onto the bumper of the car. "It was August twenty-eighth. My mother was driving me back for my third year at FSU. Sunny day. Middle of the day. All it took was one drunk driver. My ankle got banged up and Mom, well…" He rubs his palms on his jeans. "She didn't make it."

My hand flies to my mouth. "God, I'm so sorry." I want to jump up and wrap my arms around him, but I stay where I am. I don't know him that well, don't know why he opened up like he did. I'm wary of overstepping my bounds. There's some sort of connection between us, though, an unknown thing that fuels the electricity when our eyes lock. The same thing that allows me to relax in his presence and allows him to open up to me. I want to go to him; I'm just not sure I should.

Saving me from making a decision, he sits at my side. He unfurls his long legs in front of him and folds his arms. "Sorry," he says.

The tightness in his face is hard to look at. "Sorry? Why are you apologizing? I'm usually the one that does all the apologizing." *Smile, smile. Please smile.*

He laughs despite himself. "Yeah, you do say sorry a lot, Canada."

"Yeah, sorry," I say. We both grin, and I exhale.

A kid pushes by us on the street, his skateboard rocking over the uneven road.

"I don't know why I told you that," Sam says, his good humor fading. "I don't talk about it much. Sometimes the not talking is harder, though. Suffocating." He rubs his temples. "My head's all fucked-up these days."

"That's why you took off traveling, then? To get away for a while?"

He nods. "My dad's been a mess ever since. I've been taking care of him and my sister. She left for college this year, and he's getting better. He's not the guy he was, not even close, but he's getting out of bed on his own now. My uncle pushed me to go and do something for myself, promising he'd watch out for my family. So I took him up on the offer. I had an appointment with a doctor in Toronto." He flicks his head toward his legs. "Another possible surgery to fix the limp, but it doesn't look like it'll help. I booked my flight there, bought a used pack…that no longer has a Canadian flag,"—he nudges me—"and now I'm here, traveling with you."

He doesn't even try to blink his tears away, and my heart breaks for him. I may joke about how insane my parents are, but my mother is and always has been my best friend—the only person I trust unconditionally. If I lost her, I don't think I'd recover.

He leans back and squeezes his eyes shut. With a shake of his head, he sucks a breath and exhales, his shoulders lowering with the movement. "I maybe should've had you sign a disclaimer or something before forcing you in the car. You sure you still want to travel with this fucked-up guy across New Zealand?"

Hooking up with the Trifecta of Cool didn't work out for me, not the way I'd intended. It only took three days until I sprouted my third head. I'm not sure I'll be any less freakish with Sam, but I trust him when he says he won't laugh *at* me. I shrug like I don't care. "Now that you mention it, *Florida*, maybe we should call it off. I am, after all, pretty together. Wouldn't want you spoiling my stellar reputation as a well-rounded, accident-avoiding, normal girl."

A deep chuckle moves through his chest, and the sound travels up my spine. "Excellent point, Canada. So we're a fucked-up guy and disaster-magnet girl ready to take on a country with more sheep than people." He nods decisively. "Yeah, we got this."

I nudge him with my shoulder. "Thanks for telling me, though. It's nice to get to know you better, even under the circumstances."

As I'm about to stand, a gust of wind blows down the street, on it the unmistakable smell of rotting eggs. Not the passing-wind variety. The kind of stink that simmers in filth until it's a thick, bubbling mess. The kind that coats every follicle in your nose. My knees slam together, my arms pulled to my sides. "Osmophobia," I squeak, my eyes darting wildly.

He looks at me like I sprouted that third head. "Osmo-*what*? Are you some weird medium, like those people who can speak unknown languages with ghosts?" He glances around nervously.

"Is there…" He drops his voice. "Is there one behind me now?"

I elbow him in the arm. "No. It's just, I have this *thing*." Here I go getting stranger by the second, Pininfarina back to claim her rightful throne. For four hours I was halfway normal. Now it's a resounding, *not*.

"Thing? You have a thing? Like what kind of thing are we talking here?" He leans forward to catch my eyes. I glance away sharply while twitching my nose to shake that god-awful stench still lingering in the air. He takes that as his cue to keep needling me. "If by 'thing' you mean you play word games in your head and shout out random syllables, I can live with that. You know, still travel with you. But if your eyes roll in your head while you chant out psychobabble, we might have to cut our ties."

"Honestly, Sam. You're ridiculous."

"*I'm* ridiculous? Which one of us is shouting out random verbiage?" When I groan and roll my eyes, he shakes his head. "Okay, fine. I can handle the silent treatment. But riddle me this, Canada. How is it you were able to spend four hours with me confessing all sorts of hilarious, yet embarrassing, shit about your family, but you shut down when asked a simple question? So let's try this again. What's with the word choice?"

"You're *relentless*." I try to dirty-look him, but I'm pretty sure I'm making my angry-old-lady face. "Fine, just promise you won't laugh."

"No."

"What do you mean no?"

"No, as in I can't promise not to laugh."

"Seriously? Why would I tell you now?"

"Because what I said before still stands. I'll never laugh *at* you, but if the occasion calls for it, I'll laugh *with* you. So, like I said, no promises."

"You're infuriating."

"Yeah, I've heard that before." He scoots an inch closer, his elbow pressed to my arm. "We're not leaving this spot until you open that pretty mouth of yours and give me the dirt on your *thing*."

This guy has already witnessed three I-can't-be-from-this-planet incidents, and he knows about my family's uniqueness. Why not add another quirk to my growing pile of peculiarities? Why quit while I'm ahead? "Okay. Fine." I groan as I press the heels of my hands into the cement curb. I really am a total freak. "I have this *thing*," I say and pause, digging my palms harder into the curb, "where, like, I don't know…I kind of list my phobias. Like the ones that prevent me from acting normal."

He dislodges a tube of mints from his front pocket, pops one in his mouth, and tilts the pack toward me. I shake my head, still pressing my hands into the sharp little rocks on the curb until they're embedded in my skin. He rolls his mint around and finally says, "So this is your *thing*?"

"God, yes. It's my *thing*."

The mint clinks against his teeth a couple of times as he sucks on it. "Do you have an actual list? Is it written somewhere? Can I read it?" When I growl and knock him over on his side, he laughs and rights himself. "I'm fucking with you, Nina. Let's back up to the actual phobia you blurted out. What's osmophobia?"

This keeps getting better. First I have to confess to my lame list of phobias, now we get to dissect them. I could jump up and leave, thanking him for the ride and wishing him safe travels, but this is the guy who chased me to Waipu to make sure I was okay. The same one who knew just what to say to ease my embarrassment about the Hot Soup Incident. The one who shared with me the deeply personal fact that his mother died. I lift my hands and pick off the tiny shards stuck to my skin. "Fear of smells," I say, my focus on my palms. "I mean, it can't just be *me*, right? You did smell the waft of stink that blew past us?"

He slaps his knee and chuckles. "Right. We're in Rotorua." He looks at me like that should explain everything, but it explains nothing. I roll my hand as if to say, carry on. "*Rotorua*," he says emphatically. "Didn't you read up on New Zealand before you left?" I shake my head, and he frowns. "Anyway, Rotorua is sometimes called the Sulfur City. This place is like a geothermal hotbed with geysers and mud baths. You really didn't read a guidebook or anything before you booked your ticket?"

I brush the remaining dirt from my hands on my skirt. "I kind of left in a rush."

He pulls back to study me. "Define rush."

"Rushed like, I packed a bag, took a cab, and threw a dart at the departure board to choose my destination. Metaphorically, of course. There wasn't like an actual dart."

"Thanks for clarifying that. I'm pretty sure if it were an actual dart you'd still be sitting in a windowless room at the airport being grilled under hot lights after a week of no sleep. Back to this sudden departure of yours—did it have something to do with your tendency to invite disaster?"

I didn't realize I was this transparent. Or maybe it's Sam. He seems able to read me so easily. As much as I hate talking about this stuff, it's nice to have someone to confide in besides my mother. "Something? More like everything. Let's just say I thought university would be a fresh start. A brand new me. It was anything but." I grab the lip balm from my purse, his gaze seeming to follow the movement as I apply a layer. "Actually," I add, "probably not everything." I snap the cap back on, press my lips together, and put the balm away. "I have no idea what I want to do, you know, career-wise. I registered for U of T because it's the way of things: school, university, job, married, two-point-five kids." I shrug. "I didn't put much thought into it at the time, and it seemed pointless without any direction."

He stares at me so hard, I look down. He clears his throat. "Yeah, I get that. I delayed going back to school this year for the same reason. Rethinking my career path." After a beat, he jerks his head away, slaps his hands together, and holds them up to the sky. "Well, Canada, today is your lucky day. Know why?" When I roll my eyes for what feels like the millionth time, he lowers his lips to my ear. "Because you and I are gonna forget all that future crap and live in the now. It's *now* my life's mission to help you chase down and conquer every phobia on your list." He jumps to his feet and tilts his head toward the hostel. "Let's check if they have beds. We have a big day ahead of us tomorrow."

When I don't move, he grabs my hand and yanks me up. He leans in close, the peppermint on his breath erasing the memory of the Sulfur City's aroma. "Tomorrow, Canada, we chase the crazy."

I nearly choke. Chase the crazy? My crazy? In front of Hot Guy and all of New Zealand? I stumble after him, head spinning and panic rising, as I try to figure out how I ended up traveling with my worst nightmare.

Nine

SAM

Either this was a kick-ass idea or Nina's going to kill me. I've been planning it since we started tackling her phobias. We've made good progress, too. Over the past four days, we've conquered just as many fears. Her consecotaleophobia was easy—fear of chopsticks. The hardest, hands down, was her katsaridaphobia—fear of cockroaches. That one sucked, even for me. I'm just hoping I didn't go too far with this stunt.

I read about these evenings in my guidebook. Aside from the sulfur smell, Rotorua is a cool place, kind of the cultural center of New Zealand. Tonight we get to experience native Maori rituals, from their traditional songs and dances, to their *hangi*—a meal cooked on hot stones in the ground.

As we wait with thirty-odd people outside one of the sacred meetinghouses for the performance to start, Nina leans closer. "This was a great idea. Thanks for arranging it." She does that thing where she fidgets with her hands when she can't contain her excitement.

I shrug like it's nothing, not wanting to let on that there's more to this evening than she suspects. "No worries. Just thought it'd be fun."

Holy shit, is she going to kill me.

I latched onto her phobias as a way to keep my focus off all the things I want to do *to* Nina and *with* Nina. Not that it's helping. This girl is a different brand of crazy with her hippie folks, her tendency to flash people, and this whacked-out phobia list. Still, I'm consumed by her. Every quirk I learn makes me want to know more. Luckily, she's open to a fault, but, apparently, only with me. Every admission from her about her family or her fears is followed by, "Oh my God, I'm such a freak." That's when I lean in to say, "Own the crazy," and she looks ready to hug me. It's painful to keep my hands to myself.

And other parts under control.

I have to remind myself over and over to keep my distance from her, keep my jeans on and my legs hidden. My dick, however, didn't get the memo. I've had to adjust my stride to account for the constant tightness. My body's desperate for her, but when I look at my legs now, imagining what she'd see, they look more deformed. Uglier. Like Freddy Krueger's face.

With another lame shrug, I say, "The other option was staying at the hostel for me to cook you another five-star meal."

She tilts her head and raises her eyebrows. "Cook? You don't cook, Sam. You melt cheese on stuff."

"Wow, Canada. Those are some harsh words. If you weren't so hot, I'd leave you to travel on your own."

She juts out her hip. "Hot? *Please.* I'm wearing the same shirt I wore yesterday, my hair's a ratty mess, and I forgot to put on eyeliner. Maybe you have some corneal disease and need to get your eyes checked."

"Interesting," I say while I tap my chin.

This girl is too much. Part sexy, part adorable, and all irresistible, she has no idea how appealing she is. Totally clued out. I'm not sure the pre-accident Sam could've gotten past her long list of quirks, but there isn't much about me that's like it was. My emotions rule to the point I worry one of my doctors shot me up with estrogen. The guy who was once okay with going to business school and working for his dad's consulting firm to make a pile of money isn't sure it's what he wants anymore. After the time I've spent in rehab, I keep thinking physiotherapy could be cool. Like it's more important to love what I do than to be driven by the almighty dollar.

Then there are girls.

Before, I was down with the Reeses and the Laceys of the world, pretty packages with not much inside. Now, I'm not so sure. Lacey's rejection shot my ego to shit, but I'd be lying if I said I hadn't been thinking about ending things, too. Her idle gossip and clothing obsessions had lost their amusement. If we couldn't talk about who was banging whom and who was wearing what, it left a lot of dead air. The kind that suffocates you.

But Nina? Fuck. We spend days together and I'm never bored. Our silence is always comfortable. Maybe I would've been into her before, maybe not. Either way, I'm so wrapped up in wanting her now and terrified to have her, I'm floating around in no-man's-land, flirting like I'm in high school but letting it go nowhere.

She nudges me with her elbow. "Interesting *what*? Why are you tapping your chin like that?"

Damn, she's cute when she puckers her lips. "I believe I've discovered another phobia to add to your list."

She whacks me lightly. "That's not how it works. They're *my* phobias, so it's my list." She crosses her arms, and it pushes up her breasts.

I try not to stare. She looks amazing in whatever she wears, never trying to impress. In a plain yellow skirt and simple white tee, she looks awesome. Not the kind of girl you have to worry about smearing you with lipstick when you want to steal a kiss. I drag my gaze up to meet her eyes. "Yeah, well, the rules have changed. I don't have an official name for this fear of yours, but…ready?" I do a drum roll on her shoulder.

"God, you're annoying."

"Yeah, again, I've heard that before. Anyway, since you're on pins and needles, the new phobia on your list is: fear of compliments. It's nuts the way you turn every nice thing I say into a detailed rant about how wrong I am. Is that something you've perfected over time? Like some New-Age tactic to lower the bar in case people think you're cool?"

"Just so you know, there are several curse words I'm shouting in my head, and they're all mean. Really mean. I hope you can feel them."

I grab my chest and stumble back. "Wow, Canada, that's some dangerous voodoo."

An older lady next to me chuckles. She studies Nina, then

me, and gives us a knowing smile. I'm not sure what that look means, but she sure as shit thinks Nina and I are more than friends.

Wanting to pretend for a second we are, I straighten up, walk behind Nina, and place my hands on her shoulders. I bend so my lips graze her ear and flash to the feel of her body flush against mine in that tiny bikini. "Next time I tell you you're hot, you might want to say thanks."

A whimper escapes her lips, and she falls against my chest. I don't move an inch. It's a sickness, my need to touch her. Any excuse I get, my hands are on her body. A pat on the arm, a brush against her hip. I know she likes it. That's often when she looks up at me with *those* eyes. The ones that get my heart racing and my dick lengthening and my head screaming at me to stop whatever it is I'm doing. You can't look at a guy with eyes like that and not want to fuck him. Hard. I'm a total dick for encouraging her when I know full well I won't do anything about it. Not since I have a "girlfriend." *Asshole.* But I'm addicted to her and to that look.

I can still feel the lady watching us, and I like it. I want people to think Nina's mine.

"Sam," Nina says quietly, her back expanding against my chest with a deep inhale, "don't you have a girlfriend? I'm not sure guys with girlfriends should be saying stuff like that."

There she goes, calling me on my bullshit. This is my chance to tell her Lacey and I broke up. Slide my hands around her waist and run my tongue along her ear like I did that day in Pahia. Live in the moment. Any second, it could all be ripped away. Instead, I lean in and say, "I have a girlfriend, Nina. I'm not dead. And you're beautiful." My hands are still on her shoulders, her pulse ticking beneath her cotton tee.

She pauses a moment, leans farther into me and says, "Okay, thanks."

A loud grunt from ahead makes her jump, and she moves away from me. I stop from reaching for her and stand to the side, cursing myself for being such a pussy. *Again.* I focus on the six Maori men on the grassy field in front of us as the opening ceremony starts. I focus on them, because it's impossible not to.

These dudes are huge. Incredible Hulk huge. My nuts almost crawl into my stomach at the sight of them. The Maori are a warrior culture, and these guys look like fierce Polynesian men about to do battle. Swirling tattoos cover their faces, some real, some not, and even though they're wearing nothing but black-and-white fringed skirts, you couldn't pay me to crack a joke about it. No chance in hell I'd pick a fight with one of these monsters.

"I'm so excited," Nina whispers as she bounces from foot to foot.

"Yeah, me too," I say, but not for the same reason.

Seriously, she's going to kill me.

The warriors put on a show chanting, grunting, smacking their limbs, and making insane faces that has Nina grabbing my arm in fear. Like a total douche, I flex, and she grips me tighter. I may as well enjoy this. Odds are she'll want nothing to do with me in a few minutes. Soon, the Maori men and women will be performing traditional dances in the meetinghouse, but not before a volunteer is chosen to take part in a number with the group. *Fuck, yeah.* Phobia number five is about to be destroyed. Chorophobia—fear of dancing in public.

The guys finish their ceremony, and a woman steps up to ask for a volunteer. The request is barely made before I grab Nina's elbow and shoot her hand into the air. Holding her arm high, I whisper, "Chorophobia."

She all but faints.

"Oh, my God, no! No, no, no! Sorry. I can't. I just…oh my God, please—*please* drop my arm." She tries to wiggle free, but I don't let go. Not that it matters. I spoke with the organizer when I booked our spots and told her it was Nina's birthday. Told her she'd always wanted to try the traditional Maori dance. I take my role as Phobia Slayer seriously.

When the largest Maori guy smiles and strides toward us, my grin fades. He stops a foot in front of Nina and holds out his hand. She tilts her head back to see his face.

So do I.

"Come with me, pretty girl. Let's start your lessons." His gaze rakes up and down her body, and I want to tear his head off. Unfortunately, I'd have about as much luck with that as swimming in a blood-filled shark tank. This dude is a giant.

Her tiny hand sinks into his, and he leads her away, terror on her face, a deep frown on mine. The sight of her hand in his makes it hard to swallow. This girl has me so upside down, I can barely think straight. I want her but can't risk her rejection, so I end up sitting here watching as Conan the fucking Barbarian drags her off to probably flirt with her and do God knows what else. If she doesn't kill me, I might kill myself.

She glances back once, glaring. I cup my hands around my mouth and holler, "Chase the crazy, Canada. Let your freak flag fly!" That gets a smile tugging at her lips, but I'm still frowning.

* * *

I sit on the foldable chair, my knee bouncing restlessly as I wait for the show to begin. I distract myself from worrying over that Maori dude hitting on Nina by studying the carved walls. The native Maori culture is evident all over Rotorua, but this sacred meetinghouse is awesome. The walls are thick with reddish-brown carvings, legends and stories told through art. I wish I knew how to read them.

Seconds later, a woman walks on stage barefoot in a traditional Maori costume: a fitted tank top with patterned diamonds in red, white, and black, and the same fringed skirt the men wear. A band is fastened around her forehead in a similar pattern. Nina's ushered on stage with a few other women, the men standing behind them. They've given her a headband, too, and her red hair hangs loose over her shoulders.

She looks pale—paler than usual—her lips pulled tight, her eyes darting over the audience. When she spots me, she gives me her angry, squinty face. *So damn cute.* I shrug back, smirking.

The same lady who was watching us outside is sitting at my left. She leans over and asks, "Your girlfriend?"

"Yes," I say with my sights locked on Nina. The word drops without hesitation. It feels great to say it, to pretend she's mine. To pretend I'm the old Sam with the pumped thighs and smooth skin that powered me on the football field. The guy who would've put the moves on Nina by now.

The lady chuckles and taps the purse clutched on her lap. Her bracelets jingle. "Looks like she's not exactly thrilled about her impending performance. How'd you convince her to get up there?"

I cringe. "Do forcing and convincing mean the same thing?"

She looks up at Nina, then back at me. She laughs again. "Good luck with her later. You might need to work extra hard to earn her forgiveness." Then she winks at me.

Nice. This lady is pushing sixty and basically told me to have sex with my girlfriend. And work extra hard at it. *My girlfriend.* It doesn't even feel like a lie, not with the time we've spent together. I've decided travel time is like dog years. Four days of traveling together is equivalent to hanging out for four months. I already have a list of adorable stuff I love about Nina. The way she hums when she's eating something she likes. The way her teeth scrape her lip when she's deep in thought.

Jesus, am I in trouble.

Suddenly, Nina's gaze drops as she smiles shyly. When I realize it's because that Maori dude is behind her whispering in her ear, I crumple the pamphlet I've been holding. His massive hand moves to rest on her hip, and blood rushes in my ears.

The lady next to me pats my arm. "Don't worry. I saw the way she was looking at you outside at the ceremony. That girl only has eyes for you." She mumbles something like "Young love," as she shifts on her seat.

Now I feel like an even bigger asshole. I'm the reason she's up there with that fucker's hand on her hip, facing a fear that's got her all freaked out. I'm pretty sure she's as into me as I am into her, but I keep playing the girlfriend card to keep my distance while finding ways to string her along. Like I said. *Asshole.* It's one thing to have Lacey cringe with undisguised disgust when

I showed her my legs, but to see that on Nina's face? Christ Almighty, kill me now.

The women onstage chant a song, a hypnotic rhythm, and Nina looks panicked. She's stiff, wide-eyed, and she jerks a few times as she struggles to remember the steps. It's not a complicated dance, the same few moves repeated with the guys stomping and singing behind them, but I'm guessing her chorophobia has her drawing a blank. I give her a thumbs-up and whistle on my other fingers. She bites her lip, smiles, and loosens up.

By the end of the song, after only one almost-fall-on-her-face moment, she's smiling so wide it's contagious. Until Conan comes up behind her, whispers in her ear again, and leads her offstage. The show continues as I wait for her to sit beside me, but it's hard to focus with the way I'm grinding my teeth.

* * *

"I still can't believe you made me do that and didn't even warn me." Nina's red hair looks black in the darkness, the backdrop of the fire sparking in her eyes. She tips her head back to sip her beer, still smirking.

At least she's not pissed. I crack open my can and take a generous gulp while our group mingles around the sparsely wooded area beside the meetinghouse. The charred barbeque smell from the deep pit in the ground lingers from our tasty meal of roast chicken and potatoes. "If I'd told you about it, would you have come?"

She wraps both hands around her can and sways her shoulders. "No. No way. Not a chance."

"And was it fun? Do you feel invincible? Like you could write a girl power song and star in your own video?"

"Yeah, Sam. That's exactly how I feel. Actually…I feel a lyric coming on." She snaps her fingers and leans over her beer like it's a microphone. "R-E-V-E-N-G-E, find out what it means to me. R-E-V-E-N-G-E, don't get cocky, wait and see." She sings the whole thing to Aretha Franklin's "Respect."

I practically snort a stream of beer through my nose. "I think you've missed your calling. But revenge? Does that mean you're gonna try to conquer your fear of being mean on your own? What was that one called again?"

"That one I had to make up. I couldn't find a term and decided on canuckaphobia." When I squint at her, she shrugs. "You know Canuck, as in Canadian? Like we're always so polite and stuff. Always neutral. We're the Switzerland of North America."

"Right. Canuck." I nod a few times. We sip our beers and watch one of the Maori leaders with a small group explaining how they cook the food in the underground pits. Another guy adds some logs to the fire and it roars back to life. I nudge her with my elbow. "What's next on the list, anyway?"

She looks over my shoulder and gives a little wave. I turn as Conan the Barbarian waves back. I move to block him from view. Fat chance with the size of him.

She faces me, a mischievous glint in her eye. "How about androphobia?"

"Definition, please."

"Androphobia." She drops her voice and looks around like a spy about to share a world-ending secret. "Fear of men." Her eyes dart back to the giant.

And I almost crush my beer can. Is that why she looks at me the way she does, because she wants something she's never had? With me? Or with that mutant of a man? "Please tell me you're messing around. Conan the fucking Barbarian? You must not value my life."

"*Your* life? What does this have to do with you? And his name, by the way, is Cliff."

Cliff? Shit. Didn't see that one coming. "Look, if you go over there and talk to…Cliff, and he does anything to make you uncomfortable, I'm gonna have to WWE the dude. You did see his size, right? You'd be responsible for me having to get my jaw rewired. You sure you want that on your conscience?"

The amusement falls from her face. She studies me a beat. "You'd do that for me, Sam? You'd stand up to a guy like that? For me?"

I've known Nina for two weeks, spent four days traveling with her, and I can say without a doubt I'd let that giant pummel me into the ground if it meant protecting her. But I keep it light. "Like I said before, my pops would skin my ass if I let a girl like you get hurt. So the choice is yours. Are you gonna go over there to flirt with the guy who'll likely pulverize me, or do I get to hang out with you for the rest of the night?"

"I'm yours," she says softly, and it almost kills me to hear those words.

The older lady who sat beside me in the show touches her on the shoulder. "You were great earlier. Enjoy the rest of your evening, you two." She winks at me and leaves.

I look away from Nina, wishing like hell we'd be doing exactly what that lady thinks, the two of us naked and sweaty under my sheets. To do that, I'd have to be honest with Nina. It felt great to tell her about the accident, about my mom. It was hard. Always is. But it felt good not to hold onto it like some dirty little secret. Still, I pussied out when it came to my legs. "I banged up my ankle" is the understatement of the century. I got twelve stitches in my chin, another twenty in my scalp, my front right tooth was knocked clean out, and my face swelled so bad I could barely see.

My legs were the worst. Most of the bones from my left knee to my ankle were shattered, and I'm lucky I was dragged from the wreckage when the fire engulfed my feet, working up my calves. They stopped the flames from claiming more of my body, but not before the fire chewed the shit out of my legs. It's a damn good thing I was unconscious.

Nina nudges my arm. "What's the plan for tomorrow?"

I blink the ugliness away, tired of reliving it. It's not as hard as it once was, not with those green eyes on me. "Actually, I was planning on going to Taupo. Spend a night there, then head on a hike. Or what do they call it here, a tramp? The Tongariro volcano is there, and there's a one-day crossing. I was thinking of splitting it into two days and staying at a hut overnight."

She looks down at her feet and says, "Oh."

"Oh?" I ask. "What does 'oh' mean?" God, I hate when she looks sad, and that's how those frown lines read.

Nina, the open book.

She scrapes her teeth over her bottom lip, releasing it with a sigh. "Nothing. I mean, it's been fun hanging out. I'll just, I don't know, hop on another Kiwi bus. I still have my pass."

She thinks I'm ditching her. Like it's possible for me to leave her on her own. To not have her next to me every minute. When

I go to my dorm at night, when I get stuck in my head like just now, heaviness settles in my heart. The weight of the last year. The second I see Nina, though, it dissipates. I don't know how this happened in four days—make that four months in travel years—but I'm not letting this chick out of my sight, fake girlfriend or not.

"Hey." I place two fingers below her chin and tilt her face toward me. "I didn't mean I was taking off. We're traveling together, remember? The fucked-up guy and disaster-magnet girl taking on the world? I've been planning to do that hike since before I got here. It just came out wrong. Besides, I'm not hiking that thing on my own. I'll need someone to carry my pack for me." When she doesn't laugh, I drop her chin and inch closer. "Is that cool? To do the hike, I mean."

She frowns at my damaged legs. "You're sure it's not too tough for you? I overheard a group at the hostel talking about it. It sounds like an intense climb."

"Nina, I was this close to taking on King Kong a second ago, and you're not sure I can go for a hike?" She doesn't look up. I grab the hand hanging at her side, her fingers moist from the beer bottle, but soft, too. She keeps her focus on the ground. "Thanks," I say. "It means a lot that you care. Seriously. The hike might be tough. I'm not an idiot. That's kind of why I want to do it. I'm ready for the challenge. I *want* the challenge. You just have to be okay with taking it slow. If I rush things, I'm bound to get hurt. So we'll take our time, okay?"

I'm not sure if she can read the meaning between my words, how badly I want to rise to the challenge of being with her. I'm just not ready yet. Maybe if she gets to know me better, if I show her how awesome things could be with us, it won't be so easy for her to turn away when she sees my scarred flesh.

She weaves her fingers between mine and runs her thumb over my skin. It's such a simple gesture. Any other girl, on any other day, and I'd barely even notice. Maybe even be annoyed. But *this* girl, on *this* night, in *this* amazing country, and I'm falling to my knees.

She looks up at me with something I'd swear is adoration. "Okay. Let's do this hike of yours." She rises on her tiptoes and plants the softest, sweetest kiss on my cheek. "Thanks for tonight. Really. It was fun. I'm going to use the bathroom, then maybe we'll head back. Get an early start tomorrow."

She drops my hand and walks away, and I can't catch my breath. I shut my eyes and inhale deeply, the scents of earth and fire heavy in the air, but it's that hint of coconut from her hair and the cherry from her lips I want to capture. Is this how my dad felt when he fell for my mom? Desperate for the slightest scent or touch? The type of yearning that leads to love and forever.

I should hop in my car and get the hell away, but knowing it and doing it are two different beasts. Especially when she eases my heavy heart. I run my hand up the back of my neck, visions of my dad in his dark room all I see. But I'm not him. I survived my mom's death and helped take care of him and my sister. I'm stronger than he is. I can open up, be with Nina, and say good-bye at the end of this trip. I glance down at my jeans. If she can get past my legs, that is.

Ten

NINA

After the hour-long drive this morning, Sam and I dump our stuff in the dorms, tour the town to get our bearings, and buy the food and clothes we need for our hike. Then it's dinner at a pub, which turns into drinks, which turns into live music, and now I'm sitting bleary-eyed on my bunk as I try to process what happened this afternoon.

What's about to happen tomorrow.

We stopped in a tourist center earlier to buy the passes that allow us to stay in the hut along our two-day "tramp," as the Kiwis call it. Sam's had fun using that word in all sorts of sentences today. He keeps stopping to say things like, "Are you sure your folks are cool that you'll be 'tramping' with me?" and, "I could give you 'tramping' lessons before we head out." If I roll my eyes one more time, they might get stuck that way. But I keep laughing, so he keeps doing it. *Frickin' Hot Guy.*

We were at the tourist office earlier trying to book our passes, but all the bunks were full. Sam glanced at me, rubbed his chin like he does, then he swung back to the guy at the counter to ask if they rented tents. I didn't clue in at first, didn't think twice about the question or the implication. It wasn't until I was two steps out the door, a tent bag tucked under Sam's arm, that the reality of what was going to happen sank in. For one night, I'd be sleeping in a tent with One-syllable Sam. A game of freeze tag ensued with him staring at me like I was a moron while horns honked and people shouted until he dragged me to the other side.

For the life of me, I don't know how I let this happen.

I tuck my legs underneath me on my bed and grab my phone from my purse. I sent a message to Mom last night and have been dying to hear from her all day. These time zones aren't easy to navigate. I just couldn't hold it in any longer. If I don't talk to someone about Sam, I'm likely to spontaneously combust. So I texted Mom. Even when it comes to guys, she's my sounding board.

When I was fifteen, she handed me a year's supply of birth control because, and I quote, "Your father knocked me up at eighteen, and although you are the most amazing gift he could have given me, let's hope you don't stretch that womb of yours until you're good and ready. Have fun, but be careful," she added as an afterthought. She's also the person I cried to after the infamous I'm Not Sure I Lost My Virginity Incident. She didn't get mad at me for what I did, she just said, "When the time is right, Pininfarina, when the *guy* is right, it will be nothing short of magical."

So I texted her that there's this *guy* and he's *amazing*. But there's a *girlfriend*.

Things have shifted over the past five days; at least for me they have. I still fantasize about Sam, but I alternate between wanting to rip his clothes off and wanting to cover him in a T-shirt that reads: *Property of Nina Gabri*.

I've never been so myself with anyone. Ever. This is everything I wanted when I left Toronto. Me, being a girl who can joke and laugh and conquer her fears like a ninja warrior. Me, flirting with a guy so stupid hot I still fantasize to the point of tripping over my feet. Me, having fun like a normal nineteen-year-old. All of this is because of Sam. I don't just fantasize about being *with* him anymore. I want to be his. There is, however, the unfortunate circumstance of a beautiful, blond girlfriend.

Something's up with him and Lacey. He never talks about her, never even mentions her name. He flirts shamelessly with me. And I let him.

On second thought, his T-shirt should read:

Property of Nina Gabri*

*a.k.a. Pininfarina Gabri—home wrecker and instigator of mayhem

Still, I can't stop myself.

When I power up my cell, I suck in an excited breath, but exhale, deflated, when the screen comes on. No message from Mom. No one for me to confide in about my feelings for Sam. Or about the whole hiking thing. The thing where I'll be sleeping with him. In a tent. For one night. Alone. *Holy God.*

Spontaneous combustion is imminent.

The girls in the dorm are all asleep. I grab my toiletries and sneak out to go wash up. As the bathroom door swings shut behind me, a gasping sob echoes from around the corner, followed by the sound of skin slapping tile. I swivel for the door to run and get Sam, sure a girl's being attacked. Then I hear, "Fuck it."

There's no fear in those words, only resignation.

I inch toward the bend up ahead and peek around the white-tiled wall. My mouth drops open. *Holy crap.* No way can this be happening. No frickin' way.

A girl stands in front of the mirror, metal scissors in one hand and a fistful of black hair in the other. When our eyes clash in the mirror, she says, "Fucking perfect," and I say, "Oh, God."

Leigh glares at me like I'm gum stuck to the bottom of her shoe, and I contemplate running out of here after all. Since we're all using the same guidebook, it was only a matter of time before I met up with the Trifecta of Cool. I just hoped Sam would be with me when it happened. Still, I don't bolt. There's mascara streaking her face, and she just cut a chunk of hair from her head.

Although she might be thinking of shoving those scissors in my eye, I step closer. I hold up my hand like you would toward a rabid dog. "You okay?" I say, which is literally the dumbest question I've ever asked. It's pretty clear she's not okay.

She makes a horking sound and shakes her head at the ceiling. "Run along, Nina. This doesn't concern you."

I glance toward the door and back at her tearstained face. If Sam were here, he'd tell me to swallow my fear and face my demons head on. Right now, my demon has chosen to manifest itself in the form of a not-so-nice girl giving me hate eyes. But

I will prevail. Swallowing heavily, I walk to the sink and put my stuff down. Leigh's dark eyes follow every movement. Without saying a word, I approach her from the side and reach for her scissors.

I place my hand on hers and tilt my head to meet her gaze in the mirror. "Let me. I cut my sisters' hair all the time. I'll do a better job."

She grips the metal handles tighter, but a second later, she lets go and releases another sob. I take the scissors from her and drag the garbage over. She dumps the clump of hair she's holding, the black strands floating into the trash. I don't ask her what's wrong, and I certainly don't ask her if she's okay again. I know too well what it's like to have people see you at your lowest. It makes you wish you were a turtle with a bulletproof shell. She sniffles a few more times, hiccups, and rubs her hands down her face.

Taking my time, I snip off long chunks before styling the shorter pieces. Partway through, I bite my lip. "I have an idea. I'll be right back."

She looks kind of worried when I leave her alone, but I return in seconds with a taller garbage bin. I flip it upside down, grab her by the shoulders, and sit her down, giving myself a better view. She can't see in the mirror anymore. She fiddles with her fingers, alternating between biting her nails and picking her cuticles. When I'm done, I turn her to face me. The pixie look rocks on Leigh. It makes her sharp cheekbones stand out and highlights her thin frame.

"Okay," I say. "Your turn."

She spins toward the mirror, and her hand shoots to her hair.

"Holy shit," she says and then, "Mother fuck," then, "Holy shit" again.

I knock my knees together and hunch a bit. "Sorry. I did the best I could. Honest. You can go to a salon tomorrow and get it fixed. Shoot, Leigh…I'm sorry." One of the three sinks has a leaky faucet and the drip echoes against the walls.

She runs her fingers through her short black strands. Then she grins. "This is perfect. I love it. Exactly what I needed." Black lines still streak her face, but she's looking in the mirror as though she's the fairest of them all.

Still uncomfortable washing up and leaving her on her own, I play with the hem of my tank top, rolling the blue cotton between my fingers. "So can I ask what happened? I don't want to overstep, but why the sudden makeover? And, you know,"—I drop my shirt and point to her cheeks—"why all the tears?"

She flicks her head back and throws her hands up as if cursing the heavens. "Why? That bitch Reese, that's why." She spins around and folds her knobby arms across her chest, her eyes welling with hurt. It reminds me of every time I cried myself to sleep after another supposed "peer" thought it was okay to call me names and hurl insults.

"Do you want to talk about it?" I ask, unsure what else to say.

Drip goes the leaky tap. *Drip. Drip. Drip.*

She mutters under her breath and steps from foot to foot. She makes a familiar throaty sound and says, "Fuck," like she's having a whole conversation in her head. Suddenly, she looks at me dead on and says, "I'm gay." Just like that. No pretense. I'm gay and deal with it, or get the heck out.

"Oh," I say. *Drip. Drip. Drip.*

Oh. Really? Is that the best I can do? For all I know, I could be the first person she's ever confessed that to, and I reply with a resounding, "Oh." I'll file that gem next to "Are you okay?" under the title *How to Lose Friends and Alienate People.* Leigh's no longer glaring at me. She's backed herself into the wall, one knee bent ninety degrees, her arms still folded.

I clear my throat, walk over, and lean against the wall beside her. "Must be pretty rough, always trying to be something you're not. Never feeling accepted for who you are." I don't know if I'm talking about her or me. Not that I'm struggling to come out of the closet. My self-imposed confines are due to my inability to own my crazy, as Sam says. Unless I'm with him. Then I let my crazy shine.

She looks at me from the corner of her eye and back at her folded arms. "I can't believe I just told you that. I've never even said it out loud."

I laugh despite myself, and she curls her lip in irritation. I try my best to backpedal. "No, God, it's not like that. It's just, I say that all the time to Sam."

"To Sam?"

"Yeah, well…we've been traveling together. You probably won't be surprised to learn, despite what I told you girls in Auckland, I don't exactly have an entourage of friends back home. Sam calls me out on that stuff, and I'm always confessing things I've never talked about."

She looks at me, smirking now. "Let me guess, the boob-in-the-soup incident wasn't your first foray into freakdom?"

I snort. "Not by a long shot." She rocks from side to side, her knee swinging in arcs as she presses her shoulders into the tiles.

With a deep breath, I try to get her talking. "What happened with Reese that sent you in here crying and, uh,"—I wave my finger at her head—"the hair thing? Which, if I must say, looks really cute short."

She nods. "Thanks. I had a great hairdresser." We smile at each other, then her lips tighten. "Let's see, *Reese*. I don't even know where to start with that bitch, so I'll give you the condensed version. We went to high school together. I've had a thing for her for years, God knows why, while still maintaining my 'boy-hungry' image. We made out one night a year ago—a fun experiment for her, an intense moment for me. When I tried to recreate that scene last night in Auckland, things didn't go as planned. Names were yelled. Really fucking shitty names I won't repeat.

"I lost my shit and practically tore out her stupid-ass braid. I caught the first bus south and landed here, in a bathroom in Taupo, in fucking New Zealand, hacking at my hair because it's exhausting trying to be something I'm not. So that's the short version, and for some messed-up reason, I'm sharing it with you. The boob-in-the-soup girl." When I squint at her, she swats the air by my face. "God, whatever. I'm sorry. And I'm sorry I took that stupid video of you. It was kind of a dick move."

I roll my eyes. "Kind of." I should be angrier with her than I am, but everything about her makes more sense now. Especially her sour expression that deepened every time Reese tried to turn me into her own personal Barbie. I deal with my insecurities by playing my own version of *Where's Waldo?*, expertly blending in with the scenery. Leigh, on the other hand, lashes out. It's not fun to be on the receiving end of said lashing, but I get it. I try to choose my next words carefully. "Were you serious, though? Is this the first time you've ever told anyone that you're gay?"

Drip. Drip. Drip. Drip.

Then finally, "Let's just say my family isn't what you'd call supportive, and my high school was filled with carbon copies of Reese and followers like Brianne. I guess it's a hell of a lot easier to say it out loud to a virtual stranger who I never have to see again, in a place I never have to visit again. So, yeah, you're my first." She snorts at the statement.

"I can relate. I mean, not that I'm gay. Just, it's easier to be myself with a slate I can wipe clean at any given moment. Sam's been kind of making me own my insecurities. He tells me to chase my crazy." Every time he says it, his eyes sparkle and his lips twitch. Those are the times I want to cover him in that T-shirt.

"What's with all this Sam talk? Does he have something to do with your magical transformation from boob-in-the-soup girl to halfway normal?"

I want to give her my squinty face at the mention of that nickname, but when I glance at her, she's smirking, not sneering. Like Sam, I think she's laughing *with* me. "Yeah, I'd say he's responsible for the Cinderella version of me."

"What's the deal? You two getting all hot and heavy in the backseat of his car?"

My cheeks flame, along with my ears, chest, and neck. "Of course not. We're just friends." Friends who flirt a lot. Friends who will be sleeping in the same tent. For one night. *Together.* A friend who tells me crazy is better than normal.

"I don't get it. I sensed something between you two that first night in Auckland. And let's be honest here—the guy's a ten."

When my jaw practically hits the floor, she shakes her head. "If I were a switch hitter, I'd tap that. But you don't have to worry about your precious man-candy. I vowed to stop faking it with guys six months ago. That night on Todd's couch was enough to have me showering for weeks. Anyway, I digress. Man-candy, you—no hanky-panky. What's the deal?"

I've never confided in anyone but Mom. Unless you count One-syllable Sam, who in no way qualifies as the shoulder for me to lean on when needing to discuss his flirtatious self and my growing obsession with him. That leaves the formerly surly Leigh. The slim possibility of letting out the confusion clouding my brain has my ankle bouncing and my lips pursing while I try to hold in the flood of confessions that wants to flow free.

Drip. Drip. Drip. Drip. Dripdripdripdripdripdripdrip.

Reminder to self: I can always grab my pack and leave. Nothing and no one is keeping me here. If she turns all *Mean Girls* on me, I simply have to wake Sam and drag him to another hostel.

She's playing with the short strands by her ears, not bothered by my internal meltdown and how long it's taking. Then the word vomit flows. "I seriously don't know what to do. It's just, Sam's amazing. So great to hang out with, and…well, *hot*. Obviously. Like really hot. And I'm not a total freak with him. A bit of nut-job, sure, but not my usual scale-tipping insanity. Even if I were, I don't think he'd care. That's the crazy part. He's seen me at my worst, like *my worst*—you don't even know what happened on that airplane. Anyway, it's like he almost likes me, even with all that other…*stuff*. He flirts with me. At least I'm pretty sure it's flirting. Touching me a whole lot, telling me he thinks I'm hot.

It's only been like five days, and I'm so wound up over him my head's about to explode." My chest heaves as I catch my breath.

"I'm not sure I follow." She swings around to face me, her shoulder pressed into the wall. "You're drooling over the guy, and he's all handsy with you." She wiggles her fingers in the air. "Why all the drama?"

"He has a girlfriend."

She frowns. "No shit. I guess that's why he didn't seal the deal with Reese. But why is he leading you on? And why the hell would you want to be with a guy who's willing to screw around on his girlfriend?"

There's the million-dollar question. I shouldn't entertain the thought of being with Sam, but I can't shake the way he looks at me and looks out *for* me. And, most important, I'm more than ready to tackle my androphobia. More than okay with putting my trust in him. Even if I geek out in some horrifying way, I don't think he'll treat me the way the last guy did. In fact, I know he won't.

So this is me trying to convince myself all is not well on the home front with One-syllable Sam and his picture-perfect girlfriend. This is me being a crappy person. I'll refrain from sharing the bikini-sexy-ear moment with Leigh. "I don't know. No matter how hard I try, I can't get him out of my head. And I get the feeling things aren't as good as they should be with him and Lacey. I suck, don't I?"

"You don't suck, Nina. Far from it." She points to her head. "Look at this kick-ass haircut you gave me. Besides, I wouldn't have chosen you as the first person to confide in if you sucked. I have my standards. So enough sucking talk. How about I feel

Sam out in the morning? Try to get the lay of the land as an outsider?"

"You'd do that for me?"

"Yeah, whatever. No biggie. Don't go getting all weird about
it. I don't do sappy." She pushes off the wall, goes over to the sink,
and turns on the dripping faucet.

I can't remember the last time I had a friend go out of their
way for me, let alone do such a personal favor. Maybe she's trying
to make up for the video thing, or maybe she's softer than she lets
on. Either way, I'll take the olive branch.

After splashing and rubbing her face, she grabs her towel to
wipe some of the mascara from her cheeks. She exhales heavily,
probably still freaked out about her confession and hurting over
her run-in with Reese.

Before I overthink things, I say, "Sam and I are going on a
hike tomorrow, a two-day crossing over Mount Tongariro. We've
rented a tent. How'd you like to come?"

She makes a snorting-choking sound and spins around.
"How'd you neglect to mention that fun fact during your mono-
logue? You and the guy with a girlfriend alone in a tent? What
part of you thinks I want to choke on the sexual tension between
you two? The answer is a resounding no, but the sentiment's
nice." She stops, pauses, then plants her hands on her hips. "Actually…what if I hang here and maybe head south with you guys
when you get back? If they stick to their plans, Reese and that
pack of losers won't be here for a couple of weeks. Would that be
cool?"

I nod, my heart suddenly full. Leigh and I just had a real
conversation, no video-game-like animatronics from yours truly

where I have to stop and think before I do or say anything. Just two girls, both a little messed up, trying to figure their stuff out. "Yeah," I say. "That would be cool."

* * *

In the morning, Leigh and I sit kitty-corner on the end of the kitchen table, eating bowls of fruit salad and talking about where to go after the hike. Sam appears in the doorway, stops short, and cocks his head. His brow furrows. He seems to recognize Leigh, but maybe can't place her with the haircut. When his face darkens and his jaw ticks, I'm pretty sure he makes the connection. I wave him over, and he approaches slowly.

Instead of sitting down, he hovers over her with crossed arms. "I'd say it's nice to see you, Leigh, but that would be a lie. Nina, why don't you get your stuff? We'll leave right away." He glares at her, never looking my way.

I put my fork down. "It's cool, Sam." I attempt to catch his eye, but he's too busy trying to burst Leigh into flames. "Honestly. Leigh and I got caught up last night. She apologized for the whole video thing. We're cool. Okay?"

"Yeah, Romeo." She bites the strawberry from her fork, chews, and swallows. She waves her utensil at his face. "Back off with your creepy staring. Another minute and I might accidentally stick this fork in your eye."

He blows out a breath. "One move and I shave your head." Then he looks at me. "You really want to hang out with this sorry excuse for a human being?"

I nod quickly, none too sure how to broach the next subject.

It doesn't look like Sam and Leigh are about to trade friendship bracelets, but she needs me. I decide on being direct. "Yeah, I'm sure. Actually…this *wonderful* excuse for a human being is going to be traveling with us after the hike." I slap a toothy grin on my face until he snorts.

His good humor doesn't last long. "No way. This bitch isn't getting in my car."

Leigh drops her fork on the metal table with a loud clatter. "Oh, this bitch *is* getting in your car, and this *asshole* will let her. Last I checked, your travel partner has some say on who she hangs with. Or have you turned your car into a dictatorship?"

"You can fuck off, Leigh. And when I shave your head, your eyebrows are going, too." He faces me. "Come on, Nina. Is this for real? You seriously want to spend time with the girl who spread a video of you all over the Internet?"

I smile weakly. "Yeah." I promised Leigh I wouldn't tell Sam about her confession. Not that I think it's a big deal, and not that he would either, but she has to do this in her own way.

He huffs and pushes his hand through his mess of curls. "Fine. Give me your phone first." He holds his palm out toward Leigh.

"No friggin' way, bucko. Not on your life."

"Then consider yourself traveling solo." But he doesn't pull his hand back.

She swings to me and mouths *What the fuck?* When I shrug, she rolls her eyes, grabs her phone from the table, and practically tosses it at Sam.

He thumbs the screen then scowls at her. "I don't see it. Did you erase the video?"

"Yes. That masterpiece of theatre is forever destroyed. I deleted it last night. Happy? Can I have my property back before you invade more of my privacy, *Mussolini*?"

He leans down low, his face inches from Leigh's. "You can travel with us, because it's what Nina wants. But you do one thing that makes her uncomfortable, you even look at her wrong, and I will open the door while driving ninety and kick your ass to the curb. Are we clear?"

Instead of biting back with what I'm learning is a typical Leigh foul-mouthed comment, she narrows her eyes and tilts her head. After a prolonged pause, she nods decisively and says, "Crystal." She holds out her hand, and he drops the phone in it.

He straightens up and rakes his hair again. Deep grooves linger where his fingers were, and I can't help but wonder if it feels as soft as it looks. "Now that I have *that* to look forward to," he says, "what do you say we head out, Nina? It's looking like it's gonna rain. We should get a move on."

Leigh offers to clear our plates, and I'm a few steps away when my phone vibrates. A text from her lights my screen.

Man-candy is into you. Don't know what the girlfriend deal is, and he's a bit of a douche. But he's hot for you. Good luck in the tent. Kirk out.

First thing I do after reading the text is laugh. *Kirk out.* I didn't peg Leigh for a Trekkie. It makes me like her even more. Second thing I do is almost have a coronary. It's one thing to *think* Sam's into me with some mysterious girlfriend getting in the way. It's quite another for someone to confirm my suspicions on the day we leave for a "tramp." The same day we'll be sleeping in a tent.

The two of us.

Together.

Alone.

That spontaneous combustion thing starts up again as I try to put one foot in front of the other on the way to get my pack. This is going to be a long day.

Eleven

NINA

Sam. Oh, God, *Sam*. I…I can't. Oh, my God, I just can't."

Panting. Burning. Aching limbs. Lungs sure to collapse.

"Don't crap out on me now, Canada. Five more steps and you've made it."

I don't look up. That would mean moving my head. *That* requires energy. I suck a breath, oxygen raking through my lungs, and I take another step. Then another. After the promised five, I can tell I'm not at the top.

"Five?" I manage to shout. *Endless* would be a good word to describe this climb.

Or infinite. Or illimitable. Or plain horrible.

"Okay. I lied. Just don't stop moving. You're so close. And we're not setting up camp on a ninety-degree cliff. Keep your eye on the prize. You're almost there."

Frickin' Hot Guy and his stupid hike. He thought his limp

would slow us down, but I'm the one huffing and puffing, trying to figure out how I ended up on Mount Everest while in New Zealand. I chance a glance up, using the moment to inhale a mouthful of air. Sam leans over the edge, hands on his knees, grinning down at me. If there was ever a reason to summit a mountain, that face is it.

Sam, who I'm falling for. Sam, with *that* jaw.

Sam, who I'll be sleeping with. In a tent. *Alone.*

Another five agonizing steps later, he's got me by the shoulders, helping me up. In the blink of an eye, he has my straps undone and is easing the bazillion-pound weight from my back. The air still feels sharp in my lungs, like it could slice through me.

"Keep moving around," he says. "Come on, let's walk it off." He grabs my hand and leads me over the rocky ground, the two of us walking in wide circles.

After a few laps, the air is less daggerlike and my breathing slows. I blink at my surroundings. So focused on my aches and pains, I didn't stop to soak in the landscape, if that's what you'd call it. This is probably what the moon looks like. A few hikers passed us on the climb, but we're alone in this crater, surrounded by jagged outcrops of brownish-black rocks and yellow tufts of grass, low mountains on all sides. It's majestic and eerie and otherworldly, and I'm here because of Sam.

"Beautiful, isn't it?" he asks. He's still holding my hand as the silence engulfs us, my heart pounding in my ears.

The air is cold and damp. It alleviates the heat from that insane climb but doesn't do much to quell the warmth between Sam's hand and mine. Still, I don't let go. And he doesn't let go. I could stand here forever.

"Yeah, beautiful," I finally say, no longer referring to the scenery.

He drops my hand and folds his arms as he studies the darkening sky. "We still have a ways to go. We'll break for lunch after the Emerald Lakes. The Blue Lake is after that. Then I'm guessing it's another hour or so before we reach the hut. How are your legs doing?"

I plant my hands on my hips. "*My* legs? My legs are fine. I could run a marathon. Make that two."

"Okay. Want to race? I'll give you a thirty-minute head start and make sure I limp extra bad." He wiggles his eyebrows. *Frickin' Hot Guy.*

"Whatever, Sam. I'll live. With the way that sky's looking, we shouldn't linger too long." I zip my jacket higher and say a silent thank-you to Sam for making me buy long underwear. "Let me get my hat first."

Nodding, he says, "Sounds like a plan."

He strides toward our packs, his limp looking more pronounced. He doesn't complain and doesn't stop, but I'm sure his ankle hurts. If I slow down, maybe he'll take his time instead of pushing harder.

With our knit hats on, I slather on some cherry lip balm. Sam hoists on his pack before helping me with mine. Once I have the buckles done up around my chest and hips, he lets go. A ton of bricks is probably lighter. I teeter once, twice, but don't fall.

He moves in front of me, his brown eyes roaming my face. He tugs the front of my hat playfully. "This is a good look for you."

I shake my head. "Good look? The hat's about a size too big—"

"Hey," he barks. "I thought we had a talk about the compliment thing. Let's try that again." He runs his finger along the edge of my wool beanie, skimming my ear in the process. My knees almost give out. "This, *Nina*, is a good look for you." He pronounces each word, his voice roughening. "It gives you a hot, outdoorsy vibe." He lets go and drags two fingers over his scarred chin, the thing he does when he wants to say something but isn't sure he should.

My lips part as I watch the movement, knowing exactly how his arm looks underneath his jacket. The bulging of his bicep. The way his forearm flexes. I've gawked at his T-shirt–clad arms countless times, those tan muscles forever tattooed on my brain. Sex-goddess me takes over. In my head, Sam strips me until I'm in nothing but my hat and hiking boots, and I do the same to him. He plunges into me. Hard. Fast. Greedy. The sound of skin slapping and my cries are all that can be heard for miles.

I'm not sure when I lose my balance. It could be when I picture his thickness entering me, or the deep thrusts that follow. Either way, the weight on my shoulders wins the battle for uprightness. I fall. Undignified. Flat on my back. Thankfully, my ten-ton pack breaks the impact.

Remembering the compliment, I force a smile and say, "Thanks."

He snorts. "My pleasure." He leans over me. "You want to revisit that statement about the extended marathon?"

I laugh with him while I lie like a beetle flipped on its shell. I'm happy to let him think my tiredness is the reason for my fall. No matter how much time I spend with Sam, I can't seem to shake the fantasies he inspires. Or maybe I don't want to. With the way he flirts, he makes me think there's something between us. But there's this *girlfriend*. "Maybe my legs are a bit weak, but I can make it." I extend a hand toward him. "Please, kind sir, could I have a lift?" I ask in my not-very-good English accent.

He winks. "As you wish, m'lady." His accent isn't much better.

For the second time in the past ten minutes, my hand sinks into his as he helps me up. I can't imagine what he thinks of me, the way I can barely control my limbs around him. When I'm up, I avoid his eyes. I don't want to see amusement in the form of mocking on his face. I could never handle that. Every other living being on the planet can point and stare and laugh in my face, but not Sam. Never Sam.

He leads the way and I follow, thick clouds gathering above us.

* * *

The rain starts after lunch. We inhale our peanut-butter-and-jam sandwiches, knowing the downpour is imminent. Even with the fog, wind, and rain, the volcanic lakes we pass are mesmerizing. I try to find the right word to describe the color of the crystalline waters in the middle of this vast volcanic land. Viridian? Cerulean? I settle on perfect.

Sam stops regularly, often to make sure I'm okay, but to rest his leg, too. A five-hour hike seemed breezy when we discussed it this morning. No *problemo*. I hiked the Grand Canyon with my folks—the rim of the canyon, anyway. A flat trail. With no backpack. And I thought the tai chi kept me fit. *That* theory's been shot to bits. With each passing hour I breathe harder, the straps of my pack dig farther into my shoulders, and blisters form on my heels. My legs cramp up, and the steady drizzle has me chilled to the bone. When the hut appears in the distance, I gather whatever energy I can muster and pick up the pace.

A few steps later, a large puddle splits the path ahead of us. Sam stops at its edge. When I get to his side, he takes my hand and looks at me. "Ready?"

I know that glint in his eye, that mischievous sparkle. I try to tug my hand back. "Ready? No. Definitely not. Whatever you're thinking, I'm pretty sure I'm not ready."

He tightens his grip, and says, "Excellent," ignoring my answer.

Just like that, he tugs me forward, the two of us splashing into the puddle. Dead center. I sputter out a series of *oh, my God*s and *holy heck*s as he drags me through the calf-deep water.

I stop at the other side and push at his chest. We both stumble, water squishing from our boots. "Are you insane? What were you thinking?"

A wide grin splits his face. "Tell me, Canada, were you dry before I dragged you in there? Did I ruin your stilettos?"

"No. Sorry. It's just…" Just what? Just too much fun? Just too crazy? I've spent so long trying to blend in and not get noticed, it freaks me out to do something so bold. Something that would make people stare. But no one's here. No one but me and Sam, the guy who makes me feel invincible.

"Race you to the next one?" I ask.

He winks. "You're on."

That's exactly what we do. Before each puddle, we grab hands and run through like five-year-olds. We even stop to jump in a deeper one, splashing water everywhere. I've never laughed harder, or smiled more, or felt more carefree. I've never felt so alive. We run through the last muddy pool and stop to catch our breath, the hut a few strides away.

I lick the rain from my lips and stomp my sodden feet, still giggling. I lean back to feel the rain on my cheeks. "Sam, that was awesome."

He touches my face then, wiping strands of hair away. "You're awesome," he says. The way his fingers graze my cheek, barely making contact, sends tingles down my spine. Standing upright is once again a challenge. I could latch onto his strong shoulders, claiming dizziness, any excuse to feel the expanse of his muscles. But he walks into the hut and leaves me, heart thundering.

I don't know if it's the air up here, but the oxygen seems to be thinning. Fast. In a few short hours, I'll be sleeping next to Sam. My head is sure to explode, a side effect of my overactive imagination and the naked images that are bound to swell to the point of detonation. I'm beyond freaked out, but, if I'm honest, I'm excited, too. *Sam thinks I'm awesome.* He's here, in New Zealand, with me. Flirting with me. He can't really love his girlfriend, can he?

I'm the worst kind of person.

The hut is clean but sparse with a couple of wooden tables and benches, a counter with a sink and gas cooktop, and the thing I was hoping to see: a woodstove to heat the place. And me. A separate room to the side houses twenty-six bunks. People are spread out in the two rooms, reading, eating, and playing games. Everyone nods hello and smiles at how wet we are. Wet, and really cold now that the fun of running through puddles has worn off.

Sam and I take turns in the outhouse, swapping our soaked

clothes for dry ones. I make our packaged soup while he braves the wind and rain to set up our tent. "Sweet Home Alabama" rocks from someone's radio.

If I weren't so nervous about tonight, I'd probably sing along. This is Mom's Brownie Song. A few times each week, Mom and Dad burst into my room around nine o'clock and dance around chanting, "Brownies! Brownies! Brownies!"

Nine p.m. is munchies hour.

Although Mom's the one writing the never-ending cookbook, it's me everyone comes to when wanting something edible. Soup was my first foray in the kitchen, then pasta, stews, cookies. I couldn't wait to get home from school, thinking about what new dish I'd create. I've barely cooked while traveling. Sam's always too quick to melt cheese on whatever receptacle he can find. Hearing "Sweet Home Alabama" reminds me how much I miss it, though. It's Mom's go-to song when I'm baking, and I belted it out while making my last batch of brownies: dark chocolate with lavender and pink salt. They disappeared in seconds.

I spend the rest of my time at the stove reprimanding myself for lusting after some girl's boyfriend and reminding myself this is what guys do. They flirt. It's harmless. It's like scratching an itch. I'm reading into things with Sam because it's what *I* do: fantasize. I've for sure imagined this connection between us. Although Leigh said she sensed it, too.

Mom didn't help, either. I finally got a text from her before we left, and her confession shocked me. She said when she met Dad, he was in a relationship. An unhealthy relationship. Still, a relationship. She said she let things unfold naturally. Since there's a serious time delay, I didn't bother with the million questions that surfaced. Like how long did it take? Did they talk about their feelings before he ended things? Did they hook up *before* he ended things? Then I started thinking about my parents and hookups and a whole lot of grossness, so I imposed a blackout. But her words encouraged my ridiculous notion that Sam might, maybe, possibly like me.

Later, I sit with him and eat and chat with the nice Italian couple at the table. The whole while I'm transfixed by the way his jaw works when he swallows. The way his elbow grazes mine. The way his curls bounce when he laughs. There's a lot of transfixing going on. My porno soundtrack is on low, a constant steady hum I can feel everywhere. It doesn't help that his honeyed eyes linger on me. Or maybe I'm imagining that, too.

By the time we head to our tent, I'm dizzy from the day we've had and the night ahead. We crawl into our sleeping bags, me in a long underwear top and bottom, him in loose flannel pants and a tight, long-sleeve shirt. It grips his muscles in all the right places. He turns on his headlamp, puts it to the side, and the tent glows dark blue.

We both pull our sleeping bags up to our chins, the warmth from the hut fading fast as a deep chill takes hold. Sam rolls his head toward me. "That was a great day. Thanks for making it so much fun." His voice is quiet as the rain patters on the tent.

I kick my legs in the bag to prevent hypothermia. "Don't thank me. You're the reason we came here. You made me run through those puddles. Which, by the way, I'm regretting. It's likely we'll freeze by morning." I exhale and a puff of vapor escapes my lips. I kick my feet more.

Soon, he's wiggling in his bag, too, both of us trying to keep warm. Before I know what's happening, he unzips his bag and reaches for mine. The zipper slides down at breakneck speed, my heart pumping faster. "Hey, wait, Sam. What…what are you doing?" I can't move. I can only watch his fingers as they finish undoing my sleeping bag. Strong fingers. Long fingers. Fingers that could…

"I'm hooking our bags together. It's too damn cold." He doesn't even look at me.

Holy God. Our bags. *Together?* "Are you sure that's a good idea?"

"What? Sharing our body heat because we're in the mountains? In a tent? On a cold, rainy night? I'm pretty sure it's a perfect idea." Ignoring my hesitation, he shoves me out of the way to zip our bags together.

"That's not what I mean."

"I don't follow, Nina. Use your words."

Either he's clueless or he's messing with me. The sexual tension between us has me ready to snap, tension I've been conjuring if he thinks this is a good idea. "Sam…you have a *girlfriend*." I whisper the word like I'm cursing.

"And?"

God, he's infuriating. "And…" He settles into the bag and drags me against him, flipping me over to spoon against his chest. *That chest.* All rational thought leaves with the next burst of vapor from my mouth, a soft whimper with it. He tightens his arms around me. "*And* what?" he asks again, his hot breath in my ear.

Something digs into my back then. Something thick. Long. *Hard.* This is bad, right? Like really bad. It either means my attraction isn't one-sided or he suffers from priapism—an uncontrollable state of persistent erection. (I happened upon that term while Googling fear of penises.) Please, God, let it be priapism. He has one hand on my ribs, below the swell of my breast. The other is wrapped over my chest, his fingers clutching my raised shoulder. We inhale in sync and exhale slowly. Then I remember his question. The one about why I thought spooning against his erection was a bad idea. Yeah, *that*. I find my voice. "You have a girlfriend, Sam. Doesn't spooning, you know, lead to…*forking*?" Again with the whispering.

His whole body shakes behind me. "Holy shit. Did you just say *forking*? I need to preserve this moment in a time capsule."

I move my hips forward, just enough. The dampness gathering in my long underwear is too distracting to properly defend myself against his teasing. "I don't know what's so funny."

He tugs my hips to his, right into his priapism. It sends a bolt of heat between my thighs. "Let me get this straight," he says. "You're worried I might, what? Eat off your fork later? Or that you might eat off mine…and like it? And sorry about the hard-on, you're just too hot."

"Oh, my God." I tug forward and dive under the sleeping bag, pulling it over my head. "You have no shame," I shout through the nylon. The heat between my legs inflames, spurring on my perpetual dampness, the chill from earlier gone. I squish myself as far as possible into the side of the sleeping bag, away from Sam and his raging hard-on.

He crawls under with me. *With me.* "Here's the situation, Nina. Fact is, it's cold, and I'd like to stay warm. Under the circumstances, this is the best option. I can't do anything about my reaction to you. You'll have to deal with it. So, please, get up here and into my arms before we freeze to death." He breathes, I breathe—both of us impersonating a horny Darth Vader. Leigh was right. You could choke on this sexual tension.

My multiple-choice answers are as follows:

Choice A: "Sure, Sam. I'd love to cuddle with you and your hard-on. I can't imagine your girlfriend will mind."

Choice B: "No, Sam. I'd like to become a human Popsicle that scientists will dissect to learn how it's possible a Canadian girl couldn't brave the cold.

Choice C: Say absolutely nothing. Run from the tent and disappear, leaving a trail of hormones and unanswered questions as to how the strange girl in all those embarrassing videos vanished. They'll write a book about it.

Unfortunately, I can't run away from Sam even if I want to, because, well, he's *Sam*. Choice B is out of the question. I've had an issue with dissection ever since Kyle Turner flicked frog guts at me in the middle of our bio lab. He called me Slime Girl.

That leaves Choice A.

Slowly, I crawl over to him and inch my head out of the bag. His hands are on me again, my back to his chest in seconds, his hard-on still *hard* and settled against my backside. "That's better," he whispers, tugging me closer. He doesn't apologize again for his blatant arousal. He chuckles softly. "That was hilarious, by the way. Forking? I plan on adding that to my book of Cute Things Nina Says."

Tired of him and his flirting, I grind my backside into his erection until he says, "Christ," and stills my hips. "What the fuck was that?"

"Nothing. Just, I was planning on writing this whole scene

into my how-to book on the best ways to lose your girlfriend." I move forward a millimeter, shocked at my nerve to rub against him. Shocked at how good it felt. A series of short, sharp breaths hit my ear.

Instead of tugging me closer, his voice drops to a whisper. "I could add a few things to that book." His tone is different. Tight. He moves farther away, and I roll onto my back. He's propped on his elbow, gazing down at me.

"You okay?" I ask, placing my hand on his chest. It looks small and pale on his black top. When I flatten my palm, he closes his eyes. One, two, three heartbeats later, he opens them up and all jokes vanish. The tent swells with unspoken words, hunger etched on his face, darkness in his eyes. I've never wanted anything as bad as this. *Sam*. His mouth on mine. His hands on me. To feel like I belong to him, if only for a minute.

Not knowing why, my hand floats from his chest up to his chin, to the scar embedded under his stubble. I trace the indentation, the way he often does, and our lips part at the same moment, his eyes burning into mine. Fierce. Beautiful. Perfect. Those are the words that describe this man. "God, I wish you were mine," I say. *Like out loud?* Those words were supposed to be on mute. Unspoken. A silent prayer.

That's when he growls.

Twelve

SAM

She's touching my face, tracing my scar, and I'm not sure how we got here. I'm not sure of anything anymore except how badly I want to dive into Nina. This girl, on this night, in this tent, is the most beautiful thing I've ever seen. My chest spasms from the tightness, and I've never been so hard and desperate for a girl. Ever. I swear, if I could bury myself inside of her, she could make me whole again.

I knew I was asking for trouble, renting this tent and sleeping next to her. I must've been on crack thinking I could hold back. Resist her. I want her so damn bad, but I'm realizing with each passing minute her rejection is bound to kill me. I can't let her see the flesh beneath my flannels.

Then she says, "God, I wish you were mine."

My self-control snaps. A growl rips from my throat and her lips part—an invitation. A plea. I can't stop myself. Our lips connect, those soft, pink lips, and she tastes like cherry and sex. I slide my tongue against hers and she responds willingly, her hands tugging my neck closer, pulling at my hair. *Jesus.* I try to take it slowly, be gentle. With her phobias, I doubt she's had much experience, and I don't want to frighten her. Apparently, she has different ideas. She arches her breasts toward me and claims my mouth, her teeth on my lips, her tongue unforgiving. I match her intensity, driving my tongue deeper, clutching her roughly to my chest.

I thought I was hard before, like a teenager with my dick digging into her ass. But this? It's like I've been pumped with steel, and I need to get closer. I slide on top of her, and her legs part for me. Invite me in. Her hips jerk upward as my name falls from her lips. "Sam," she moans. "Oh, God, Sam."

I devour the words, wanting to preserve them, knowing I'll relive them for days to come. Her hands are on my back, kneading the tension in my muscles. I grind into her, rubbing my length where it counts, nothing but thin fabric between us. And I get harder. There's no rain, no cold. There is only her. The tent fogs with our heavy breaths.

"Nina," I murmur, needing to hear her name. "Nina," I say again, as I taste the length of her neck and take her ear between my teeth. "You don't know…" I tug her ear harder. "You have no idea…" She rocks her hips up to mine. The movement causes my dick to slide lower, and it comes to rest at her center. We both still, ragged breaths drawing us closer. She sucks her lip into her mouth, and something in her eyes shifts. Still heated, still hungry, but brimming with trust. I should be able to do the same. Trust her. Show her all of me the way she's opened herself up. But I can't. Not yet. Not when I only have half a heart.

The breaking gets that much worse.

With my dick hovering at her clothed opening, she says, "Sam." It sounds desperate. Needy. I lean forward to kiss the mole on her cheek, the place I've been dying to lick. As I taste her skin, I nudge my hips forward an inch, and we both moan. *Holy shit.* With two bits of fabric between me and the heaven that is Nina, I press in farther, only as far as these confines will allow, and I almost come.

Her hands glide down my back and dip into the waistband of my flannels. Her nails claw against my ass. It's too much. She's too much. And no fucking way am I taking off these pants. I adjust my length over her and grind so hard she cries out. We rock together, clothes on, eyes locked, both of us chasing our release. I palm her breast over her shirt, her nipple pebbled and as coiled as the rest of her. Her head drops then, her thighs tightening around me.

A few thrusts later she cries, "God, yes."

I growl, "Nina," as I come hard and fast, still shuddering a minute later.

We're fully clothed, our lips swollen, limbs spent, my release seeping through our pants. It's ridiculous and juvenile, and it's the hottest thing I've ever done. I'd like to say I'm sated, that my craving for her has been quenched, but I'm already hard again. It wasn't enough. With Nina, I doubt it ever will be.

Her eyes widen at the feel of me thickening, and her body tenses. I push onto my knees, my hands still caging her shoulders, the sleeping bag hanging over my waist. "Hi," I say.

She stifles a laugh, still breathing heavily. "Hi," she whispers. Then her brow puckers. "Was that normal?"

I shake my head. "No. Not normal."

Instantly, she curls in on herself. Her gaze slides from mine, shifty, like she's scanning for the exit, and she moves to get up. I lock my knees on either side of her hips, pinning her in place. "Nina, this is me. You're not allowed to get embarrassed with me. Ever. Okay?"

She inhales deeply, swallows, and finally opens her mouth. "What did you mean though, not normal? I haven't been with guys much, and this was…different."

Different? I'm no saint. I lost my virginity to Mark Baylor's older sister. She was eighteen, I was fifteen, and, man, did she have good hands. I'd blame her for kick-starting my lust for women, but that would be a lie. I like sex. Plain and simple. I like to think about it. Have it. Talk about it. I like everything about it. I experimented a lot in my younger years with as many willing partners as I could find, and when I hooked up with Lacey, she was game. I'm not one to cheat. I'm a one-woman guy. But I like to fuck. A lot. So it means something when I say *hell-fucking-yeah* this was different.

"Let me rephrase my earlier answer. Was that normal? Yes and no."

She cocks her adorable head. "Explain, please."

I'm still on my knees, leaning over her, both of us wet from my release, but I can't move. My dick is hard again, and I'm not ready to go clean up. "Okay. Yes meaning, that was dry-fucking and it's normal. It's a thing people do. Mainly sixteen-year-olds, but still, a thing. No, it wasn't normal because never in the history of man has dry-fucking ever felt that good."

I lower over her again, desperate to feel her, when she says, "What about Lacey?"

There goes my hard-on.

I roll away from her, kick my feet out of the bag, and sit hunched over my bent knees. The rain slaps against the side of the tent, the fabric billowing with a gust of wind. She watches me, those catlike eyes zeroing in. She deserves some answers, but I need to get my head straight. I turn and force a smile. "You okay if I go clean up and change? We'll talk. I promise. I just need to wash up."

She nods and says, "Sure." But the trust in her gaze wavers. Can't say I blame her. A horny guy with a "girlfriend" just dry-fucked her and now he's bailing. *Asshole*. I fumble for another pair of pants in my backpack and brave the wind and rain on my way to the outhouse.

Although I need to clear my head and figure out how to confess to Nina that I've been lying to her and that I'm scared, fucking terrified, to tell her the truth, it's too cold and gross to extend my stay in the outdoor shitter. I get back too fast.

She's in our joined bag, the nylon held up to her chin. Her head is on her makeshift pillow—a pillowcase filled with lumpy clothes. I zip the tent shut, kick off my shoes, and dive into the other half of the bag, facing her nose to nose.

She drags her teeth over her lip. "So."

"So."

"We were gonna talk."

"Yeah." I stop myself from reaching for her and settle on inhaling her scent; cherry, coconut, and the smell of sex. The smell of us. A guy could get high on that. She waits patiently, barely blinking. I need to man the fuck up and tell her the truth. Without warning, her palm comes to rest on my elbow. I cover her hand with mine.

She exhales with a quiet, "Hi."

I almost crumble.

Emotion claws at my throat, raw and unfamiliar, like I'm breathing underwater. This girl says hi to me, and I'm falling to pieces. I can't tell her. Not yet. I need more time—with her, with us. Blind her with how awesome we are so she can't see how damaged I am.

When I pulled back the covers of my hospital bed and Lacey saw the mutilated flesh clinging to my legs, she looked ready to puke. She actually gagged a bit. My confidence, my manhood, walked out the door with her that day. She got more distant, stopped visiting, and rarely asked about my mom. She disappeared from my life. Good riddance, as far as I'm concerned. But what if Nina freaks out, too?

I move an inch closer. "Lacey and me, it's complicated."

"Yeah, I gathered. But I need specifics. We can't do *that* and not talk about it. I mean, unless you're messing around with me and, like, not interested. Which is totally fine. We're traveling. We barely know each. And well…the tent and everything. Just forget I asked. Sorry. It was stupid. I'm stupid. I'm going to disappear now." She tugs the sleeping bag over her head.

I want to laugh at how cute she is, stumbling over her words—words that couldn't be more wrong, but I'm not about to let her go on thinking I'm not into her. "I can still see you, Canada." She pulls the nylon tighter around her head. I join her in her safe place under the sleeping bag and press my forehead to hers in the dark. Her breaths are deep and heavy, practically filling my lungs. "I'll get to the Lacey thing, because you're right; we can't raise the dry-fucking standards and pretend it's nothing. Before we get to that, though, I want to be clear about something." I feel for her hands in the dark and lace our fingers together. Everything amplifies in our cocoon, the heat, the smells, the sensations. I'd kill to hit pause. "I'm into you, Nina. *Very* into you. This isn't casual for me. It hasn't been since that first night at the hostel, and what happened tonight meant something. To me, at least. Whatever else happens, I want you to know that. It's been more than a little challenging keeping my hands off of you. Tonight, it was just too much."

"Okay." Her soft voice fills the space between us. "I'm into you, too. Very. I'm just a lot scared."

I kiss the hand I'm holding. "Join the club." A truer statement there never was. "What do you say we surface for the rest of this conversation?"

She wiggles her head out, and we pull the lip of the bag to our shoulders.

I give her a wink. "Hi."

"Hi." She giggles quietly.

I kiss her forehead and she sighs. The rain has lessened outside, the steady patter now random drops. There's a glow in her eyes. Not the lust I sometimes see—something deeper, something more. Maybe it's the soft light playing tricks.

I drag in a breath as I build the lie I can't seem to shake. "So,

Lacey. Things got rough for us after the accident, strained for a bunch of reasons. It changed me, what happened. Can't say if it's for the better or the worse, I'm just…different. And things weren't the same with us. I was close to ending it a couple of times, but Lacey's been dealing with some family stuff. She's in a tough place. I care about her, and I'm worried what'll happen if I cut her off. I'm not sure she can handle it. So I left on this trip, knowing, theoretically, we were done, but holding back from telling her. She's pretty fragile right now."

This is me being a pussy. This is me sucking dick. I'm like that guy who goes to the pharmacist on behalf of his "friend" to ask about his crotch itch. *Lacey* is vulnerable. *Lacey* is fragile. *Lacey* might break if she gets dumped. Me. Me. Fucking *me*. I want to wring my own neck. I watch Nina for any telltale signs she knows I'm the biggest douche alive, but she's dragging her teeth over her bottom lip, deep in thought.

"Okay," she says.

"Okay? Like, okay what?"

"Okay, I get it. And thanks for telling me the truth." She hitches her shoulders higher and shivers from the cold.

Truth. *Spineless asshole.* The irony of the situation isn't lost on me. Here I've been forcing her to take control of her life and own her crazy, while I'm running from my shadow. I hate being this guy. The Sam before the accident never would have shied away from Nina. That Sam was fifty percent cocky, fifty percent charm, and all precision on the football field. Now I'm more fifty-fifty coward and menopausal woman.

In time, I'll tell her. In a week or two. When I have her where I want her, I'll show her my legs and hope for the best. Hope revulsion doesn't blanket her face. I have a sinking feeling it would make the downward spiral I hit after Lacey's rejection feel like a kiddie ride.

I nudge her shoulder. "What do you say we try the spooning thing again to warm up?"

She purses her lips. "There are rules now."

"Rules?"

"No, sorry, *rule*. One rule."

I raise my eyebrow in question.

"No forking," she says. "None whatsoever, dry or otherwise. Keep your horny bits to yourself. If, or when, you end things with Lacey, we can revise said rule."

"Just the one rule?"

"Yeah, but it covers all sexy stuff. It's a blanket rule."

"Okay. Fine. Blanket rule. Now get over here." I tug her against my chest, my erection already straining for her. I shove the loose covers of the sleeping bags between us. "I can't control my dick, though. He's got a mind of his own and thinks you're hot. If he nudges you from time to time, I'll try to rein him in."

"God, Sam. You're breaking the rule after barely a minute."

"No I'm not. There will be no forking. Scout's honor. But I can *talk* about forking. And *imagine* forking. I think about us forking a lot."

"You're impossible." I can tell she's smiling.

"Yeah, I know." I hug her tighter.

We breathe in time, her back swelling into my chest.

"Sam," she says suddenly. "Tell me something about your mother. Anything. One of your favorite memories."

A gust of wind billows the tent, the rain picking up again. She clasps my hand and threads our fingers together. The fingers I didn't realize I was clenching.

I press my chin to the top of her head and swallow. "Twelfth grade. I was grounded because she found out I skipped a bunch of classes, but there was an epic party that night. Just down the street. No way was I going to sit in my room while my friends were partying. So I snuck out my window, almost killing myself in the process. A few beers into the party, the entire room fell silent, the people parting like the Red fucking Sea. My mother stood with her arms crossed, glaring at me."

I shake my head and find myself *smiling*. It's nice to think about my mom, to remember her and not turn it into a cry-fest like often happens with my cousin James. He's the only person I can talk to about her, but it's always so draining. I can't bring things up with my dad, unless I want to watch the man fall apart. My sister deals with her loss by burying it. She avoids the subject at all costs. Although my friends are cool, silence descends if the topic of mothers comes up. Or football. Or girlfriends. That's another reason I needed this trip. I couldn't take the worried looks and awkward moments—everyone treating me with kid gloves because I can't play ball anymore. Because Lacey dumped me. Because my mother died.

I'm not sure if Nina senses my need to talk about this shit, to remember my mom, but I'm grateful she asked the question. I hold her tight as I recall that night. "So my mom dragged me out by the neck of my shirt, still hadn't said a word, and we were down the street about half a block when she sat on the street curb. She pulled me down beside her. I was still holding my beer.

I mean, I was shitting bricks at the sight of her in the house and was too scared to do anything but follow her out the door. Anyway, she grabbed it and chugged the entire thing. Like a pro. It was awesome."

I sandwich her hand between both of mine, and she leans farther into me. "Go on," she says.

So I go on, rain pattering, heart pounding. I relive the moment. I allow the memory to *be*. "She threw her arm around my back, and I'll never forget her words that night. 'You're getting older, Sam. I know that. It won't be long until you're off at school, and I won't be there to keep you in line. You're going to drink and party and break the rules from time to time. I did. Your dad did. I just hope you know which rules are breakable and which aren't. I hope we taught you that. And I'm sorry about tonight. I know the party was a big deal. I just needed to feel like I was still your mom. Like I still had some say.'"

I give Nina's hand a squeeze. "That was the first time she spoke to me as an adult, an equal. And I got it, you know? What she was going through. It's one of those moments that sticks with you." I inhale the coconut scent from her hair, exhaling slowly. "Thanks. It's nice to talk about her like this. The good times."

Everything about Nina is beautiful. The gray wool hat she wore today pulled low on her forehead, her usual ponytail over her shoulder. But like this, on a cold, rainy night in New Zealand, her beauty is in her ability to ease my heavy heart. I lift her hand and kiss her knuckles, because I have to. Because she needs to know how important that question was. "Now it's my turn. I have two things I'd like to ask."

Her breathing stills as I brush my lips over her fingers. "Two?" she finally says. "That hardly seems fair. I only asked one."

"Sucks to be you, Canada. Question one: You've mentioned your folks live in a swanky area of Toronto. I'm struggling to put together how two eccentric hippies have afforded that lifestyle. I don't mean to be blunt. Just seems odd is all." The rain is heavier, a rumble so constant you could tune it out. Actually, when I'm around Nina, I can tune everything out.

She rolls back, shifting to see my face. "Technically, that wasn't a question. It was an observation. But I know what you're getting at. My dad is a hoarder, pot-smoking, hippie freak, but he's also a computer-slash-math whiz. He was part of the HTML-five team that created some robot language us human folks can read. If you get him talking about his work, he throws around words like interoperable implementations, syntactic features, and scalable vector graphics, so I don't ask about it. He made a pile of cash and still freelances. Actually, if you think about it, he's part of the reason my high school life sucked. His algorithms helped build YouTube, the vehicle that houses my humiliation."

"You could look at it like that, *or* you could thank him for your exceptional physique. You wouldn't have made it up that first hike if it weren't for the tai chi he forced on you."

She tries to push my arms away, but I don't let her. She settles on slamming her elbow into my side. "You suck."

"I know." I draw her closer, spooning her against my chest again. "Question two: Your siblings all have cool car names. Don't get me wrong, I love Nina. It suits you. But I don't get why you missed out on the chance to rock a kick-ass name."

"Again, Sam, that was a statement, not a question. You sure you've done two years of college?"

I squeeze her thigh in that sensitive spot that makes her jump. She squeals and pushes to the other side of the sleeping bag, breathless. Instead of biting back with one of her funny comments, she stiffens and quiets. This is the Nina who gets embarrassed. This is the Nina who shuts people out. This is the Nina I thought we banished.

I lift onto my elbow and place my hand on her shoulder. "Did I hit a nerve?" I run my thumb down her neck, my hand settling near her collarbone. Near the dip I kissed. The place I want to graze my teeth on right now. But I can't break her rule. Or maybe it's *my* rule. A familiar heat stirs in my flannels.

She stiffens under my touch, but something tells me it has more to do with my question than my closeness. "Yeah," she says. "I guess I lost the lottery on the name thing. My dad got into cars after I was born, hence the cool names. So I'm just Nina. Two syllables. Boring, plain old Nina."

She shrugs all nonchalant, but I can read her plain as day. Her brows are furrowed, her eyes glassy. She's chewing on her cheek. Everything about her screams she's lying. And she's upset. I can't imagine why she'd lie about the origin of her name, but I won't push her. Not yet, at least. I lie down and tug her against me. "We should sleep. I was thinking we might do that side trail on the way out tomorrow."

She shakes her head. "No. I'd like to get back earlier. I'm looking forward to seeing Leigh."

Great. Not only do I have to sleep in my own bunk without Nina tomorrow, but I have to share her with the Wicked Bitch of the West. I don't know what Nina suddenly sees in her. Chicks like that don't change overnight. I need to get rid of Leigh and save Nina from whatever crap that girl's bound to pull. More important, I need to travel with Nina alone. I need to imprint myself on her and ditch this lie festering between us before I mess things up for good.

Thirteen

SAM

After traveling with Leigh, the Wicked Bitch of the West, for two weeks, I have since changed her name to the Raging Bitch. It just has a ring to it. Our first argument happened the minute she sat in my car and told me flat out, "You smell like month-old cat litter. New car rule. No wearing the same clothes for more than two days."

Yesterday, our enlightening conversation centered on cheerleading and whether or not it's a sport. My vote: no fucking way. Leigh's vote: of course, asshole.

After the Raging Bitch rebutted my claim that any activity involving a guy using jazz hands is not a sport, she kicked my seat and demanded I toss her my phone. She wanted to find a video to prove her point that palming a chick's ass before flipping her in the air trumps the jazz hands. I still say no fucking way.

So the Raging Bitch had my phone for a while, a hell of a lot longer than it takes to look up some stupid video, and she's been bitchier ever since. And quiet. Evil-genius quiet. Something feels off. I keep checking the rearview mirror as we drive into Nelson—our first stop on the South Island of New Zealand. Leigh makes eye contact each time, glaring so hard I'm surprised the mirror hasn't cracked. Tired of trying to figure out her bullshit, I shift the mirror and glance at Nina, who is texting her mom as usual. I have to force my eyes back on the road. The curve of her neck and her low-cut tank top are hypnotic.

It's been two weeks since I rocked against her in that tent. Two weeks since I tasted her lips. *Two fucking weeks.* Aside from interruptions by the Raging Bitch, Nina and I have been inseparable. And I'm ready to explode. Every time I try to ditch the girlfriend lie and tell her about my legs, I make up another excuse. *This hostel's dirty. She looks tired. I'll do it tomorrow.*

It's gone way beyond infatuation. Sure, I jack off to images of our dry-fucking escapade, and I spend most of my time trying to figure out how I can touch her skin or borrow her cherry lip balm just to taste her. But it's my chest Nina affects most. The constant tightness. The ache. She's infiltrated my bones.

She still looks at me like I'm a human Popsicle, but I need a sign she won't freak when she sees my legs. Something, *anything*, to give me that last push.

I park outside the hostel, the ocean and beach across the road. Salt inflames my nose, waves crashing and seagulls squawking as I walk to the trunk. It would be peaceful and calming if I didn't hear that nasty throaty noise Leigh makes as she mutters from behind me, "Hurry it up, gimpy."

Heads are going to roll.

Instead of helping Nina with her pack into the hostel, which is what I should be doing, I swivel around. Leigh's features sharpen. I try to match her glare, but this chick gives the Grinch a run for his money. "What did you call me?"

She taps her chin. "Dumbass? Gimpy? Asswipe? Which time, exactly?"

God, I want to rip her heart out, but Pops's famous sayings are always at the back of my mind: *You ever hurt a girl, son, and I will beat your balls with a cactus.*

But I'm done with Leigh's attitude and snide remarks. I call ahead to Nina, "You mind signing us all in? I just need a word with…Leigh." *The Raging Bitch*, I don't say.

Her sexy green eyes dart between my ticking jaw and Leigh's narrowing gaze. She hikes her pack higher on her shoulders. "Sure. Just don't dismember each other or anything." Her eyes land on me for another second before she lumbers through the front doors.

Once she's out of sight, I drag Leigh by her arm to the side of the hostel. We stand facing each other, arms crossed, lips pursed, while the mother of all staring contests ensues. Finally I say, "What the fuck is wrong with you?"

She pulls her head back. "Me? What's wrong with me? What I'd like to know is why you've been lying to our ginger friend all this time." With raised eyebrows, she smirks at me.

This is no normal smirk. This is the Raging Bitch's evil-genius-plotting smirk. Fucking hell. *She knows.* I stare at the ground, blinking, until it sinks in.

It must have been my phone.

I'm always logged onto Facebook, connected with friends back home. Lacey's been posting pics of her new boy toy, one of the dipshits from Delta Tau Delta. I couldn't give a crap, but my buddy Xander messaged me to say he thinks Lacey's stock has tanked since we broke up. *Since she dumped me* is what he should have said, but like all my friends these days, he avoids the subject.

Back to the Raging Bitch. The only explanation for her intel is that she must have scrolled through my messages when she borrowed my phone, learned I've been lying about Lacey, and now she's waiting for the perfect moment to ruin my life. She hasn't told Nina yet—I'd know if she had—but she's probably dying to infect her with loads of crap about how big of a dick I am. "You went through my cell yesterday, didn't you? You know I don't have a girlfriend."

She shrugs her bony shoulders. "Is this you showing off your above-average intelligence? Yeah, I scrolled through your phone. Your friends look as douchey as you."

I scrub my hands down my face and pace. "I have reasons for what I did. And…*fuck*. It's none of your business anyway."

"I'd love to hear your reasons for making Nina feel like second-hand laundry."

Hearing the words guts me. Even coming from Leigh. Nina tells her stuff and it means Nina said something to that effect. Maybe not as blunt, but my lying has hurt the one girl I'd do anything to protect. My chest aches again, deeper this time. Like if I don't make things right with Nina, it might suffocate my heart. I'm an asshole for letting things go this far.

I stop pacing and face Leigh. "Look. I just need to talk to her and explain. She deserves to hear it from me. I think even you can agree with that."

"Give me one good reason why I shouldn't march in there and tell Nina you're as worthless as the residue below scum."

To avoid her glare, I glance down the street. There's a couple by the road, the girl's arm secure around the guy's waist, his hand hooked over her shoulder while they study a map. I can't count how many times over the past few weeks I've wanted Nina in my arms, held tight to my side. It was never like this with Lacey. Sure, I liked being with her. The touchy-feely stuff just never entered into the picture. But Nina? These days, it's a constant obsession. And my "accidental" touching of her body isn't enough. I know she wants me, too, but my phantom girlfriend keeps her away.

I'm so done with this.

If I don't tell Leigh about my legs and she barges into the hostel, ranting about my lying ways, I'll lose Nina for good. But I can't. Not like this. If she sends me packing because of my scars, then I'll have to deal with it. But I'm not letting her cut me loose because I'm too big of a pussy to tell her the truth. Looking back at Leigh, I grit my teeth. For some messed-up reason, Nina trusts her. Confides in her. I suck a deep breath and look the Dragon Lady dead on. (The Raging Bitch wasn't cutting it.) If she's my only way, then so be it.

I nod to the picnic bench by the sidewalk. We walk over and sit on the top, our feet on the bench below, both of us leaning our elbows on our knees. Her knees are sharp and angular, like her face. My knees look like raw hamburger below my jeans, and I'm about to share that with the bitch who called me Gimpy.

"You know about my accident, right?"

She nods while she bites at one of her nails. "Yeah. Nina told me about your mom, which, you know, sucks. And"—she flicks her head to my ankle—"the I-can't-play-football injury."

I snort and glance up the street. That same couple from before is coming out of a shop, hand in hand, both of them in shorts on this warm day. I'm in jeans. Always in jeans. Would Nina be okay by my side with my deformity on display for everyone to point and stare? Would I be? That's one thing I haven't done since the accident. I live in Florida, and I haven't put on a pair of shorts in more than a year. And I'm a guy. Who sweats. Not a good combo.

I grab a twig from the bench and start breaking it into pieces. "The ankle injury is more involved than I told her. Most of my left leg was shattered, and I had extensive third-degree burns."

"On your leg?"

"Both legs, just past my knees. It's pretty horrible, and I'm…" I toss the rest of the twig on the grass and drop my head in my hands. "I'm scared shitless, Leigh. If you want the truth, there it is. I've never fallen for anyone the way Nina twists me up, and I lied to her so we could get close before I unveil my messed-up legs. Things didn't go so well with Lacey when she saw the damage. I'm a little sensitive about it. It doesn't excuse the lying, but whatever. It's not like I can take it back. The question is, will you help me or not? Will you go inside and ask Nina to come out so I can talk to her?"

All I get is silence. Then, "I think I need to see them."

I snap my head up sure she's smirking, but her face is dead serious. "Are you out of your mind? A minute ago you called me Gimpy. No chance in hell."

"Sam? It is Sam, right? I call you so many names it's hard to keep track."

I shake my head in awe of her nerve.

"So anyway, *Sam*, I know Nina pretty well. It might help if I can see what you're working with. I mean, I still haven't removed you from my douchebag list, but you're no longer at the top. So let's head to the guys' washroom."

Like hell. "No fucking way. Not happening."

She runs her hand up her neck and tugs her hair. A seagull swoops down to scoop a crust of bread from the road. The smell of barbeque floats over from behind the hostel. Then she says, "What if we play a version of 'I'll show you mine, if you show me yours'?"

I fist my hands, wanting this conversation to be over. I need to talk to Nina and make things right. "I've seen your legs plenty. They're…fine. The answer is still no."

"What I mean is, if I share something with you, something personal, will you tuck your mangina away and show me your fried legs?"

Un-fucking-believable. The Dragon Lady returns with a vengeance, and she wants me to put myself on display for her. Probably so she can tear me to pieces. Knock my ego down until it can't be resuscitated. And mangina? Is it really that obvious? Damn those doctors for whatever they did to me. "Let's put it this way, Leigh. Unless you're about to tell me you're a hermaphrodite with no discernible sex, and I get to see your lack of genitalia, there's nothing you could share that would change my mind."

"I'm gay," she says.

"You're what?"

"Gay. You know, I dig chicks. Not in the happy sense."

"Really?"

"Yeah."

"Seriously?"

"Are you asking me to tie your nuts in a knot? 'Cause it kind of sounds like you are."

I wouldn't have pegged Leigh for gay. My cousin James came out a few years back, and we practically threw a party. It meant we could all stop pretending we didn't know. Aside from being effeminate, he was always checking guys out, and girls *never* came up. When he finally opened up, we got closer. He'd picks me up stumbling drunk from parties at ungodly hours, and I'd rescue him from bad dates by posing as his scorned lover. He's also the only person since the accident who doesn't treat me like I'm about to break.

I assumed James was gay, but Leigh's confession is surprising, especially the way she flirted with Bruno and Callum at the first hostel. "Sorry. You caught me off guard. But gay, huh? Does that have something to do with why you left Reese and Brianne?"

She nods. "Long story. But you, Sam, are the second person I've shared that tidbit with. Nina being the first, the night she helped with my makeover. I don't suggest you take that lightly. If you ever breathe a word to anyone, I will light the rest of you on fire." She pushes off the table. "Now get your pansy ass up so we can get this over with before I change my mind. To the men's shitter we go." She struts toward the hostel.

I groan and follow her. She may be a blunt bitch, but, in a weird way, I'd rather deal with that than the way my friends tiptoe around me. And she can help me with Nina. Apparently, I'm willing to get eaten alive for that girl.

By the time I'm standing, legs wide, arms crossed, with the bathroom stalls at my back, in nothing but my T-shirt and boxers, I'm feeling less confident about my decision. I mean, *Christ*. How did I let her talk me into this? My shoes, socks, and jeans are in a pile to my right, and Dragon Lady's in front of me, studying my legs. She's been staring for a good five minutes and hasn't said a damn thing.

She *finally* cocks her head. "Yeah, so, you're kind of right. It looks like they put the flames out with a fork."

"Jesus fuck, Leigh. What the hell is wrong with you? You think maybe I'm little vulnerable here? At least you can hide your shit. You're not walking around with an 'I'm gay' tattoo on your forehead."

"If you're done being sensitive, I can give you some cream for your itchy mangina."

"Screw you."

"That's sweet. Can I finish my assessment now?"

"Whatever. Let's get to the part where you help me with Nina."

A guy pushes into the bathroom, and I reach for my jeans as Dragon Lady hisses at him. "Not a step closer, dude. Back out the way you came, unless you want my foot so far up your ass I can kick out your teeth."

The guy pales and scurries away.

She swings back to me. "Where was I?"

I know exactly where she was. Gawking at me. I've stared in the mirror enough to know every horrifying inch. The hard white patches that belong on a lizard. The puckered sections, red and lumpy. The rectangular scars up my thighs from the skin grafts. I'm the beast to Nina's beauty.

"Here's the deal," she says. "It is pretty awful. You're right about that. But you're not giving Nina enough credit. That girl is a walking disaster. She *gets* different. She knows what it's like to be a freak. If she cares about you, she'll get past the legs."

I shift on my feet, frowning. "That's why I lied in the first place. To build something between us so she'd be able to deal with…this." I flick my hand toward my legs. "Honestly, if she looks at me like I'm a leper, I'm gonna hurt something. I know I need to tell her; I just have to find the right time."

She walks over to my jeans and tosses them to me. "Get dressed, Man-candy. I won't tell Nina you've been lying. But you need to come clean. She's fallen for you. Hard. I'm pretty sure your shredded legs won't be the deal breaker."

As she leaves the guys' washroom, I call, "I'm gonna head to the Internet café down the street first. Can you ask her to meet me outside in an hour?"

She gives me a thumbs-up and pushes out the door.

I need to get my head on straight before this goes down, and James is the guy I go to when things get heavy. He sees this relationship stuff clearly. Can't say the dude dates good guys, but with Lacey, he warned me she was a waste of space way before it ended. My life was so upside down at the time, I didn't do anything about it, but he knew she wouldn't stand by me when it mattered. Maybe if I e-mail him about Nina, get it all out on a page, it'll help. I get dressed in a hurry.

* * *

I slide into one of the plastic chairs at the café and power up my account, pumped to get this weight off my shoulders, but the incoming message from James deflates me:

Don't go hopping on the next plane back, but I thought you should know there's been a setback with your dad. He's kind of barricading himself in his room again, but we're on top of it. Don't worry. AND...on a happier note, I've got a hot coffee date tomorrow. Trevor is his name, and even you would approve of this boy. I'll keep you posted on your dad. And seriously. DON'T. WORRY.

As a general rule, people only say "don't worry" when there's something to worry about. I reach for my phone by the keyboard, but it's four a.m. at home. Squeezing my eyes, I drag my hands down my face. Dad was on the mend when I left, getting up and getting out. Not back to work or anything, but not sleeping the days away. Part of me wants to book a flight and head home, but my uncle's last words before my trip stop me. "You can't shoulder all the pain for your dad," he said. "You need to live your life. Get your ass on a plane, get away, and I'll look after my brother. Don't make me tell you twice, or you'll be spending the next few months living with your pops."

As much as I love my pops, the idea of living with the forever chauvinistic, cut-to-the-chase Larry Cannon is up there with those naked exam dreams. Highly unpleasant. If I show up at home, that's exactly what'll happen. And I still haven't decided if I'm going to ditch the idea of working for my dad's consulting firm and get into physiotherapy. Every time I do my exercises, I picture myself helping other people. Making a difference. But my dad's counting on me to take over his company. With everything that's happened, I don't want to let him down.

Needing to purge the guilt and nerves and thoughts over-crowding my brain, I hit compose and start typing.

For the next thirty minutes, I let spill everything that's been getting in the way of me moving forward with that school crap and with Nina—the girl I think of as mine even though I've been too scared to do anything about it.

She turns me sideways in the most awesome way with her crazy stories, awkward moments, and those eyes that reduce me to a horny mess. With her, it's like I'm a virgin all over again—the anticipation, the wanting. The twenty-four/seven erection. Not having had sex in over year isn't helping. But *this girl*?

The dread of potentially reliving what I went through with Lacey hasn't vanished. But everything about Nina makes me feel *more*. More grounded. At peace. Happier than I ever thought I could be since the accident. If she doesn't freak, we could be epic. Even if it's just for now, while we travel this amazing country, be-ing with her could be exactly what I need. It might not be what I was looking for, but I can do this. I can be with her, say good-bye when it's all done, and not fall apart. Walk away a better man.

I'm not my father.

By the end of my e-mail to James, after making it clear I need constant updates on my dad, my hands are cramped from typing, but as soon as I hit send, my nerves subside. No more bullshit. No more hiding who I am or what I look like. The lies have to end.

Fourteen

NINA

"You in here, Nina?" A scowling Leigh struts through the bathroom door. With the time we've spent together, I'm learning a Leigh scowl is akin to her smiling. "Paige said you walked in here ten minutes ago." The second she says Paige's name, though, that scowl tips upward.

We were at a bar yesterday, Sam and me playing pool—more like Sam playing and me smacking balls around—when I noticed Leigh at a nearby table chatting with a girl. I don't know how one girl knows the other is gay, but I'd say those two were getting *acquainted*. The girl in question was pretty in a natural way with shoulder-length brown hair and minimal makeup. When she leaned back and I glimpsed her T-shirt, I knew why Leigh was drawn to her. Just below the *Star Trek* logo were the words Go Trek Yourself. After spending the night hanging out with Leigh, Paige changed her travel plans to meet us in Nelson.

I finish washing my hands and rip off a sheet of paper towel. "Sorry. Just couldn't bring myself to use the gas station washroom. Then the check-in took forever, and I got stuck talking with a girl in the dorm. I better not have a bladder infection from holding it in." I took one look at the situation that was the public restroom in the grimy gas station and decided reaching stage three of the have-to-pee stages was preferable to catching a rare disease. "What was up with Sam, anyway?" I ask, curious about their private chitchat.

She crosses her arms and leans against the bright blue wall. "Nothing. The guy thinks I have a bad attitude or something."

I choke on my laugh. "Can't imagine why he'd think that."

"Wow, Nina, is that sarcasm? My little girl is all grown up." She winks at me and glances around. "You know, the last time the two of us were chatting it up in a hostel bathroom, you gave me this rockin' haircut." With a wry grin, she runs her hand up the back of her short hair.

"Yeah, it rocks, but you should be thanking the salon that fixed my hack job. I'm not sure I should be signing up for beauty school anytime soon." I crumple the paper towel and toss it in the trash.

"Nina, do the words 'thank' and 'you' sound familiar? I swear you've got some compliment complex. Or inferiority complex. Or a fear-of-being-cool complex. You need to stop with all the self-deprecating crap."

If I hadn't heard that exact same stuff from Sam, I might be offended by her tirade. But Leigh is Leigh, always honest and quick to point out the stuff most people avoid. And Sam is Sam, always trying to get me to see the best in myself. And make me laugh.

"Okay. *Thank* and *you*. Better? Between you and Sam, I might actually leave this trip a functioning member of society." I lean toward the mirror and drag my fingers through my hair. "Did you hear Sam at the gas station? Pretending he was local with that god-awful accent he was putting on? For sure they thought he was mentally challenged." When he winked at me after his performance, my laughter took a backseat to the heat in my belly.

She makes her favorite throaty sound. "Honestly, you guys need to fuck already. I'm tired of trying to breathe through the sex pheromones fogging up the car. It's been two weeks since the 'dry-fucking incident' I'm not supposed to mention, and every time you talk about him, you look ready to come."

I duck as if I can avoid being hit by her bluntness. "Oh, my God, *Leigh*." I check under the stall doors to make sure no one's here. "What are you even talking about?" Conversing with her is like being subjected to spontaneous rounds of dodgeball, said ball being swapped for the naked truth.

She bites at her cuticles, unfazed. "Whatever. I know you know what I mean. Man-candy can't keep his hands to himself whenever he's near you. It's worse than watching mating rituals on the Nature channel."

My jaw practically hits the floor. It doesn't matter how much time I spend with Leigh, her tell-it-as-it-is attitude never gets less shocking. I just wish she'd channel some of that brutal honesty toward her own life. Every time I suggest she tell her folks she's gay, I get shot down. She won't confess to Sam, either. Although the way those two are always hurling subtle, and not-so-subtle, digs at each other, I can't say I'm surprised.

I shrug when I recover from her straightforwardness. "You're crazy. Sam isn't into me, he's with Lacey." My tone is unconvincing, even to myself. I've dissected his reasoning for staying with her a thousand times. *"Lacey's fragile. If I end things, it might push her over the edge."* It doesn't fully make sense. Not with the way things are progressing between us. There's the constant touching—his hands on my hips, arms, back, or anywhere whenever he's close. The heated looks I *thought* went unnoticed before this talk with Leigh. I've also felt his priapism against my backside on more than one occasion when he's standing behind me. And he still likes to talk about forking. A lot. It seems the enjoyment he gets from making me blush hasn't been diluted under present circumstances.

For me, it's been two weeks of reliving that night in the tent. I change our position, the clothes we *are* or *aren't* wearing, and how far we let things go, but it's always Sam and me and a cold night in a tent. I've come up with various titles for my erotic short films. Some of my personal favorites are *Battlestar Orgasmica*, *Fast & Curious*, and *Position Impossible*.

Still, there's this *girlfriend*. "Seriously, you're crazy," I say again.

"*I'm* crazy?" She snorts. "Let's not dissect that one. You'll forever take gold in crazy. I'll just say this. I'm pretty sure there's more to Sam than meets the eye." She kicks off the wall and heads for the door. "Speaking of Man-candy, he's waiting outside. Said something about wanting to speak to you *alone*. I'll head out with you. Paige and I are gonna check out that Thai place in town." She glances back then. "Give him a chance, Nina. Let him explain." A blush warms her cheeks as she adds, "And you're on your own tomorrow. I'm kayaking with Paige."

I raise my eyebrows. "Paige, huh?"

She makes her throaty sound. "Yes, Nina, *Paige*. Say one more thing, and it'll make my conversations with Sam sound like nursery rhymes." But she can't keep from grinning.

Still unsure what her cryptic "let him explain" means, I follow her outside.

Sam is leaning against the driver's side of his beat-up station wagon, thumbs hooked into his pockets. He's in his gray T-shirt, dark jeans, and his scuffed, heavy boots. I watch him for a moment, remembering the feel of his weight on me. The way my whole body clenched when he was between my legs. I wanted to rip off his pants and feel the length of him. I wasn't scared, wasn't awkward. I was the sex goddess I've imagined, and it's because I was with Sam. Because I trusted him. Knowing he wouldn't laugh at me for doing something wrong gave me the confidence to let loose.

Things got out of hand in the tent, and as much as I've wanted to give in to the fantasies that night inspired, I don't want to be the *other* woman. I just wish I knew why it was taking so long for him to leave Lacey. He can't go on protecting her forever, and he can't keep stringing me along, either. I'll have to put an end to his flirting soon or take off and travel with Leigh. My belly falls. *Sometime soon.*

Unsure how long I've been staring at Sam, I look down sharply, taking my lip between my teeth. His boots are in front of my sandals in seconds. "Can we walk for a minute?" he asks.

Leigh pipes up beside me. "Nina can walk. You, however, will likely hobble."

He shakes his head and pins her with a dark look. "Bite me."

She doesn't bat an eye. "I would if I could find your junk. Unfortunately, I left my magnifying glass in the hostel."

Sam doesn't miss a beat. "Is it the same one you use to make sure your dick's tucked between your legs when you pull on your pants?"

Holy crap. I step back as I wait for Leigh to go grenade on Sam. Twice, I've witnessed her at her worst. The explosion of curses and comebacks that followed had me ducking in the car to avoid being hit by insults. When she gets started, no one's safe.

Thankfully, her fury is focused on Sam. "No, needle dick. It's the one I use to channel the sun and burn fuckers who piss me off. And as much as I've enjoyed participating in this stimulating battle of wits, I don't like taking advantage of the handicapped."

The staring contest on the heels of Leigh's words is enough to have Sylvester Stallone begging for mercy. This won't be good. It won't end well. As I struggle to breathe, the unthinkable happens. The two of them grin. *At each other.* This is…different. Maybe they bonded earlier when talking by the car. Maybe they laughed while recounting my many tales of humiliation.

I think I prefer Grenade Leigh.

"Catch you later," she calls as Paige comes out of the hostel.

I turn to Sam and drag my eyes up his muscled chest, wishing he'd taken off his top in that tent. Blinking, I say, "Walk sounds good."

He places his hand on the small of my back to guide me forward. Every time he touches me, I become hyperaware of my body: the bend in my knees, the position of my hands. The length of my breaths. Slower. Deeper. *Heavier.* Everything magnifies. He laces his fingers into mine, and I almost melt. The smart version of me should pull my hand away. Smarter me should paraphrase

Leigh and say, "Shit or get off the pot, bucko." Sex-starved me, however, stumbles forward.

He leads me to Tahuna Beach, a short walk down a path across the road. It's early evening, and he's quiet as we walk, our fingers still bound, the shivers spreading down my spine having nothing to do with the cool breeze. He's been quiet a lot the past couple of days. Still joking like he does, but thoughtful in his silence. I'm not sure what's up with him, but I'm hoping it has to do with him finally deciding to end things with Lacey.

When we reach a secluded sandy spot, he tugs on my hand and turns me to face him. "Hi," he says.

My heart skips a beat. "Hi," I say shyly, recalling where we were when we last spoke like this. By the way his eyelids lower, I'm guessing he remembers, too.

"I've been wanting to get you alone for a while. Not easy with Leigh around all the time."

I cringe. "Sorry. I know you two don't get along great. I just think it's better for her not to travel on her own. So thanks, you know, for putting up with her." I wish I could explain Leigh to him. She's so used to laying it on thick and putting on a show that she can't tone it down and let people in. Where I crave anonymity, she craves attention—both of us trying to convince people we're someone else. We're two halves of the same whole.

He crosses his arms and digs his boot into the sand. "She told me, by the way. That she's gay. I thought she was like the Rizzo to your Sandy just waiting for the right moment to humiliate you. I get her now. She's still a raging bitch, but I can deal with her."

I exhale, relieved, that he finally knows, but I can't imagine what changed her mind. Grenade Leigh wouldn't confide in

Sam. She also wouldn't share a smile with him after a verbal thrashing. I try to puzzle it out, but it's hard to focus on anything besides *Rizzo* and *Sandy*. "Did you just make a *Grease* reference?"

He looks around as if I must be talking to someone else in this crowd of two. "No, Canada, you must have misheard me. What I said was she's like the rock to your scissors. You know, like the game rock-paper-scissors. She'll crush you every time."

"Actually, I have above average hearing, and my understanding is you love movies with well-choreographed scenes and heartfelt ballads. I just want to know, for the record, which is your favorite: *Mamma Mia* or *High School Musical*?"

He shakes his head, his focus on the ground. "My sister watches that stuff. Not me. I just, maybe, get sucked in from time to time." He looks up, smirking. "And the answer I'm not admitting to is definitely *High School Musical*. I'm also not admitting that I played Kenickie in my school production of *Grease*."

"You didn't?"

"I did. There was a certain Marci Fray playing Sandy. Unfortunately, she fell for Danny. Totally predictable."

"Sounds heartbreaking."

He agrees with a solemn nod. It's fun when we joke like this, the easy back-and-forth. I feel my whole face smiling. "Is there a video I can watch?"

"Only if I get to see the 'Age of Aquarius' number."

"Never going to happen. But let me get this straight…you watch musicals and you starred in one. Do you belong to a book club, too?"

He shoots me a mock glare. "You just started a war, Canada."

Next thing I know, I'm on the sand with Sam above me tickling my ribs. I squeal and wiggle and twist until he smiles, triumphant. Then his grin fades. He's straddling me, both of us breathing heavy, his unmistakable erection pressed between my thighs. *Shoot.* This wasn't supposed to happen. Not unless he brought me here to tell me he and Lacey are done. If that *is* why I'm here, then I should be wearing my nice pink bra, not the plain white cotton one I've been in all day. I should have showered and brushed my teeth and, I don't know, worn my skirt instead of borrowing Leigh's ridiculously tight jeans.

"Quiet," he says. "I can hear you thinking."

Frickin' Hot Guy.

With a groan, he pushes off of me and onto his butt. We sit face-to-face, his bent legs over mine, and he lies back to stick his hand in his front pocket. When he sits up, he unravels a thin leather necklace, a white bone pendant hanging from the end. Holding it in his hand, he leans forward. "It's the Maori Koru design inspired by those ferns we see everywhere. The way they unfurl. It represents peace, tranquility, personal growth, and positive change." He fastens the leather around my neck, his hands coming to rest on my collarbones. "It's how I feel when I'm with you. At peace. Better. And…" He brushes away the hair blowing across my face and tucks it behind my ear. "I hope it's how you feel with me, too."

There must be a screenwriter hidden in his car. Maybe in the trunk? Or on the roof? It's the only explanation as to how Hot Guy has just rambled off the most romantic words since the writers from *Jerry Maguire* penned, "You had me at hello." As far as I'm concerned, Sam had me at the terminal in Toronto.

I trace the smooth bone resting on my chest, the thick curves spiraling in a circle. "It's beautiful, Sam, but you shouldn't have."

"Yeah, I should have." He leans forward and cups my cheeks. "You have no idea the effect you have on me, and I want you to know. Really want you to understand." His tone is different, desperate. Like he thinks he's losing me. Is that what this is about? The perfect words? The necklace? Is he letting me down gently because he's decided to stay with Lacey?

Panic sets in. I'm not ready for the "it's not you, it's me" talk. Not when I haven't been given the chance to experience him fully. *Us* fully. The past couple of weeks have been too perfect. *He's* too perfect. And I'm not good enough. I'm Pininfarina Gabri, disaster-magnet, and I don't even have the courage to tell him my real name. His hands are still on my face, and I think he wants to kiss me. One last hurrah. *God*, do I want to taste his lips again. Then he leans closer. The smell of salt is pungent, seagulls riding the air currents above us, and I almost give in. *Almost.*

Quick as I can, I scurry backward through the sand like an injured crab. "Sorry. Gotta go. I promised my mom we'd Skype tonight. In, like, ten minutes. So, yeah, thanks for the necklace and, uh, I'll see you in a bit. Just gonna go to the Internet café. Down the street. For some privacy." I nod a bunch and scramble to my feet. "Sorry," I say again.

Damn Polite Tourette's.

"Nina, wait," he calls as I hurry toward the path.

I stop and hunch forward, breathing hard, trying to figure out what the heck I'm doing. Sam goes out and gets me a necklace to show me how much I mean to him, and I crawl through the sand to get away. My haywire brain could only compute one reason for such a meaningful gesture—he's dumping me, which in itself is ridiculous. We're not even a couple, so, technically speaking, I can't be dumped.

And if we're getting technical, I think I just proved Newton's third law of motion: When one body exerts a force on a second body, the second body simultaneously exerts a force equal in magnitude and opposite in direction on the first body.

Sam's force: Make a grand gesture to prove his affection toward me.

My equal and opposite force: Run away, making him think I'm not interested.

Frickin' perfect.

I straighten up as I wait for him to make it over. He was trying to tell me something, and there's a possibility he was about to tell me he wants us to be together. Like *really* together. He's opened up to me over the past couple of weeks, sharing stories about his mom, smiling at the memories. That takes trust. Not the kind you give away when getting in a cab. The kind of trust people offer to show their faith in you. And I crab-walked away. I trust Sam more than any person I've ever met, outside of my family, and he needs to know that.

When he makes it to my side, I hunch and whisper my trademark, "I'm sorry."

He runs a hand down my arm. "The only one here who needs to apologize is me." A deep, shuddering breath moves through his chest. "I don't…" His eyes slide away before locking on mine, resolve shining bright. "I don't have a girlfriend. Lacey and I broke up months ago."

The light in his eyes dims as I shake my head, frowning. "You don't have a girlfriend?"

"No," he says, one word laced with guilt. His hand falls away.

As the news sinks in, my first reaction is: *Yes! Sam is single!*

My subsequent reaction is: *Sam lied.*

He's been all over me but holding back, and he's let me go on thinking I'm a crappy person for having designs on some girl's boyfriend. Does Leigh know? Was that what her cryptic "let him explain" was all about? My temples throb. "I don't understand. I thought, you know, the way we were, the way *you* were…" I lower my voice. "I thought you wanted me."

He takes my hand and places it over the necklace he gave me, covering my fingers with his. "I want you, Nina. I swear to God, I've never wanted a girl the way I want you. I'm sorry I lied. Part of it was to make you feel more comfortable traveling with me, but that's not the only reason. I'd like to explain…if you'll let me."

When I step back, his hand drops and he flinches. Unable to look at his stricken face, I study the sand at my feet, cataloguing the twigs and rocks among the grains.

If any other guy had led me on like this, I'd leave right now. I may not have the confidence to yell and scream, but I wouldn't stick around to find out why he thought so little of me. But this is Sam. We've opened up to each other in ways we haven't with other people. You can't fake that kind of connection. That kind of bond. There has to be a good reason why he lied. Besides, Leigh told me to let him explain. The last thing she'd do is side with Sam without good reason, and she wouldn't have come out to him if she didn't think him worthy of the knowledge.

It's time for some answers.

When I nod, he exhales. He intertwines our fingers and leads me to the hostel. We don't talk. We glance at each other from time to time, our palms sweatier with each passing second, my heart hammering so hard I'm sure he feels it in his fingers.

Fifteen

SAM

We push into the hostel, and when I tug Nina to the right, she stops. "Where are we going? The lounge is up ahead."

This should be interesting. After deciding to come clean tonight, I booked a private room in addition to our dorm beds. I'm not about to strip in a bathroom like I did with Leigh. I need some privacy to show Nina my legs and deal with her reaction. If things go the way I want, if she doesn't look at me like I'm a freak, then she's sleeping in my arms and waking up with me, whether she likes it or not.

I squeeze her hand. "I booked a private room. I'd like to talk in there."

She frowns a moment, then says, "Okay."

Once inside, I release her sweat-slicked palm and turn to lock the door. We stand side by side as she studies the small room with its queen-size bed, tiny adjoining bathroom, and gray walls decorated with New Zealand photos.

I nod to the bed. "Have a seat."

She sits on the checkered gray-and-black comforter and fiddles with her fingers. She opens her mouth as if to speak, but when I start undoing my belt, she clamps her teeth shut. Her eyes almost pop out.

I've gone over a million ways to tell her about my legs: describing the accident in detail, explaining about Lacey and her reaction, even talking about burn victims and the road to recovery. None of them felt right. In the end, it's all about owning my baggage the way I've forced Nina to own hers.

When I finish with my buckle and release the top button of my jeans, she finally finds her voice. She holds up her hand. "Sam…I thought we were going to talk. Like now? There's a massive lie you need to explain, and I'm not sure I can concentrate if you take this *Magic Mike* show any further. In fact, I'm not even sure what I just said."

I'm on the verge of maybe losing her, and still, she has me smiling. "This *is* me explaining, Nina. I need to show you something, and it's not the raging hard-on I usually have when you're around." Actually, this is one of the few times I'm not hard as a rock in front of her. Fear and libido are not fast friends.

She swallows slowly, and I lower my zipper.

With a huge breath, I bend down to unlace my boots and kick them off. My socks follow next. I keep my focus on the maroon carpet as I slide my jeans past my hips. She gasps before I step out of them. This is it. This is my worst nightmare realized. I don't know what I'll do if I look up and her face is twisted in disgust. The expression Lacey couldn't hide when she came to the hospital.

"Oh, God," is all I hear. Then, "Was it the accident?"

I nod, my focus never wavering from the pull in the carpet about an inch long, the material frayed at the edges. This is my moment of truth. To be chosen or discarded like the deformed freak I am. I glance up, no longer able to take not knowing. Nina's hand is at her mouth, but the look of revulsion I expected isn't there. Sadness? Empathy? Normally, I'm not one for the puppy-dog eyes I get from well-meaning folk who offer condolences, but I'm so relieved she's not curling her lip and wincing, I practically fist pump.

She lowers her hand, gets to her feet, and approaches until she can intertwine her fingers with mine. Her touch does weird things to my throat until I have to gulp down the lump threatening to rise.

"Is this why you lied about Lacey?" she asks. "You were nervous to show me your legs?"

I run my thumb down the back of her hand. I don't speak until I'm sure my voice is steady. "I know it wasn't fair to you. But the more time we spent together, the harder it got. I've fallen for you, Nina. Fucking hard. Not sure how else to say it. I love the way you ramble when you talk, and how you fill every drive with rounds of I Spy and Twenty Questions. I can talk to you about my mom without falling to pieces, and I can barely be around you without needing to touch some part of your body. I didn't feel half this much with Lacey, and the way my legs went down with her sucked. She couldn't handle it. That's not why we broke up, really. Still, it sucked."

I grip her hand tighter, wishing she had known me before this trip so she could see how much she's helped me, understand how

I feel. I move a fraction closer. "I lied, Nina, because I was scared. I'm sorry I did it, and I have no right to ask this now, but…I want you. Us. This. If you can't forgive me or be with me the way I want to be with you, it's okay. I'm a big boy. I can handle it. I just need to know."

It's a relief to say it out loud, get it all out in the open, but she's studying my face with tight features, and for the first time ever, I can't tell what she's thinking. She may not be freaking out, but that doesn't mean she's still attracted to me. That she'll forgive me and stay in my life. She unlaces our fingers, steps back, and I almost crumble.

So this is it. This is my undoing. *No*, screw that. Getting in deep with a girl was exactly what I wanted to avoid on this trip. And here I am, practically falling apart over Nina. My happiness, my state of mind, doesn't depend on her. I need to get away before she says *I'm sorry* and *I just can't*. That shit's too much.

"Okay," I say. "Fine." I snatch my jeans from the floor and fumble with them, my foot missing the opening. I never should've gotten involved with her. I should've let her run off after that crap in Pahia. I need to meet another Reese.

That's when her hand comes to rest on my forearm.

At her touch, I slump forward. I should get out of here before I fall harder and she rips my heart out, but that one touch has me hoping. She grabs the jeans still clutched in my hands and tosses them on the floor. "Will you take your top off for me?"

That gets my attention. I straighten up, and those goddamn eyes are on me. The eyes I thought I'd lost forever are burning into my chest. "Are you saying what I think you're saying?"

She blinks a few times and quirks her lips into a sexy grin.

"You're not getting rid of me that easy. I've wanted to see that chest of yours since I sat across from you in the terminal. I think I can make a better decision about what I can and can't do with you if I actually see it. You know, an informed decision."

This must be divine intervention. Mom must be smiling down on me. She's seen my legs, knows the score, and she's still here. My dick wakes up. Big time. "How about a deal?" I ask.

"A deal?"

"Yeah. A deal. I lose my shirt if you lose yours." I'm desperate to see her creamy skin and count every freckle.

Instead of answering me, she rips her top over her head. The chubby I'm sporting springs to attention, that pale skin ready for my teeth to mark her as mine. I'm not used to her being so bold. So forward. It's a side of Nina I haven't seen, but, man, do I like it.

She waves her hands to hurry me up. "Come on. I've been waiting for this for forever. You have no idea how many times I've pictured it."

A laugh bursts from my throat. I thought I was about to lose her, and now I'm smiling and horny as hell. And the evening's just begun.

I stretch my shirt over my shoulders and toss it on the floor.

Her jaw slackens. "I have to touch it," she whispers.

"It?"

"That chest."

"Just my chest?" I ask, smirking.

"Other things, too."

Hell, yeah. "In that case, go ahead."

She runs her hands over every dip and curve from my collar-bones to the lines of my pecs, and down the ridges of my abs. My stomach muscles tighten at her touch. I close my eyes, getting lost in the sensation. "God, Nina," I groan when her fingers make it to the waistband of my boxers and run along the fabric. Soft lips land on mine. I keep my eyes closed and enjoy the taste of cherry and her. I let her lead while I still have the willpower to hold back. When I get my hands on her there won't be any stopping me, and I'm not sure I can be gentle.

Her tongue brushes against mine, and she nips my lower lip. Then she says, "You know you're beautiful, right?"

If she only knew how much those words mean.

I open my eyes to make sure I'm not dreaming, to make sure she's really here. Is she ever. The way her lips part and her breasts rise and fall, there's no question I'm awake and she's all in for what I have to give her. No longer able to keep my hands to myself, I stroke my thumb over the beauty mark on her cheek and draw a trail along her jaw and neck down to the cleavage I'd like to bury my face in. She shivers.

"You don't know beautiful, Nina, until you've seen yourself through my eyes."

She pauses before saying a quiet, "Thank you." No smart remarks rebutting my compliment. No self-deprecation. Just a perfect thank-you.

I cup my hand over the cotton of her white bra, needing to touch her but still holding back with everything that's in me. I'm as hard as I've ever been, my balls tight and aching for her, but I don't want to scare her by unleashing my pent-up sexual frustration.

She hisses out a breath when I tweak the hard bud beneath her bra. "Sam, sexy stuff needs to happen soon. Like now. Or I might explode. Rupture from the inside out. I seriously can't take it."

Enough said.

Our lips collide in a flurry of teeth and tongues as I grope her ass, my hips grinding into her. I drag my hand up and unlatch her bra. It pools on the floor, and I lower my mouth to the taut peaks begging for my attention. Every inch of her skin is as silky as it looks. We both moan, a heady sound, until I'm not sure who's enjoying the foreplay more. I walk her until the backs of her knees hit the bed. She falls with a soft bounce and reaches for me.

Before I join her, I need to do something about the tight jeans standing between me and the heaven that is Nina. "Those need to come off."

"Yes, please," she says. The always-polite Canadian.

She'll be swearing before this night is done.

Needing to taste her again, I nudge her thighs apart and dig my fingers into her denim-clad hips. I kiss and suck along her slim waist and belly button.

Her back bows off the mattress. "Please, take them off."

I press the heel of my hand against the apex of her thighs. Her hips jerk, and I suck on her belly until a red mark blooms on her milky skin. I love seeing it there. Knowing I left it. Knowing she's mine.

It's time to lose the jeans.

I pop open the top button, drag the zipper down, and try to tug the fabric below her hips. Jesus, are these jeans tight. I get them below her ass, below the white lace underwear begging to be ripped off, and the things get stuck.

She wiggles. "Harder, Sam."

Harder. Hearing that word from her pretty pink lips makes me all kinds of crazy. There's a wide rip in the knee of her jeans that would make this mission a hell of a lot easier. Without a second thought, I grab the fabric and tear it straight to the ankle.

She squeals and pushes up on her elbows. Wide-eyed, she stares at the destroyed denim. "Leigh's going to kill me. These were hers."

As far as I'm concerned, that's an added bonus. "I'll get her another pair."

With that, I find a slit in the other leg, rip the shit out of it, pull off what's left of the jeans, and toss the tattered material on the floor. She giggles at the sight. All humor fades when I hook my thumbs in her underwear and guide the material down. Standing above her, I get choked up again, my emotions always grazing the surface. *So damn beautiful.* She has the hips of a woman, not the waiflike lines I often see on chicks. A smattering of freckles decorates her pale skin, constellations guiding me home, and the necklace I gave her rests between her breasts.

I wish I had Nina's gift for words. *Beautiful* doesn't cut it.

I need to get closer, feel her against me, but tonight's not the night I lose myself completely and sink into her. I'm not sure where this self-control comes from, but I know she hasn't had much experience. I want to ease her into things.

Gripping her waist, I toss her gently across the bed. She lands with a soft "Oof," and I'm on my knees prowling toward her in seconds. When I have her caged below me, my hands on either side of her head, I devour her swollen lips again and lower my dick where it was in that tent all those weeks ago. This time she's wet and bare below me with nothing but my boxers between us. Her knees spread wider. Her lids flutter. I press my dick against her. Hard.

I rock forward, and she cries, "Sam."

My raspy name on her lips, her soft skin under me, the way her hips move in time with mine. *Christ.* Knowing I'll likely come in my boxers again, I push to the side, never taking my lips from hers. Her small hands drag up and down my chest until I press closer. She winds them around my neck.

I flatten my palm on her belly and slide it down, down, down. Soft. Slick. Drenched. *Holy fuck.* "Do I do this to you, Nina? Is this how wet I make you?"

"Yes, yes, yes," she chants, arching her hips from the mattress, urging my fingers where she wants them.

Sucking a trail down her neck, I explore every inch of her perfect breasts while I slide one then two fingers into all that beautiful wetness. My fingers glide in and out, and I work her into a frenzy with my thumb. She pants and moans and bucks. Her knees fall farther open, and her leg slides against mine—against my rough flesh.

I freeze.

Those catlike eyes launch a thousand silent questions at me, but all she says is, "Sam?" My gaze darts down to our legs, and she follows the movement. "They're perfect. You're perfect," she whispers and rubs our legs together.

I can't believe I ever doubted her.

Her hips move, asking for more. I press the flat of my thumb against her best part and glide my fingers deeper inside, wanting her to explode around me.

Next thing I know, she's tracing a pattern down my abs, under my waistband, and I groan. She fists my throbbing length, and I hiss out a breath. Then we're moving in time. Together. I rock into her soft hand, and she circles her hips to guide my fingers deeper. Faster.

"God," she cries, and it almost sends me over the edge. With one last buck of her hips, her belly convulses and she pulses around my fingers.

Getting her off is an addiction I'll never kick.

Her hand is still on my cock, her thumb rubbing circles, and I'm about ready to explode, but she pulls away and pushes me on my back. I lift my hips as she grips my boxers and drags them off, tossing them to the floor. Her teeth graze her lip, and my dick twitches. She settles between my legs as I wait, impatient now, for her hand to get back to business. Excitement dances in those satisfied green eyes. "My turn," she says. She bends down and drags her tongue up my hard-on. Heat spikes along my flesh, my abs contracting instantly.

This is not what I expected from inexperienced Nina.

Breathing heavily, I push up onto my elbows. "You don't have to do this. We can take it slow." Her smooth ass is perched in the air, her lips hovering over my dick, and I wish like hell I'd kept my mouth shut.

She lifts up, her eyes flashing mischief one moment and turning down, shy, the next. Her thumb traces the line her tongue just left, and my head tips back as a groan rips from my throat. "Sam?" My head snaps up at her questioning tone.

She runs the flat of her palm up my cock, exploring it like she's found gold. I clear my throat and try to concentrate. "Yeah?" My voice sounds hoarse as hell.

Her gaze flicks to meet mine. "Will you tell me what you like? As I do it. Will you tell me if it feels good?"

Mother of God. My dick gets harder as her grip tightens. "Nina, baby, I guarantee whatever you do will feel amazing, but if you want to know what I like, I'll guide you." My hips move of their own accord, my dick sliding against her palm, and a spasm runs through me. "You sure, though?"

She bites her lip, nods, and lowers her mouth exactly where I want it.

Odds are I won't last long.

Her hot tongue drags up my length once, twice. Then again. My whole body tenses, heat gathering in my core, and I can't stop watching her. Her red hair over my thighs, her shy curiosity. I've never been so entranced by a girl going down on me, but her innocence and excitement have me hypnotized.

When her mouth engulfs me, my vision blurs. "Use your hand, too." A low groan moves up my throat as she fists my dick. "Tighter." She obliges, and I roll my hips to set the pace. Steady, even thrusts. Little sounds of pleasure vibrate between my legs, and I drop my head again. "So fucking good, baby. Just like that…but deeper." I grip the sheets. "Use your tongue on the tip," I ground out.

The rest is so intense I can't stop from grunting and calling her name. I mean head is head, but this is Nina. She's between my busted legs, wanting nothing but to give me pleasure, and nothing has ever felt this good.

"Faster." With my one word, she brings me to the brink, lips tightening, tongue circling, hand gliding until every inch of my body feels ready to combust. I fist her hair and thrust my hips to demand more. No more being gentle. No more easing her into things. "I'm gonna come." The words sound strangled, and she moans between my legs. Heat barrels down my spine as the longest, hardest orgasm I've ever had floods out of me.

When I catch my breath, I scrub my hands down my face and shake my head to make sure it's still attached. "You're a quick study."

She licks her lips. "That was fun."

"I'm game whenever you are."

Her gaze drops to the bed, and she bites her lip.

Now she's embarrassed? Now she gets all shy with me? "Get your naked self up here."

A smile creeps up her flushed cheeks. She nestles her body against mine, all our dips and curves fitting perfectly. I kiss the top of her head and stroke her side. "Everything about you is awesome, Nina, but that was…" Her back expands with an inhale as I search for the right word, her breath tickling my chest when it rushes out.

"So it was okay? You liked it? It's just, I've pictured it a bunch, and I was kind of nervous."

I chuckle against her. "If my ten-minute orgasm and temporary blindness were any indication, I'd go with yes. You blew my mind tonight, in more ways than one." I don't tell her how much her acceptance means to me. I don't tell her how I feel reborn. I just press her against me, and she cuddles closer. "But I'd like to revisit the part where you said you've pictured it a bunch. Like how often? And what exactly have you pictured?"

She tucks her head down.

"Come on, Canada. You either let it out or I tickle it out of you."

She kicks her legs and wiggles around. Although I can't see her face, I'm pretty sure she's scrunching it up in that way she does.

Fucking adorable. Still, she stays mum. I lock an arm around her waist and graze my fingers toward her armpit. That's all it takes to have her shouting, "Okay, okay, okay!"

Mission accomplished. "Let's hear it."

After a lengthy pause, her soft breath hits my neck. "A bunch probably means, like, an unhealthy amount. I don't have an actual number or anything. And I guess I have this thing I do. A lot."

"Thing? I thought we covered all your things. You have another?"

"I doubt we've scratched the surface."

"Do tell, Canada. This sounds like the type of thing I might like." She traces my abs again, but I clamp my hand on hers. "Spill."

"Okay." She sighs. "It's not that big of a deal, I just have a lot of fantasies. About you. Like all the time. And tonight, with you all naked and hot and manly, I needed to, you know... *taste you*." She rubs her nose against my neck, squeezing closer to my side.

This damn girl. She has X-rated fantasies about yours truly, but she has to whisper "*taste you*." Although I plan on reenacting every last dirty film, the way she's clamming up, I can tell she's not ready to voice them. *Yet*. "I'll let you off easy tonight, but we're not done talking about this particular *thing*. I'm pretty sure those fantasies happen every time your eyes burn into my body. It makes it hard to function around you."

She giggles. "Deal. But what about *your* thing? You're not exactly easy to be around."

"*My* thing?"

"Yeah, your thing."

"I don't have a thing."

She lets out an exasperated huff, meaning she's rolling her eyes. "Your thing's worse than my thing."

I rub at the scar on my chin, trying to figure out what my tell is.

She groans. "You just did it again."

I squint down at her, confused.

"Your fingers," she says. "*Over your scar.* The way your arm does that hot guy, flexing thing? You have to know it makes me wet." She reddens, her hand flying to cover her face.

I blink slowly, a long swallow moving down my throat as my dick hardens again. "What did you just say?"

"Nothing. Nope. Not a thing." She buries her head into my chest and sighs.

As much as I want to get busy with her again, I'm pretty sure she's content to fall asleep like this, in my arms. Can't say I mind. Having her close eases the ache under my ribs that flares when she's not around. Anyway, I'll be scratching my scar most of the day tomorrow to get her ready for another unforgettable night.

Shifting so she's partway under me, I drape my leg over her, and that dreaded lump settles back in my throat. Thoughts of our limited future invade my mind. I've been so focused on making Nina fall for me while keeping her at arm's length that I haven't stopped to think about where we go from here. If my uncle can't get things sorted with my dad, I'll have to go home earlier than planned.

Nina and I live in different countries, lead separate lives. Losing her isn't something I want to consider. Sure, I can walk away. I always need to know I can walk away from her and be okay. I'm just not sure I want to. Not when she's the first girl to want me, scarred legs and all. The first girl I've talked openly with about my mom and my uncertainty over working for my dad. Everything with her comes easily. With no secrets between us, it'll be that much better. After the year I've had, I deserve *better*.

I hug her tight. We'll have to muddle our way through this.

Sixteen

NINA

I have a boyfriend. A sweetheart. A beau. A specimen of manly perfection. Sam was worried I'd be turned off by his legs, but something about them makes him more human, less flawless. More like me. With my help, he's learning to accept himself, too. He's even wearing shorts again. If anyone stares too long or makes a face, I fist my hands in his hair and pull his lips down to mine. Now he tries to get noticed.

According to him, we're perfect in our imperfections. Leigh's take on us is less diplomatic. When she ditched us to travel with Paige, she said, "Being around the two of you is like watching circus freaks trying to mate. If I don't leave, I'll end up plunging hot needles in my eyes." Sam growled, I laughed, and we decided to meet up in a few weeks in Christchurch.

Now Sam's all mine. That chest. That jaw. Those tasty lips. I can barely believe it. I sent Mom a text that first morning, and she practically blew up my phone with replies—twenty-seven in total. The last one made me shriek and had me fumbling to hit delete, but Sam pinched my knee and snatched the phone away. Even *he* blushed while reading her text:

If he asks if you'd like a pearl necklace, the answer should be no.

He took one look at me and burst out laughing, telling me over and over how awesome she is. Sam and I talk a lot about our families. He asks about my mom without the resentment you'd expect, and he seems genuinely happy to remember his. I've grilled him about the accident, too. About how badly he was hurt. Every word tears me up, but I need to know, and I get the feeling he needs to let it out. We've spent hours discussing his hospital stay, the surgeries, the pain, the recovery. How we feel both young and old and how the choices we make in the next few years will define us.

It sounds as though Sam is leaning more and more toward physiotherapy instead of working for his dad, but I'm still muddled over what to do with my life, what career would suit me best. When I think about it too long, my head hurts. Instead, I plan meals, cooking and laughing with Sam, staring at Sam, *fantasizing* about Sam. I do things that come naturally to me and make me happy.

All this talk and time has spanned a week that feels more like a year—seven years in travel time, as Sam says. Our conversations are set against a rotating backdrop of kayaking, beach walks, hikes, and one surprise dinner at a local winery, all in and around Nelson. We've grown closer, so close I can barely stand it when he's out of sight. By the way he curls his hand around my waist and nuzzles my neck at every opportunity, I'd say he feels the same. We've progressed, my *boyfriend* and me, in every department…but the sexy department.

Since the night of the big reveal, we've swapped our separate bunks for a private room. Unfortunately, and fortunately, my monthly friend paid a visit that same night. Unfortunately, because it meant Sam and I had to tone down the sexy stuff while we were together. Half naked. In a bed. Not an easy task. And fortunately, because Sam and I had to tone down the sexy stuff while we were together. Half naked. *In a bed.* There's only one explanation for my debilitating fear to go further with him: The I'm Not Sure I Lost My Virginity Incident scarred me more than I realized.

When I went down on him that first night, I was nervous as anything. But Sam put me at ease. He let me know what I was doing felt good, and I loved being in control, knowing I could make him fall apart. I was *almost* the sex goddess I've imagined—still fearful, but experimental. Since then, I've had too much time to overthink things. Letting go enough to be with him is twisting me up to the point of immobility. I'm still turned on. Constantly. On the verge of a colossal explosion so epic it'll make the Mount Saint Helens eruption look like a spurt. I want him in every way, but fear has me frozen. I lied, too. I told him my period is ever-present even though it ended two days ago. Shark week, as Leigh calls it. I just can't stop reliving that awful incident. I know this is Sam, and Sam won't yell at me or call me names if I spaz out, but that doesn't erase the horror of what I went through.

My *boyfriend* is a few strides ahead of me on the Copland

Track, a rocky trail that weaves around crystal-clear creeks and riverbeds, the steady incline leading us up to our destination. It's our first overnight hike since the trek over Mount Tongariro. Tomorrow, we'll be hiking out the way we came, but not before we spend one night. In a tent. As boyfriend and girlfriend. I've stumbled over my feet four times the past hour, once landing sideways in a puddle. My mind keeps spinning back to the feel of his girth in my mouth, the roll of his hips as I took him deeper.

When my toe smacks a branch and I lurch forward, Sam spins in time to save me from sprawl five. The first thing I see when I right myself is the hefty bulge in his hiking shorts. He lifts my chin with two long fingers. "You're doing it again, Canada."

I look left and right, then at his honeyed eyes. "Doing what?"

He pushes the curls from his forehead and touches his scar, flexing every muscle along his arm, probably just to drive me crazy. *Frickin' Hot Guy.* "You know what. If you want to see me naked, all you have to do is ask." He snakes his hand around my waist, stopping me from toppling backward. "I'm all yours tonight," he says. "And you haven't gotten away with not divulging those naughty daydreams of yours. I'll fork it out of you, if need be."

Oh, God.

This past morning, the period myth met its demise. I had no choice. Sam was bound to check me into a hospital for a blood transfusion. So tonight there's nothing stopping all that raw male power from pushing into me.

Nothing but the appearance of Pininfarina Gabri.

He lets go, adjusts himself, and gives me a kiss that fuels me for the next few hours.

After dumping our packs by the hut and setting up our tent, he takes my hand and leads me through the bush. "You're gonna love this," he says as he drags me farther from the few people we just met. A devilish grin sharpens his jaw, and I wiggle my hand away.

That's the look he wore before he none too discreetly decided to cure me of my hippopotamonstrosesquipedaliophobia. My fear of long words. (Although I like using them in my head, in public—not so much.) Sam's proposed cure: Distract a cashier at the grocery checkout so I can scream his handwritten list into the microphone. "Is this a phobia thing? Because I think I've conquered most of them. And I'm excited to cook dinner tonight. Don't go ruining the moment by scarring me with your phobia-slaying skills. You've done some permanent damage."

"You'll thank me later. And yes, this is a phobia thing, but it's also something I'd like to do. So you know—two birds, one stone."

He grins like Lucifer himself.

There's a break in the bush ahead and we enter a clearing with a few shallow-looking ponds, lush green mountains rising behind them. Every new landscape in New Zealand tops the last. More dramatic, more breathtaking. It's no wonder *Lord of the Rings* was filmed here. Where else could you find this otherworldly imagery?

He leads us to a rocky outcrop, turns, and pins me with his warm gaze. "Keep your eyes on me, Canada." He points two fingers at my eyes, then at his. "Your focus right here. Got it?"

I tense my elbows to my sides, my knee bouncing restlessly. Nothing looks odd about this place. There aren't any people here, no audience to witness whatever phobia he has it in his head I should eradicate. "This isn't cool. I need some warning. Some kind of a hint."

He bends down to kiss me, slow and sweet and perfect. With our lips still touching he says, "Trust me." I will until the end of days. "Eyes on mine," he says again.

I gulp.

Next thing I know, he's removing his top and tossing it on the ground next to his small pack. When his fingers reach for the fly of his hiking shorts, I whip my head around, sure thousands of people will appear.

"Hey. Nina. Eyes here." He cups my chin until we're face-to-face. "These are hot springs, okay? We're going into them. You and me. Together."

"Bathing suit?" I manage.

He shakes his head, that darn smile curving his kissable lips. "Gymnophobia—your fear of being naked in public. With your track record, I thought it was an important one to conquer."

I feel the blush creeping up my neck, splotches no doubt forming. Did the sun get hotter? "What if people show up?"

"That's kind of the point. But you're with me. I've got you. And it's not abnormal to go naked into a hot spring. It's an actual thing people do. So as I said, keep your eyes on mine."

A few minutes later, he's buck naked in front of me, his priapism at attention in broad daylight while I try to remember why I lied about my period and haven't allowed all that manly perfection to fill me up.

"Nina. Eyes."

Where am I supposed to look? Is he frickin' serious?

"Nina," he says again.

I peel my gaze away from his thick flesh, sure I've burned a hole through my underwear. "Okay, what now?"

"Now it's your turn."

I've fallen for the one guy on the planet hell-bent on throwing me smack-dab in the middle of the most embarrassing situations. I am head over heels for his mayhem-inducing self. No matter how I feel about him, it doesn't make the idea of stripping in the open any less mortifying. Sweat gathers under my arms. My heart palpitates. While I play the Statue Game, Sam closes the distance between us and makes the decision for me. He goes to lift my top, and that erection of his helps his cause. It's like a solar eclipse—I know I shouldn't look, but I can't stop myself. The second I do, I'm pliable enough for him to undress me while I gawk helplessly at his manhood. It's that distracting.

I reach to touch his rigid flesh, but he grabs my hand. "Save that for later. We're on a mission." He winks, grips my hand tighter, and the two of us run, naked, to the hot springs. Warm mountain water splashes around us as we sink into the steaming pond.

"You're crazy," I cry.

"I know," he says. "That's why you like me."

I sit facing him with my knees to my chest, our feet touching. The water barely covers my breasts. I place my toes over his. "No. I have a thing for guys with weird tics. That's why the scar-rubbing thing drives me mad."

He moves his legs outside mine, and his feet come to rest beside my backside. He massages my calves in the water. "I'll be sure to develop a few more eccentricities when I get home." His face falls then, just for a second. But I catch it.

We've talked about everything under the sun, everything but *home* and what happens when this trip is over. I refuse to think about us ending. I won't. I can't. The thought alone is suffocating. Since things are up and down with his dad, and he wants to be there for him, the only way for us to stay together would be for me to go to Florida. But does he want that? I'd be depending on him, leaving my family in a more permanent way. I don't even know what I'd do there. Study? Work? It's like I have to make every monumental life decision at once or I lose him.

Sensing my turmoil, he scoots forward and tries to pull me onto his very naked lap. Rings of water circle us, but I dig my hands into the mucky earth. God, do I want him over me, on me, in me. Everywhere. But fear has me clenching and pushing away.

He locks his feet against my hips, pinning me in place, dipping his head down until we're eye to eye. "How is it that the girl who fucks me with her eyes and has endless dirty fantasies freezes up when I get too close?" Birds whistle. A fly buzzes. A breeze ripples along the spring. But I don't speak. "Come on, Nina. What's up?"

I run my hands up the flayed skin of his legs. He lets me touch him, lets me explore. I'm fascinated by the way it pulls taut in some areas and puckers in others, the marvel of modern medicine that could transplant skin from his thighs to his calves. It never grosses me out. Doesn't make me want him less. It's simply who he is—One-syllable Sam, the guy I'm in love with. I'm not sure precisely when this happened. Maybe the first night we met, or when he chased me from Pahia, or when he showed me his legs. Whatever the moment, it's been building for a while, and it's the truest emotion I've ever felt. Undeniable. Pure. Thinking it, *knowing it*, makes me want to open up and let my guard down. He's trusted me with everything and I have to do the same.

"I don't have much experience," I say, easing myself into the truth.

He's looking at my breasts, the way they float on the surface, but he blinks and runs his hands up my thighs, stopping before he enters make-me-panic territory. "Are you a virgin, Nina?"

Here it comes. "I'm not sure."

He quirks a half smile. "That's like being kind of pregnant."

I lean forward and punch his shoulder. "Don't make fun, Sam. I don't know, okay? It was awful. He was awful. It's the reason I'm scared to death of being with you."

That drains the humor from his face. "Hey." Still clutching my thighs, he runs his thumbs back and forth, a steady motion that has me wishing I could be as brazen as Reese and take him right now. He leans closer. "I'm sorry. I just don't understand and need you to explain it. The last thing I want is for you to be nervous or scared with me. In any way. Ever." His thumbs stop suddenly. His jaw hardens, his breath stills. "Did someone hurt you? Did some fucker do something you didn't want?"

I shake my head quickly and place my hand over his hammering heart. "No. It's nothing like that. Actually, I think it was me who hurt him," I say more quietly.

He glances heavenward on an inhale. "This might kill me, but..." He levels his thick-lashed gaze on me. "I need to know what happened. The idea of you being with another guy is right up there with having my chest hairs plucked out, but this is something we need to discuss." With gritted teeth, he nods. "Let's hear it, Canada."

I slouch and trace watery circles over his heart. Time to let my freak flag fly. "We were *naked*." I whisper the word, of course. "At a party. But in a private room—not like *at* the party. Anyway, there was no *foreplay*." Forever whispering. "And he was rolling on his *condom*. I stiffened by the second, totally freaking out. The rest happened really fast." Sam gnashes his teeth together but doesn't stop me. He grunts for me to go on. "He pushed in hard, didn't give me any warning…and I was pretty, you know…*dry*. It hurt, badly. I kind of jerked up, like in those reflex tests the doctors do, but instead of kicking my leg, my forehead cracked against his nose. Blood poured out. He flew off me, calling me a bitch and a freak and other horrible things. I think I broke his nose. So he was in me for like a second, but I'm not sure it counts, and I'm petrified I'm going to do something awful when we're together." I bite my lip and scrunch my face as I wait for his reaction.

"One," he says, "let's make that the official last time you ever talk to me about another guy being near you. Ever. Two, you could knee me in the balls, and I'd still want you. I'll never call you names. I'll always have your back. Three, there will be enough foreplay that when I *do* slide inside of you, slowly, you'll be begging for more. And four, my vote is you're still a virgin. That cherry is all mine."

The thrumming of my heart is as potent as the steady pulse between my legs, the fear from moments ago fading to the background. Funny how I can be terrified one second and relieved the next. A confession and words of comfort are all that's needed to ease my mind. Sam is my church.

A sudden need to prove how much I want him emboldens me. "Okay," I say. "Virgin it is." I wrap my legs around his waist, lift my hips, and slide forward, greedy to feel his length. I land spread open against his hard-on. He grunts and I whimper, his eyes going wide then falling heavy. But I'm not done yet. *Go big or go home* is what I'm thinking. "I'm always wet with you, Sam. Always ready."

Suddenly, he thrusts up, a ragged groan ripping from his throat.

Long live sex-goddess me.

My breasts are pressed to his chest, his breaths coming faster, sharper, matching my own. When I rock forward, he says, "Fuck," and digs his fingers into my hips, holding me in place. "This was a bad idea." The veins in his neck look ready to bust.

"What could you possibly mean, Samuel?" I like being the one in control, the one reducing him to a quivering mess for a change.

Still, he doesn't let me move. "Aside from the fact that I'm a guy, and I haven't had sex in over a year, I'm pretty sure sleeping with you will set the rest of my skin on fire. So when you say I make you wet and climb onto my lap, acting like the fuckable pinup girl you are, I'm gonna lose my self-control unless I get you fully dressed."

"What if I want you to?"

"To what?"

"Lose control."

His erection thickens and heat spikes through me. "Jesus, are you serious? And don't do this for me, not that I want to talk you out of it. But are you sure?"

When I nod, he doesn't ask again. He grinds against me, our lips crashing in a desperate frenzy until I'm thoroughly kissed and out of breath. It's freeing. Liberating. I never thought being naked in the open would make me feel anything but humiliated. But *this*. This is Nirvana. My own personal Shangri-La. Shangri-La that transforms into hell at breakneck speed when laughs and shouts from the bush have me locking my knees into his waist. My eyes are so wide they sting. "Holy crap. *Crapcrapcrapcrapcrap.*"

He stares at my breasts and licks his lips. "Screw gymnophobia. I'm taking you to the tent."

I stiffen. I can't speak. He scoops me up as three travelers streak toward us in their birthday suits. He holds me against him, covering all the important bits, and carries me to our clothes and his pack. Barely wrapped in the towels he brought and juggling our stuff, we try to hurry to the tent, but we stop every few steps. We grope and kiss and laugh as we drop our clothes and clutch our towels. When I accidentally kick his shin, he winces…and laughs harder.

Perfect One-syllable Sam.

Before I know it, we're in the tent. My boyfriend and me. He lays me down on the sleeping bags and unwraps my towel, spreading it wide below me. Normally, I'd be flailing about trying to cover up, but there's something in those chocolate eyes that calms me. He stares unabashedly. Soaks me in. I'd swear there's worship in his gaze. He inches forward until we're chest to chest, all his hard lines and firm ridges pressed against the soft swells of my breasts.

He kisses me lightly and pulls back to study my face. "I'm dying to be inside of you. But if you want to wait, if you're not ready, you just say the word."

His concern melts me even more. "I'm ready, Sam. I trust you. I want you, too. I'm still nervous." I swallow as I remember all the times he helped me face my fears, persistent yet patient. The way he guided me when I went down on him, easing my apprehension. "But I really, really want this."

His forehead drops to mine. "Thank God. I meant what I said, but seriously—*thank God.*"

Shivers rack his body as I unknot the towel from his waist and toss it aside.

Instead of guiding himself to my center, he dips to my collarbone, sucking and biting. I arch into him as his lips drag down my skin. My lids flutter, my pulse ticks. His lips move over my breasts. "Remember my promise, Nina. You'll be drenched before I'm done with you."

"Please, Sam. Yes." My belly clenches.

He strokes, kisses, and bites, all in perfect places, every inch of me lost in the sensations. Strong fingers caress my thighs as little nips trail toward my center. Heat shoots through me when he drops a kiss where I'm throbbing for him. His brown curls brush my thighs. With the first lick, I spasm. "God." *Like He can help me now.* I'm clenching so tight my calves burn, and Sam doesn't relent. That liquid fire he induces returns, consuming me. Lighting me up. I want this man. I'm still nervous as anything, but I can't wait a second longer to feel him inside of me. I want to be his everything.

"Now," I pant. "Please. I want you in me."

His head snaps up, fire in his eyes. "Are you ready?"

"Yes. Sam, *please*."

He pauses, still hovering over me. "I know you're on the pill, and I've had enough blood work this past year to know I'm clean. If you want me to wear a condom, I will. But I want to feel all of you. Nothing between us."

"Sam, did you miss the part where I said I want you in me. Like now. Fuck the condom." Desperate me is bossy.

I don't know if it's the swearing or the realization of what we're about to do, but he crawls toward me, hunger on his face. He nudges my legs with his and places himself exactly where I want him, his hand gliding up and down his shaft. His tip comes to rest at my opening, but he stills and whispers hoarsely, "You have no idea."

They're the same cryptic words he spoke the last time the two of us were in a tent. "Then show me," I say.

He does. He pushes. *In. In. In.* Gentle but steady, stretching me until I have to adjust, my knees falling wider, the pressure turning delicious. He groans and drops his head. He's big, thick, almost to the hilt, filling me completely. With one quick thrust, our hips are flush.

"God, yes," escapes my mouth, followed by a guttural sound.

I jerk upward, but he's ready. He pushes up slightly. "Okay?" he asks.

Sublime. Spiritual. Transcendental. "Perfect."

I clench around him and contract as I tilt my hips. He pulls out, dragging slowly, and thrusts back in. Harder.

"Fuck, Nina." He grunts, the sound vibrating in my chest.

I don't panic. I don't hold back. I live in the moment, letting every fantasy I've ever had fuel my rhythm. Our rhythm. He rolls his hips into mine, working me into a frenzy of white-hot lust and hormonal chaos that has my vision blurring. "Sam," I cry, and he devours me.

I claw his ass to pull him deeper as I arch and moan, my teeth marking his neck and shoulders. His body writhes over mine. We grope and suck and shudder, neither of us able to hold still in the slightest. Frantic. Needy. Deeper. *More.* We're wild together, beyond what I ever pictured. Each long drag coils my already wound body tighter.

"I'm close," he grounds out.

"Yes, yes," I say. White-hot fire burns through me, building. I fist his hair, curls tangling through my fingers, and he spreads me wider. *So good. So, so good.* Tension coils low in my belly, searching for release.

I latch my legs around his waist. He practically crushes me as he drops lower, his tongue invading my mouth. When I don't think I'll survive the heat searing my belly, a tear slides down my cheek, the raw emotion gathering too much. With it, a wave of pleasure consumes me, intense and mind-blowing. Sam takes me to the moon. Stars flashing, head spinning. Convulsions rack my body.

This is surrender. This is joy. This is Sam and me.

Clenching around him, I call, "Sam. Sam. Sam."

He pumps faster, his release spilling into me. He shouts, "God. Fuck. Nina," and a string of words in short gasps. His lips fall against mine, kissing me with more passion than before, pressing his weight fully onto me until it's hard to breathe.

I'd stay here forever if I could. In my Neverland. The place where Sam and I don't have to grow up. Where we're free from the life-altering decisions that could keep us apart. He pulls back, and I whimper, still wanting those lips. "That was…" I shake my head. There are no words.

He exhales and says, "You have no idea." But I think I finally do.

He opens his mouth again as if to speak, but closes it. There's something different in his gaze. His brow puckers with what looks like…fear? My cheeks are still damp from the few tears I've shed. Tears of joy. Love.

His brown eyes shine with wetness, too. "I've never…" he starts but stops. His lids drift shut, and he rolls his hips. "Shit. I'm already hard again."

I'm languid. Loose. Leaden. Spent. Entirely satisfied. But with that one move, want spikes through me. He swallows and opens his eyes, that fear still present. I want to tell him I love him but can't seem to form the words. Something's gathering behind his stormy gaze, keeping me quiet. Instead of speaking, I tilt my hips to allow him more access, and he moves deeper, but stills, breathing hard. I've seen every emotion cross his handsome face these past weeks, from sad to serious, ecstatic to mischievous. But I've never seen him look so—conflicted. Desperate.

"Sam…are you okay?"

His breaths swell deeper, his lips part, but he doesn't answer. He blinks, and a tear falls from his brimming eyes. I brush it away with my thumb and he exhales, pressing his cheek into my palm. I bite my lip, unsure what to do or say. He takes the lead, pulling back his hips to glide forward, the two of us sighing, a shudder running down his spine.

I grab his backside and grind against him from below. He

twitches inside of me, and I almost come. Wanting to get his mind off of whatever is chasing him, I whisper, "If I let you in on one of my fantasies, will you promise to make it real?" He's asked often, slipping in the question whenever he can, hoping to catch me off guard enough to share my sometimes filthy and always indecent imaginings, but I've held out.

His shoulders flex and his nostrils flare, that haunted look from before now pure desire. He winks at me. "I promise."

I drag one hand up his back and grab his neck, then whisper in his ear. With each dirty word, he rocks inside of me. With each description, he growls until we're losing ourselves again. I don't get embarrassed. I don't get shy. Love and trust have erased my boundaries.

Afterward, in the snug tent, with Sam spooning me from behind, I struggle to fall asleep. This was the best night of my life, the most amazing I've ever felt. Still, there's one lie left between Sam and me, one I've been clinging to. The lie of Pininfarina. He brings up my siblings from time to time, joking about their names and my less-interesting one. I go with the flow, never rising to the bait. He knows there's something off with the way I skirt the subject. He can read me like that. But if I tell him my real name and he Googles me and sees the Public Speaking Incident in all its glory, I might drop dead from shame. It makes the Hot Soup Incident look like a Disney movie.

What began as a little white lie to escape my past is a ten-ton elephant now. I'm in love with One-syllable Sam, and he doesn't even know my name. His chest expands against my back, breaths steady with sleep, but my eyes are still wide.

Seventeen

NINA

"Like that, baby. Oh, yeah. Fucking perfect," Sam says from his usual position behind me.

Over the past few weeks, he's become my sous-chef in the hostel kitchens. He chops and cleans and often leans into my backside while I'm at the stove to show me just how hungry he is. Food gets the man excited. Tonight, he talks dirty in my ear while I stir my Indian curry, scents of cumin and coriander filling the air. "Like that, baby," he says again. "Stir that sauce. Oh, yeah." When I laugh and elbow him, he tugs my hips into his.

I almost burn dinner.

"If you two stop rubbing against each other for a minute, the rest of us might get to eat. Preferably without throwing up."

I lean around Sam's shoulder. Leigh and Paige are at the table in this oddly decorated kitchen, the enduring theme being floral on floral. Floral wallpaper, floral photos, floral floor tiles, and a large wall clock by the door stenciled with—you guessed it—flowers. The well-equipped kitchen and clean rooms are why it's listed as the top place to stay in our guidebook, not the decor. "Patience, Leigh," I say. "Fine cuisine takes time."

She snarls at me and turns to Paige across from her at the table, both of them wearing old-school rock shirts. "We should've gone to McDonalds," she says.

I can see their legs from here, their ankles hooked together sweetly.

This is our first night in Christchurch. Our first night with Leigh and Paige since traveling on our own, and I'm happy for the distraction. Since our most recent tent evening, I'm more consumed by Sam than ever. My love for him has reached epic proportions of the fairy-tale variety. Look out, Cinderella.

That haunted look he wore after we first made love hasn't reappeared. The fear or uncertainty or whatever it was seems to have vanished. Still, we don't talk about the future much, aside from discussing our career stresses. We don't discuss *us* much. He tells me all the time how happy he is, how special I am, and how these have been the best weeks of his life. I don't know if that spells love, but it sure spells more than "friends with benefits." I'm ready to burst, wanting to tell him how I feel, but the longer we don't talk about *us* the harder it gets to bring it up.

Leigh's barbed humor and snarky remarks are just the things I need to stop my mind from spinning out of control, and I couldn't be more thrilled for her and Paige. Like Sam and me, they're always touching in some way, sneaking glances simmering with heat. Leigh hasn't opened up to anyone back home about her sexuality, but at least here, in this far-flung land, she can be herself.

When I turn to add the last few spices to the overflowing pot of curry, Leigh says, "Fuck me," her tone none too happy.

A high-pitched laugh assaults my ears—the sound of a hyena being tickle tortured. "You ladies are a sight for sore eyes. Callum will be chuffed to see you."

I swivel as Bruno wags his thick eyebrows, his olive skin darker than the last time I saw him. Glancing nervously behind him, I exhale, relieved, when neither Brianne nor Reese walk in. Maybe he and Callum ditched the girls to travel on their own.

Bruno leans on the table to kiss both of Leigh's cheeks. "*Bellissima*," he cries.

She sits rigid, arms locked at her sides. "I thought you were British." Each word is clipped. Strained. She's been dreading running into them.

The night of Leigh's blowout with Reese, the whole thing played out in private. We've dissected it a few times, trying to guess what she told Bruno, Callum, and Brianne about Leigh's sudden departure, wondering if she outed her or fed them ridiculous lies. Since we're all on the same travel trajectory, meeting up was pretty much inevitable.

When Bruno wiggles his eyebrows and says, "Half British, half Italian—if you fancy, I can show you which half later. Love the short hair, by the way. Very Posh Spice."

Leigh snorts and I relax. Apparently, Reese kept her mouth shut.

"Interesting," she says. "I would've guessed half British and halfwit."

He barks a laugh and stands to face me.

I force a smile. Like Leigh, I haven't seen Bruno in a while, not since the Hot Soup Incident. With each passing second, I hunch lower and press closer into Sam's side. *Please don't look at my boobs.* His focus stays on my face. "Nina, luv, smashing to see you."

Bruno is a good guy. With one simple sentence, he avoids the Hot Soup Incident and my subsequent disappearance. I release a lengthy breath.

He glances from me to Sam—to Sam's hand around my hip, his legs visible in his shorts. Bruno scrunches his nose. "Sam, mate, what the hell? Those are some beastly scars."

Instead of replying, Sam leans into me. "Did you hear that, Canada? I'm feeling kind of vulnerable. Like really low. I think I need a pick-me-up."

He squeezes my hip, and I roll my eyes.

Sam's gotten pretty used to the stares and comments to the point it barely fazes him. I set the precedent, though, making out with him whenever the issue comes up. Now he takes advantage. *Frickin' Hot Guy.* "Get down here," I say as I drop my spoon on the counter and tug his neck.

With a groan, he latches onto my waist and kisses me with abandon, not a thought to our audience.

"If I light myself on fire, will Nina snog me like that?"

I try to pull back, but Sam nips my bottom lip. "Not on your life," he says to Bruno, his ravenous gaze on me.

Bruno shrugs. "Can't blame a bloke for trying. Looks like your travels have been eventful. What else have I missed?" He strides to the table, straddles the bench, and glances from Leigh to Paige.

"And this lovely lady is?" He quirks his head at Paige, who looks about to punch him. The girls aren't one of those "opposites attract" couples. Between the two of them, the dirty looks that fly would shame a death row inmate.

"She's mine," Leigh says.

Bruno's jaw drops and I spill some curry.

Leigh's definitely owning herself in New Zealand.

Bruno closes his mouth, his eyes dancing. "A very eventful time indeed." He shakes his head and studies the flower-filled room. "Looks like someone ate my nana's house and threw it up in here. And that smells divine, Nina. Any chance you'll have some extra?"

I stir the curry to keep it from bubbling over the sides. "I think I can make it stretch."

As I reach for some bowls, Callum and Brianne stumble into the room, each clutching a bottle of vodka. Brianne? *Shoot.* Leigh's shoulders almost hitch to her ears, and her lip curls; if she were a dog, there'd be a ridge of fur bristling along her back. I hold my breath, waiting for Reese to follow in behind, but the seconds tick by…and nothing.

Paige folds over the table and whispers something to Leigh, flicking her head toward the door, probably asking if she wants to leave. Leigh sets her jaw and shakes her head. She folds her arms as Brianne and Callum sit, likely readying her pointy elbows to jab Reese in the jugular. Brianne curls her pink-tipped hair around her finger and smiles at Leigh. As they get caught up, I glance at the door, but still no Reese.

Callum plants the bottles on the table and nods to each of us. "How go the travels?"

Sam grunts. "Unforgettable. You?" He situates himself even closer to me, letting Callum know I'm off limits.

Callum grins lazily, not fazed by Sam's posture. "Brilliant, thanks."

I like when Sam gets like this, staking his claim on me. Having been the outcast all my life, I revel in being with him. Being his. Our little gang of two. It makes me feel halfway normal. (If normal is floating in the clouds and being on the verge of an orgasm twenty-four/seven, the softest breeze enough to send me over the edge.) Yep, I'm feeling pretty normal.

I shove him with my hip and finish dishing out dinner. With our table growing, it's a good thing I made lots. "If you're hungry," I call to Callum and Brianne, "I can fix you guys a bowl."

Before they have a chance to answer, Leigh clears her throat. "Reese with you?"

Callum shakes his head. "She's out with some bloke. But I'm in, Nina. For the food. Love a good curry."

Leigh's shoulders drop a fraction, as do mine. I'm not sure I want to be around when she and Reese see each other for the first time since the altercation that sent Leigh hacking at her own hair. If there's one thing Leigh isn't, it's emotional. Angry, yes. Emotional, *no*. I can't imagine what happened to reduce her to that state, what words were thrown around. Her flattened lips and bouncing heel tell me she'll go full grenade on Reese if she shows up.

For some unknown reason, Brianne giggles. "Me too, Nina. I'm starving."

Our group grows by a couple more travelers from Israel, my curry gone by the end of the meal. Dinner is followed by dessert.

If you want to make friends, throw Smarties, coconut, and caramel bits into a batch of Rice Krispies squares and pass them around. We joke and laugh, sharing stories. Everyone smiles as they munch on my treats. I love how food is a common language that can bring people together, elevate a celebration, or soothe troubled souls.

Warmth spreads through my chest as the last crumbs are devoured, warmth that turns to liquid fire when Sam winks at me. One darn wink and I'm a hot mess. He's at the head of the table; Paige, Callum, and Brianne down one side; me, Leigh, and Bruno on the other. The Israelis have taken off, leaving our group to pass around the vodka.

Sam leans toward me. "I've been thinking."

Leigh snorts. "I was wondering about that pained expression. You look ready to pass a kidney stone."

He balls up a napkin and tosses it at her face. "Watch it, Leigh. I still have no problem shaving off your eyebrows." He plants his elbows on the table. "Anyway, *Nina*, as I was saying—I've been thinking, and you, Canada, rock a stove. You love it. It's all over your face when you plan a meal and when you watch these idiots devour your food. This is what you should do."

"What do you mean *do*?"

"Like *do*. As in *job*. Cook for people. If you love it that much, you should think about it as a career."

Cooking? For a living? I don't know why I haven't considered that. The usual suspects such as teacher, doctor, lawyer always top the list when I envision my future. Not because they're what I'm interested in. Because they're mainstream. Easy. Front of mind. Although Mom's writing her endless cookbook, and I cook all the time, I never thought about turning the thing I love into a job. The notion has me picturing a busy restaurant with pots clanking, chefs bellowing, and waiters rushing.

A grin stretches across my face. "Sam, have I told you recently that you're a genius?"

"Feel free to praise my genius anytime. And if you're interested..."—he rubs methodically at a stain on the table before glancing back at me—"there's a culinary institute not far from the physiotherapy school I've been checking out."

All noise vanishes. Midblink, my eyelids freeze.

"In Florida?" The words barely make it past my throat.

His broad chest expands as he inhales, a soft, "Uh huh," floating out on a breath.

"You want me to check out a school in Florida?" I ask again to be sure.

He scoots his chair closer, his knee grazing mine, both of us leaning closer to tune out our chatty group. One of his hands lands on my thigh, the other wraps around my neck. "Nina Gabri, I'd like you to come to Florida with me. I don't want this to end. I don't want us to end. Things are still sketchy with my dad, and I'm feeling like I need to be there. But I want you to come, too...if it's what you want."

I try to latch onto one of the errant thoughts running through my mind, a thousand emotions rolling inside of me. Sam—*my Sam*—wants me to move to Florida. *With* him.

He didn't use the one word I waited for with bated breath, those four letters never making an appearance, but he doesn't want *us* to end. The guy I'm in love with—the one who has officially taken my virginity and ruined me for all future sexual exploits, the one who accepts me for me, despite my ongoing list of quirks—that guy wants to live with me. My heart swells. There is, however, one part of his confession that doesn't sit well. The part where he said *Nina Gabri*. Not Pininfarina.

Flashes of the Public Speaking Incident send my full heart pounding and my stomach plummeting. I trusted Sam enough to tell him why I was afraid to be intimate with him and the only thing he made me feel was cherished. Accepted. If I move away from my family to be with him, I have to trust him one hundred percent. I glance at my purse resting by my feet, knowing my passport is tucked inside. I'm surprised it's not glowing.

Sam squeezes my thigh. "What do you say, Nina? Will you come to Florida?"

I look up from my purse, the vulnerability on his face heart-melting. Real name or not, hearing *I love you* or not, I know my answer. There's only ever been one. "Yes." I nod quickly, both of us now grinning like idiots. "Yes, yes, yes! Does that mean you've decided on physio?"

He stares at me for several long beats and steals a slow, deep kiss. Reluctantly, he pulls back. "Yeah—physio. I still have to finish my last year, but the more I've thought about it, the more I realize it's what I want. It'll be rough on my dad, but I'll regret not going for it." A mad cackle from Bruno makes us both flinch. Sam grabs my hand and leans his elbows on the table. "Look at us all adult-like with future plans and shit. Who knew I'd leave for this trip and come home with you in my life, and a career ahead of me?" Lifting my hand, he brushes his lips over each knuckle. He lowers his voice. "Lucky isn't a word I'd have used to describe myself a year ago. Not even close. But it's the only one that comes to mind now."

Sam and his perfect words.

"You have no idea," I say, stealing his line.

I'm moving to Florida. With Hot Guy. And I have a possible goal. Now I can't wait to get to a computer and research schools. Me. A chef. A culinary artist. Or a personal cook. Mom will go ballistic in the best possible way when I tell her, especially if I say my inner goddess is guiding me to become my true self. If I ever need to convince Mom of anything, I throw in the word goddess, and she's putty in my hands. Still, I'm not sure how she'll react to me moving away more permanently.

Sam turns to our friends and pounds the table, interrupting their chatter. "Pass the vodka, Callum. A toast is in order." He pushes up from the table and goes to the counter to get shot glasses.

I watch his sexy backside, barely noticing his limp. It's such a part of him it fades to the background, and I'm proud he's found the confidence to wear shorts again.

Then I hear, "Holy shit. Who chewed his legs?"

A dropping pin could shatter the silence.

"Fucking cunt," drips from Leigh like venom.

Reese. She's dolled up to the nines, her blond hair spilling over her shoulders instead of in its usual braid. She's wearing a tiny navy dress, her breasts popping out over the neckline, and her mascara's so thick, it's a wonder she can blink. She smiles sweetly at Leigh. "Who invited the dyke?"

I almost hit the deck.

Tick goes the wall clock. *Tick. Tick. Tick.* Or maybe that's the time bomb in Leigh's reddening face. Brianne slaps her hand over her mouth in shock, her eyes flitting between Leigh and Reese. Bruno shifts on his seat, frowning. Sam's the one who speaks first, his voice like rolling thunder. "Use that word again, Reese, and you'll be leaving New Zealand minus a tongue."

Leigh holds up her palm to silence Sam, spins around, and gets to her feet with precision. Each movement is controlled. Each step is calculated. Her face has become a mask of pure tranquility. But I know the storm brewing below the surface and can't understand why Leigh isn't being *Leigh*. This can't be good. Most definitely bad. The fallout will likely make the battle for Middle Earth look like a slow waltz. Paige leans back and crosses her arms, looking smug. Like she knows why the grenade has yet to explode.

"Reese," Leigh says in a sugary voice. "Remember last year at Todd's party? You know, the night you got wasted on strawberry daiquiris?"

Reese blanches. It's a barely-there whitening below all the makeup, but noticeable. "What did you do?" she says through clenched teeth.

Leigh smiles a fifty-watt smile, the brightest she's ever flashed. "Well, let's just say I had my handy-dandy phone on me with its awesome camera, so when you passed out covered in your own puke in nothing but your underoos, I decided to memorialize the moment. Wouldn't want you to forget how special that night was."

She holds up her phone. Reese reaches for it, but misses. "Give it here, bitch."

"Not on your life. Actually, I was thinking of plastering it all over Facebook. Everyone should see what a charmer you really are."

Holy crap. I should intervene. I know firsthand how it feels to have the worst circulate the globe, but when it comes to Reese, I can't muster the sympathy. She drove Leigh to a Britney-worthy meltdown. I guess when you have real friends, moral lines blur in their defense.

Leigh holds up her cell, her thumb on the send button, but in the blink of an eye, Reese whips her phone from her purse and snaps a photo of Leigh. Confused, Leigh blinks while Reese types quickly, then Reese mimics Leigh's stance with her phone in the air. "You hit send, Leigh, and I hit send. *Your* picture will read: Carpet Muncher."

We all draw a collective breath.

Leigh straightens her back. "You wouldn't."

"Try me."

Brianne pushes to her feet. "Reese, you can't. This isn't a joke."

Reese looks ready to spit. "Seriously, Brianne? You're taking her side? Remind me the next time you ask if your ass looks big in those tacky jeans to tell you the truth. It should have its own zip code."

Brianne sits with a thud, her mouth open in horror.

The phones are still held high, Leigh and Reese facing off in a modern-day duel. Something tells me the push of Reese's button could do more damage to Leigh than a knight's sword. That darn clock is once again the loudest thing in the room.

Tick. Reese cocks her head.

Tick. Leigh's fingers flex.

Tick. Reese purses her lips.

Tick. Leigh shrugs. *Shrugs?* "Fuck it," she says.

Her thumb presses down, Reese's following shortly, and then…nothing. This is the distant warfare of generals in sterile rooms giving launch codes, never once laying eyes on the detonation. The blood and the guts. But, holy God, Leigh's entire world has erupted. And she looks…unfazed. Reese, on the other hand, is shaking, a vein throbbing along her temple.

Leigh gives Paige a half smile. "Like you said, I can't run forever."

Paige bites her lip and shakes her head. "You kick ass. Get over here."

Leigh rounds the table, Paige meeting her partway, and the two of them make out like it's their last meal. Bruno hoots and hollers, drool practically dripping down his chin, while the rest of us clap and Sam shouts, "Get a room." Leigh gives him the finger.

Brianne sashays over to Reese and crosses her arms. "That was so not cool. I can't even look at you. Leave my earrings and shoes on my bunk, and don't even think of stealing my orange bikini. You can travel on your own. I'm out." She spins, the pink tips of her hair smacking Reese's face.

I didn't think Brianne had it in her.

Reese's eyes flit to each of us, the phone in her death grip looking ready to crack. She makes a strangled sound and stomps from the room.

I breathe a sigh of relief.

"That decides it," Bruno says with a clap. "Sam, pass those shot glasses. I feel a round of Never Have I Ever coming on. Drama makes me thirsty." A series of *woo-hoo*s and *all right*s rise from the group.

While they set up, I nod to Leigh, who's sitting so close to Paige they're practically conjoined. "You sure you're okay?"

Still glowing from that fairy-tale kiss, she says, "Tomorrow's gonna suck, but yeah. I'm good."

God, that girl is brave.

After the first round, my glass is still full, but Callum has admitted to an unfortunate event with Bengay and a jockstrap, and Brianne has come clean about a thin white T-shirt and a water hose. Sam's free hand stays on my thigh, inching up my skirt, whispering periodically how it's still his favorite. It's the floral skirt I wore on the airplane that gave him an unimpeded view of my nether region.

Bruno and he have spent much of the last half hour studying Leigh and Paige, Bruno wearing a typical look of male wonder, no doubt picturing himself in various unclothed positions with the two girls, both of whom would likely rather snort wasabi than be with him. But Sam looks pensive.

As if aware I'm watching him, he turns and puts both hands on my shoulders. "You ready to own your crazy?"

What the…? His look of mischief has me shrinking on the bench. "Sorry. No. Please. No. Whatever you're thinking, the answer is no."

"You can't apologize your way out of this, Canada. Check out Leigh." He flicks his head toward her.

She has such an air of ease, she's almost unrecognizable. As though releasing her truth into the world has unburdened her. At least momentarily. So she has owned herself, and Sam walks around in shorts, no longer hiding his scars. What about me? Thanks to him, I've faced down a number of phobias, but in a group of friends, I'd still rather hide behind the façade of normal than parade my eccentricities. And he's calling me on it. The guy who doesn't even know my name.

I look back at Leigh—her broad smile, the shine in her eyes. If she can risk it all and come out laughing, I can, too. Sitting taller, I grip my shot glass. "Okay, do your worst." I can be courageous. Fearless. I'm a regular Joan of Arc.

He drops my shoulders, squeezes my thigh, and holds his other hand in the air. "My turn," he calls.

All heads turn our way, and I gulp. Maybe I'm more Cowardly Lion than Joan of Arc. I doubt anyone will notice if I slip under the table and huddle in the fetal position. My floral skirt will for sure camouflage me with the floor tile. Or I could pull the fire alarm.

Sensing my imminent freak-out, Sam tightens his grip on my leg. Then he says, "Never have I ever…" *OhGodOhGodOhGodOhGod.* He won't really do it, will he? "Wet myself on an airplane, tossed out my underpants, then flashed a very flustered guy."

He sure did.

My heart shoots to warp speed, my neck so tense it might snap, and everyone looks at Sam like he's lost his freaking mind. "Own it, Canada," he whispers.

So I do. I lift my shot, drain the vodka, and slam it down, fire burning the length of my throat. While I sputter and cough, I keep my attention focused on the single drip cascading down my empty glass. Bruno's hyena laugh nearly shatters the thing. Then Leigh hollers, Callum chuckles, and Brianne giggles, the noise loud enough to wake the hostel.

"Priceless!" Bruno falls over on the bench in hysterics.

"That you are," Sam says into my ear, his nose, then lips, finding my neck. I shiver from the contact and glance at our friends. I'm no stranger to laughs at my expense, but the warm smiles and genuine humor on their faces isn't hurtful. Or mocking. As Bruno's cackle escalates, I find myself laughing with them. I snort in the process and Leigh points at me, falling face first onto the table. Sam loses it, too, slapping his knee and holding his chest.

So this is chasing your crazy. And catching it.

I'm not sure if meeting Sam was preordained, a magical twist of fate. But it's because of him I'm full to bursting with love. For him and for myself. His long lashes lower, his focus intent on me, a sliver of honey-brown darkening as his breathing steadies. "You're amazing," he says, almost to himself.

That's when I find myself reaching down for my purse, pulling the zipper back, and slowly, without hesitation, sliding my passport from its depths. I place it on the table, surprised my name hasn't burned through the pages, and I glide it toward Sam. He watches me, brow furrowed. It only takes a second for it to click, for him to understand what I'm doing. He's asked often enough about my name to know I haven't been honest.

Smiling now, he reaches for the small blue book and thumbs to the Page. I contemplate ducking under the table again, but he nods and smiles, and nods and smiles some more, and I can't look away. "It's perfect," he says. "You deserve a name as unique as you." He doesn't say my five syllables aloud. He places a soft kiss on my nose and, with it, dissolves all my fear.

Sam will never laugh at me. Even if he sees the Public Speaking Video—and odds are he will one day—he'll only ever show concern, indignation, or anger: protectiveness. Renewed warmth spreads through my chest.

I'm moving to Florida with One-syllable Sam.

Eventually, the empty glasses are filled. As Leigh and Paige cozy up together, Bruno licks his lips and rests his chin on his hands. He stares blatantly at the couple. "Never Have I Ever…fallen in love with a girl in New Zealand."

As if on cue, both girls sling their shots. The kissing starts up again, which I'm pretty sure is why Bruno asked the question, and a round of applause rises from the table. In the ensuing racket, my breath catches. That question was asked to the whole table, not just the girls. I don't dare move. Hope has me frozen. Surely Sam is as in love with me as I am with him; we've both just been too terrified to say it aloud. The way his eyes glaze when we make love, how could he feel anything but?

Look. Look. Look. Look.

Steeling my nerves, I swallow and, ever so slowly, glance to my left. Sam's running his finger around the rim of his shot glass. His very full shot glass. It shouldn't be like a dagger to my heart, but the effect is undeniable. A sharp, deliberate pang. He drags his finger in circles, round and round, never once glancing at me. Then he nudges it away.

His glass. *Away.*

Maybe it's sharing my name with him or his proposal to move to Florida, but that nudge hurts more than it should. It's not like I've declared my love, and I know his feelings for me are deep. I don't question that. I just don't know if it's infatuation, not love, me being the first girl to accept his legs. Moving to Florida with him is a big deal for both of us, making a commitment, altering our lives. But I'm giving up more. My family. My home. I'm taking a massive risk for him. If he's not in love with me the way I am with him, this could all blow up in my face. *Maybe I shouldn't go.*

My heart squeezes at the thought, the pang in my chest raw and jagged. Sam's the first guy to want me for me, crazy and all, and he doesn't want to lose us. He wants me with him. Even with the risks, that's exactly where I want to be.

Eighteen

NINA

If I could wake up every morning for the rest of my life with Sam pressing soft kisses down my belly, I would die a happy girl. Before last night, things had achieved fairy-tale status between us, each day dreamlike, but knowing we're staying together after this trip has made our happily-ever-after real. Sam's more content, relaxed. My mind's calmer, too. I've stopped overanalyzing everything we do and say, wondering if he feels the same. I don't need to hear those three words to know how he feels.

Excited to meet him in the lounge and research culinary schools in Florida, I hurry out of the washroom with an armful of toiletries. As I head to dump my stuff in our room, a guy shoulders past me, sending my soap and moisturizer flying. *Perfect.* He fumbles around to help me gather my stuff. When we stand, he hesitates. "Do I know you?" The high pitch of his voice sounds odd, the tone contradicting his height. This guy is Harlem Globe-trotter tall. He pushes his glasses up his nose.

I shrug, tucking my precious beauty products closer. "Don't think so. Maybe we've been at the same hostel or something?" But I'm pretty sure I'd remember a guy who could climb Jack's beanstalk in three strides.

He narrows his gaze and cocks his head. "Yeah, maybe…"

With a smile, I leave him staring after me. I drop my toiletries in my room and check my phone again. I texted Mom last night, gushing about Sam and Florida and all things culinary, and I still haven't heard back. When I flip over my cell, I frown. One missed call from home, but no message. Mom never calls. I thought she'd support my choice, be in my corner like always, but maybe I'm wrong. Maybe she'll try to talk me out of going. That conversation can't happen until Sam and I have a plan—schools, apartment, and a job all figured out. I need proper ammunition to defend my decision, aside from the obvious, *but he's really hot.*

Determined to make this work, I tuck my phone in my purse, practically skipping down the hallway to see my *boyfriend*, when an all-too-familiar sound floats from the lounge. I stop short. My gut churns. I almost throw up. Thankfully, time slams to a stop and prevents any actual regurgitation. I strain my suddenly bionic ears, picking up every horrifying sound, my breath now coming in gulps.

This. Can't. Be. Happening.

A deep laugh echoes from the lounge around the corner, halting my hyperventilation. I've memorized the vibrato in that sound to the point where I could write a symphony around it.

Sam's rumbling laugh is decadent, each note sexier than the last. The next sound is equally memorable, but for all the wrong reasons. It's not the words that trigger my visceral reaction. Taken out of context, they could refer to anything—a chance meeting with a celebrity, a UFO invasion, but when I hear, "Did that just happen?" in the distinctive voice that chased me around high school, my throat closes. Someone's watching the Public Speaking Video.

Then Sam laughs again.

I've seen my famed YouTube video enough times you'd think I like rubbing salt in fresh wounds. I just couldn't believe it really happened, that it was really me. I'd watch it again and again, my own corporal punishment for being such a mutant. It got to the point where Mom had to unhook the computer in my room to break the cycle.

As I approach the lounge doorway, I recognize every hoot and holler from that video as if it were filmed yesterday. Trembling, I poke my head around the corner. Two computers are at the back with three guys crammed at one and Sam at the other. Sam laughing uncontrollably. Laughing. *At me.* It's the only explanation. And it's the thing he said he'd never do.

I haven't had a migraine since that video surfaced, but spots cloud my vision, and my temples throb. Everything else numbs. Sam looks up then, deep frown lines setting in. My cheeks are hot. I feel the wetness, but I don't remember tears falling. He pushes back his chair, but as soon as he steps toward me, I retreat. I run down the hallway to the girls' dorm and crash into Leigh. I drag her back inside as he yells, "Nina!"

Wide-eyed, she takes in my tearstained cheeks and blotchy

chest—the curse of my pale skin that displays every emotion. "What did that bastard do?" Her words come out in a hiss.

I shake my head. "Nothing. Everything. I don't know." I rub my palms across my eyes and release a shuddering breath.

She grabs my arm and drags me over to her bed, one of six in the room. A couple of girls are getting ready to go out, the others probably already exploring Christchurch. As we sit cross-legged, her phone buzzes. She reads her text while I study the ceiling and try not to fall apart.

I relive the moment at the beach with the necklace and Sam's words, the euphoria followed quickly by his traitorous laugh while watching the most embarrassing moment of my life. I trusted Sam. With him, I was the best version of me. He made me believe he'd never let me fall, no matter how much I stumbled. He promised he'd never laugh *at* me.

So much for promises.

It taints every word he's ever said, every kiss he's ever given. Hearing that sound was worse than any prank or name or insult I've endured. I can't go to Florida with him now, can't trust him again after that kind of betrayal. I blink back a fresh wave of tears. At least I can thank him for putting me on the right path, helping me chase down my phobias. Pushing me to follow my passion for cooking. But our traveling together, our relationship, it ends here.

I swallow another sob.

"Man, you think loud." Leigh squints at me, her angled brows pulled together. "You need to get that shit under control. I'd recommend drugs."

"Leigh," I whisper-yell, glancing at the two other girls getting dressed. They glance our way before getting on with their routine. "Don't go shouting words like *drugs*. And how come everyone knows when I'm thinking? Is there a sign on my forehead that says 'deep in thought'?"

"First, DRUGS," she says full volume, a huge smirk on her face. I try to kick her but she blocks my feet with her hand. "Second." She drops her voice. "You drag your teeth over your lip and move your eyes a bunch. You know, like when dogs are dreaming and their eyes roll around? It kind of looks like that."

"Seriously? I twitch like a sleeping dog?" No wonder Sam laughed at my expense. "That explains a lot," I mumble.

"Actually, it explains nothing. What *does* need explaining is your meltdown just now. I already have two texts from Mancandy asking what's up."

I look over at my phone, hating the thickness building in my throat. It's buzzing, but I don't check the messages. "Just tell him I had some bad news from home, a sick dog or something. I can't deal with him right now. And aren't you supposed to be with Paige? I thought you guys were going to the botanic gardens. And...*shoot*. I didn't even ask if things are okay after, you know, Reese and the Facebook thing."

"That's a lot to toss at a girl first thing in the morning, but I'll do my best." She winks at me. "Reese took off. Good riddance. I'm getting a mix of cool and not cool replies to the post, but being halfway across the world makes it sting less. Paige is doing laundry. I just texted her that my girl needs me. So like it or not, I'm spending the day with you. And sick dog? Should I tell him it ate your homework, too?" When I give her my angry-old-lady face, she leans back, her hands raised in front of her eyes. "God,

Nina. You're pretty hot, but I don't suggest doing that around Sam. It is *not* a good look for you." I throw a lame punch at her arm. "Sick dog it is," she says.

I take a couple of Advil while she lies to Sam on my behalf, then she stares me down. "With that out of the way, the least you can do is entertain me. Begin the Nina-Sam saga." She fans her hand through the air like a conductor.

I hunch over my crossed my legs, picking at a smear of dried paint on the comforter. It matches the blue walls. Judging by the sharp smells in here, I'm guessing they were painted recently. "It's a long story," I say, still focused on the stain. She waits patiently, until it all spills out: the Public Speaking Incident. Sam's promises.

Pininfarina. How watching him laugh at me was worse than the time Tracy Evans hid a fish in my locker.

When I'm done, drained, cried out, completely exhausted, she answers as only Leigh can. "You know I have to watch it, right? I have to see that video."

I wipe my eyes and glare at her. "You can't be serious."

She winces, scrunching her nose. "That face, Nina. That face." She waves her hands at me. "You need to stop with that face."

I bite my cheek and pout. *Stupid angry-old-lady face.* Add that to my arsenal of surefire turn-offs, next to twitches like a sleeping dog, and it's all too clear why Sam so easily laughed at me.

She lets out a lengthy breath. "Look. If I don't watch it, I'll spend all my time wondering what you did, coming up with crazy stuff and blowing it up until I can't even look at you. If I see it, then I'll laugh once, and we can move on." She pins me with her dark eyes. "Resistance is futile."

It's the *Star Trek* quote that makes me cave. *Star Trek* gets me every time.

Once I agree to let her watch the dreaded video later, she lays out her plan. Callum told her about a paragliding trip happening this afternoon run by the hostel, which is totally terrifying and totally cool, and she somehow talks me into it. I'm thankful I met Leigh on this trip. Sure, she laughs at me, but she does it openly and honestly. Not behind my back. There's no pretense between us. We are who we are: two girls trying to own themselves on the other side of the world.

The plan is to tell Sam it's a girl-bonding mission. It'll give me time and space to figure out how to tell him we're over. Time to convince my heart it's the right thing to do. With the way my body aches remembering the feel of him this morning, the latter may prove difficult. I grab my phone, knowing I need to send another message to Mom. I have to cancel last night's text written by in-love me, prattling on about Florida and culinary school.

A glance down at the screen shows another missed call from her. Thinking it was Sam, I ignored it, and I'm glad I did. Calling her back means another emotional conversation, something I'd rather avoid. Plus, it's late back home. I type a rant and hit send. Now I need to deal with the other thing bound to give me a nervous breakdown.

Freaking paragliding.

This has the potential to be catastrophic on a grand scale. Monumental. Pyramids-of-Egypt grand. The idea of jumping off a cliff attached to some random guy while spiraling down mountainsides has me queasy. Combine that with my sudden fatigue, and it's kind of hard to function. I make it to the kitchen and slather some butter on toast, but my limbs turn languid, my eye-lids droop, and I can barely focus.

I've experienced this once before. As I got dressed the night of the I'm Not Sure I Lost My Virginity Incident, I was a walking zombie until I chugged my first beer. There's no doubt Hot Guy is to blame for my current state of neurasthenia—nervous exhaustion. Leigh texted him that we're doing our own thing today, and, judging by the ten messages lighting up my phone, I'd say he's looking for me.

His imminent arrival in the kitchen has me nodding off on my feet.

Nineteen

SAM

I swear to God, if Nina or Leigh doesn't tell me what's going on, I'm going to punch something. I wear a path on the pavement outside the hostel, the monotony doing nothing to calm me.

This morning everything felt right. Perfect. Sunlight filtered in through the curtains, making Nina's pale skin glow, and all I could do was stare, overwhelmed, knowing she was coming home with me. That question had been lodged in my throat for weeks, probably since the night I took her virginity—as far as I was concerned, that other dude never happened. Being with her, sinking into her, was more intense than anything I'd ever felt. It shattered me. Broke me apart. Then it put me back together.

I left on this trip wanting good times, a fresh perspective. Carefree travel sex. What I found was hope. With Nina, I feel alive again. Invincible. Desired. I found a partner who understands the shit I've been through and the struggles ahead, all while making me crack up with her craziness.

But I held back last night. Disappointment rolled off her in waves when I didn't slam that shot and prove my love. It almost killed me. I know I love this girl like I know fire burns and hope heals. I know it like I know my dad's love for my mom has him dying inside. He's lost without her, suffocating on every memory, the pain breaking his will to live. Yeah, I hurt daily. Knowing Mom will never holler at me again to clean my room or tell me she scored in the kid department is torture. But Dad? I don't ever want to know the kind of agony he's going through. Not telling Nina I love her feels like the last string keeping me from falling so deep I'll never be able to walk away unharmed.

My phone vibrates in my pocket, and I yank it out, praying Nina's name will be there. Or Pininfarina. I still don't get why she lied about her name. The guy who designed the Ferrari? That's some cool shit. Still, when I pushed her about it this morning, she held her ground, saying, "I like being Nina—the girl who messes up but owns it. And I met you as Nina. Pininfarina's tied to so much…stuff. So many bad memories."

That girl should have a name as rare as she is, but I'd call her Fred to make her happy. In fact, I'd call her whatever she wants if only she'd tell me why the hell she ran off like she did, tears streaming down her face. *Fuck.*

I tap my phone aggressively, but it's not Nina. It's Xander, wondering if he can lend out my football gear.

At least seeing his name makes me laugh. While Nina was doing her girl thing this morning, taking her sweet-ass time in the bathroom, I went to the computers and scrolled through my

Facebook page. Xander sent me some photos from rush week. They had one sucker in a bikini, his man-bush pushing out the bottoms, as he stood on campus handing out free condoms.

The sign by his feet read: *This could be your child. Use protection.*

I nearly busted my gut laughing.

Some douchebags were at the computer beside mine, one crazy tall dude with thick-framed glasses slapping his knee while watching a YouTube video, the group laughing their asses off.

That's when I glanced up and saw Nina. Nina standing in the doorway, tears in her eyes and a look of devastation on her face. My laughter died. My heart pretty much died, too. She ran from the lounge, and I jumped out of my seat, forcing my leg to keep pace as I tore after her, but she disappeared into the girls' dorm.

I clutch my phone and go back to beating a path on the pavement.

We were perfect this morning, the two of us naked in bed. *I* was perfect. Now I'm anything but. I can't imagine what happened in those thirty minutes to put that look on her face. It doesn't take much to induce one of her incidents. Something could've happened in the bathroom, but I don't get why she'd run from me. I've replayed every fucking thing that happened this morning, our whispered words in bed, the feel of her legs around my waist, wondering if I did something wrong. Said something wrong.

Suddenly, I stop pacing. My jaw locks tight. My hand pulses at my side. If some asshole hurt her, cornered her in the bathroom or something, I swear to fucking God...

My mouth goes dry, dread settling in my gut.

As I drag my hands down my face, my phone buzzes again. This time it's Leigh. Desperate for a clue as to what's going on, I hold the phone inches from my face, but her text only messes with my already fucked-up head as she spouts some bullshit about Nina's family dog. It gives me momentary relief. If some dude put his hands on Nina, I have no doubt Leigh would be as furious as me and all hell would break loose.

But this crap? A sick dog? Something's not right.

I message Xander that he can do whatever he wants with the football stuff I'll never use again, then I type my tenth text to Nina to find out what's really going on, followed by another lengthy bout of pacing when I get no reply. Tired of waiting on answers, I barge into the hostel.

When I poke my head in the kitchen and see Nina standing at the counter buttering some toast, the muscles in my bunched shoulders uncoil. At least she's not hiding out. Her back is stiff, though, her movements jerky.

I approach quietly and cage her between my arms, gripping the counter so she can't run. "I was worried about you. You okay?"

Her answering silence has my fingers whitening as I clutch the counter tighter. "Sorry about your dog. I didn't even know you had one." My tone betrays my annoyance. I can't believe she expected me to swallow that lie. Still, I don't want to push her further away. I lean over her shoulder on the verge of apologizing, when my breath hitches. "Where's your necklace?" I ask. She hasn't taken it off since I gave it to her, but the freckled skin on her chest is bare. That dread from earlier bleeds into my chest.

Her knife clatters to the counter, her eyes dart nervously, and she chews on her lip something fierce. "We have a dog," she says.

"Three, actually. Fred, Barney, and Wilma. It was a bone, I think, lodged in Fred's intestinal tract. There was a surgery and it's not good and he might die and my family isn't coping and it's really hard to deal with this far away."

The words tumble out in typical Nina fashion, but all I can think is *lie, lie, fucking lie*. And she avoided my question about her necklace.

She twists around and tries to make a dash for it, but I step closer, lifting her chin to search her eyes. They're red-rimmed from crying, her gaze sliding away from mine, like she can't stand to look at me. *What. The. Fuck?*

"What's going on, Nina? This isn't you. You're acting weird. Don't think for a second I buy that whole dog story. What happened since this morning that you're lying about?"

Instead of answering, she drops to her knees, crawls between my legs, and then scrambles to her feet.

Jesus, *this girl*. If she wasn't doing her best to avoid me, I'd laugh. I clasp her shoulders before she gets too far. "Whatever this is, don't think I'm letting you pull your bullshit. There's no avoiding me. So, I'll ask again, what happened since this morning?"

I press my lips to her ear, and her body trembles. She seems ready to answer me when Leigh appears in the kitchen doorway, a small pack over her shoulder, a familiar scowl on her face.

"Hey, bucko, back off of my girl before I ram your nostrils into your brain." She flexes her hands and widens her stance.

My breath comes faster. Sharper. "This conversation isn't over," I say to Nina before releasing her shoulders.

She hurries toward Leigh, who cocks her head and grins at me so sweetly my teeth hurt. "Always a pleasure, Sam. We're going paragliding today. Without you. I hope you get hit by a meteorite, or kidnapped by terrorists, or abducted by aliens. I hope you have a swell day."

The Raging Bitch is back.

Normally, I'd tell her where to shove her charming insults, but paragliding? I step toward Nina, hands held up in surrender. "Whatever's going on here, we can deal with it. Just don't go running off on your own paragliding. Nothing about this is a good idea." When she glances at her feet, I step closer and lower my voice. "Look. We both know the potential pitfalls paragliding holds for you. So it's pretty simple. You're not jumping off a cliff. Especially without me there."

Leigh elbows her. "You want to kick him in the shins? Or should I?"

Next thing I know, Nina hooks arms with Leigh and looks at me dead-on. No shifty eyes, no hunched shoulders. Actual anger blankets her face. Nina? Mad? *At me?* She squares her shoulders. "I don't need you, Sam. I have Leigh. And maybe I won't mess up. Ever think of that? Maybe I'll win some paragliding award for the smoothest paraglider. Maybe they'll hire me to teach paragliding lessons."

I don't need you. Each word is a sledgehammer to my ribs.

Before I can recover, she adds, "And I'm having second thoughts about the whole Florida thing. Not sure I want to live in the States." She tugs on Leigh's arm and leaves me staring after them.

I glance around at the ugly floral room, reality hitting me face-first. Heat sears my throat like barbed wire constricting my neck.

She doesn't need me. Florida's not happening. I fold forward, trying to suck back air. I have no idea why Nina's pissed at me, and I'm not sure it matters anymore. She may not need me, but I need her like I need to breathe. That's it. The plain and simple truth. I *need* Nina. *Fuck.* I'm no different than my father after all. His happiness depended on my mother. Without her, he's a shadow of the man he was, barely functioning, always remembering. This pain, right now—the gaping hole in my chest—it only leads to hurt and anguish. Heartbreak.

Nina's not worth that. Nothing is.

I storm toward the back doors, desperate for air.

Twenty

NINA

I'm a natural, a paragliding savant. Once I got over the fact that I was attached to some guy's crotch, and the waves of nausea twisting my belly subsided, I had a blast. The scenery with its majestic mountains, golden beaches, and sparkling sea were stunning. The wind rushed, my pulse raced, and I made it out alive. *Me.* Safe. In one piece. All body parts fully clothed. That kind of adrenaline was just what I needed to rid my mind of all things Sam.

Now, however, the churning is back.

I haven't seen him since this morning. He hasn't called, texted, or shown his face. His car is still at the hostel. It's probably a matter of time, though, before he takes off. I should be relieved. Happy, even. Pleased his betraying self will be out of my life. I'm still angry, hurt, and disappointed, but in the calm after the storm, I can't help but wonder if I overreacted. It's natural for him to be curious, to look me up online. And that video is a testament to my crazy. If I were beside him when he watched it, he'd likely still have howled like that, but maybe he'd get me laughing at myself, too. *Maybe.*

"Jesus, Nina. Put one foot in front of the other. That's what we normal folk call walking." Leigh shoves past me into the bar.

I don't feel like walking. Or sitting. Or existing. I'd much rather glue myself to the post I'm pressing my shoulder into. Although *I'm* conflicted over things with Sam, Leigh isn't. Callum was on the paragliding trip with us earlier, flirting with me again, asking me to meet up with him later. Apparently, he wasn't deterred by Sam's posturing last night. That's when Leigh came up with her genius idea to solve my Sam stress: shove Mancandy's loss in his face.

So I'm here, in a bar, practically naked, but I don't see Sam.

Leigh took a page from Reese's book and dressed me up. Her black skirt is a size too small on me, the thin material stretched to the max, and my black bra is visible under her sheer gray tank top. She even made me buy heels. When I looked in the mirror earlier, I felt stylish and sexy. Now it feels like I should loiter on a street corner.

Leigh is two steps ahead. She looks left, then right, probably searching for me, then spins around and juts out her hip. I try to flatten myself against the wood post.

"Just when I didn't think you could get any freakier." She shakes her head and tugs the back of her hair, a habit she's formed since chopping it off. "Stay here. I'll be right back." She beelines for the bar.

People are lined up waiting for drinks, and a dozen tables are filled with others watching muted MMA on TV. A few pool tables are at the back, and I spot Bruno and Callum with some kids our age by the retro jukebox. Maybe *hear* is more accurate. Bruno's laugh is unmistakable. The boys are busy chatting and haven't noticed me, thank God. I don't know how Leigh talked me into this.

Clutching two shots, she shoulders past a couple of older guys in denim and cowboy boots. She holds the glasses out to me. "This, Nina, is alcohol. Alcohol is your friend. It's time for some liquid courage."

She shoves the first shot into my hand. Unless we're playing silly drinking games, I don't do straight alcohol. I stick to beer or easy drinks like piña coladas, but she's right. The only way I'll be able to face Sam is by numbing my overactive mind. I tip my head back and shoot the liquid like a seasoned veteran. At least, I try. The coughing attack that follows sounds like Emphysema Betty in my tai chi class before she puts on her oxygen mask.

People look our way. *Callum* looks our way.

I snatch the other shot and down it. No hacking ensues. "I think I need another."

She hooks her arm through mine. "Let the games begin."

By the time we make it to the bar and order another round, Callum is there, leaning on the worn-out wood. "Glad you made it. This place was looking drab before you turned up." His eyes are glazed, and he's got his beer by the neck, swinging it lazily. He takes a swig and licks his lips.

I try to reply, but I revert to animatronic me. *Giggle. Don't giggle. Flip hair.*

Callum is an attractive guy, his accent alone making up

for the crooked bottom teeth and weak jaw—he doesn't have Sam's jaw. But his smile lights up his face, and he's smooth and laid back, the type of guy who surfs and plays guitar at sunset. If I can jump off a mountain and survive in one piece, surely I can flirt with him as easily as I do with Sam. My grin falters. *Sam.* Earlier today, I wanted this. I wanted to flirt with Callum and make Sam jealous. Make him feel a fraction of the hurt he inflicted upon me.

I should have yelled at him this morning for watching that video and laughing at me behind my back. I should've given him one big, gratifying slap. The slow-motion kind in those action movies with his lips wobbling and spit flying in suspended drops. Instead, I dorked up my dork factor and crawled between his legs, taking those dog traits of mine to a new level.

I wanted to be mean to Sam. I didn't want him to be worried about me paragliding. I didn't want him to be awesome, or funny, or sweet. I didn't want him to be *him.* And I certainly didn't want to be that girl who lets the guy walk all over her because she's head over heels for him. A pathetic girl who twitches like a dog.

So I threw us and Florida in his face.

My queasiness returns with a vengeance along with guilt, regret, and the uncomfortable feeling I messed things up with Sam. Sam, who I should be mad at. Sam, who should be apologizing to me. Sam, who is some kind of wonderful.

Perfect. My heart has turned traitor, rooting for Sam and Nina to make it.

Callum steps closer until we're nearly chest to chest. He leans into my ear. "You look stunning." As his gaze dips to my breasts and the visible skin through the fabric, the only thing I feel is uncomfortable. I didn't dress like this for him. I dressed like this for Sam. And he's still not here.

I slam my shot, then grab Leigh's.

Thirty minutes later, I can't remember why I'm mad at Sam or flirting with Callum. Callum's hand is on my hip, his hot breath in my ear, as we try to talk above the music and growing crowd. The tequila has loosened me up enough that I'm no longer stressing over everything I say.

He folds over the bar to order another beer, and I check out the tables. My sights skim past an older guy with a thinning ponytail and ratlike features. The creep is staring at me. He tips his beer back and winks as he swallows. The whole thing makes me want to throw on a poncho, scrub off my makeup, and swap my skirt for non–figure-hugging sweatpants. I look away quickly, and the next thing I see has the opposite effect. One-syllable Sam. He's at the door, and all I want to be is naked. With him. Alone. In a tent. Or on a bed. Or in the backseat of his car.

He scans the room. When his sights lock on me, it's like a tractor beam. We've barely seen each other all day. After traveling and spending every waking moment together, it feels like weeks since we've hung out. I should still be angry, but, *God*, do I miss him. He's in jeans and boots and a black tee. It comes to rest on top of the leather belt around his hips—hips that rocked against mine this morning.

Beam me up, Hot Guy.

The moment my gaze lands on his face, though, my lust turns to panic. His expression is blank. Deadened. That mischievous sparkle I love is nowhere to be seen.

Then his posture stiffens.

Callum rubs my knee and leans into my side. "I never stood a chance, did I?"

I swing around, not sure I heard him right. "Sorry?"

"If you looked at me the way you're drooling over Sam, I'd lock us in a room and toss the key." He kisses my cheek. "Hope he knows he's a lucky bastard."

Before I can answer, he heads toward Bruno at the pool tables.

I look back at the entrance, and Sam still hasn't moved. His dark gaze is focused on Callum. The way his fists are clenched at his side, I'd say he wants to punch Callum. Because of me? For me? Jealousy like that isn't born from infatuation, Sam struggling with his insecurities. It comes from passion. Giving me that necklace, showing me his legs, opening up about his mom...none of that was easy for him, and he chose to share it all with me. The girl who told him she didn't want to move to Florida. *Frick.*

It's time I conquer my canuckaphobia.

If I yell at Sam and get what happened this morning off my chest, we can pick up where we left off. We can talk about school and Florida and us, then we'll crawl into bed and I'll explore every inch of his tan skin. This is going down.

I run my hands through my hair, grab my wallet, and try to walk like those confident runway models. *Swing hips. Lean back. Pout lips.* Five steps into my Coco Rocha catwalk, I realize how much I've had to drink. Not enough that I can't remember my high school health class and the list of effects alcohol has on the brain, such as difficulty walking, blurred vision, and slowed reaction times. The exact ones I experience as I trip over nothing, body check an innocent bystander, ricochet into a chair, and end up on my knees.

Damn Leigh and her liquid courage.

Rough, callused fingers dig into my arms. Unfamiliar fingers. The words "Careful, pretty lady" are followed by the overpowering stench of booze and cigarettes. A quick glance left, and I'm face-to-face with the ratlike guy, the one who was ogling me before I fell on my face in front of the bar. And Sam.

"Thanks, I've got her," Sam says from above me.

I've never been so happy to hear his voice.

His hands slide around my waist, but I'm frozen on my knees with Rat Guy's fingers biting into my arms, his breath making me queasy. The last thing I want to do is top my face-plant with a regurgitation of the soup I had for dinner. I keep my attention on the floor, on the piece of green glass by the foot of the chair that sent me sprawling.

Don't breathe. No, do *breathe. Don't pass out.*

Sam's grip tightens around me. "I said, I've got her. So unless you want to lose your hands, I suggest you back away."

"Just helpin' out, mate."

Rat Guy lets go of my arms, and I breathe deep as Sam lifts me up. Actually, I turn in to Sam, press my face into his shirt, and inhale his scent. He smells like freshness and man and that lemony detergent we bought yesterday. It eases my nausea. He tucks me into his side and leads me to a nook near the bathrooms, a quieter place with a pay phone on the wall. The thing's practically an artifact.

He lets go of me and steps back to keep his distance. "You okay?"

I study my upturned palms. There's a scrape on the heel of my right hand, dirt speckling the skin around it. I wipe it on my thigh. He watches my every move, the heat from his gaze burning through the fabric of my suctioned skirt as his eyes dip lower. He can't hide the bulge in his jeans. Normally, I'm not one for PDA, especially not in a busy bar. The looks I'm getting in this outfit alone are making me squeamish. But this is One-syllable Sam, hotness personified, and I know what his chest looks like under that shirt, the sculpted abs, and that bit of hair that dips toward his belt. If I could reach into his jeans and slide my hand over his—

"Stop it with your *thing*, Nina. We need to talk."

Right, *talk*. That was the plan before my elegant face-plant. He shifts his jeans, and I drag my eyes up to meet his, giving him my best dirty look. I'm mad at him. Enraged. Wrathful. It should be easy to raise my voice and tell him how small he made me feel. I try to access the sober centers of my brain.

Unfortunately, there's that other effect of tequila I haven't considered. The Pininfarina Effect. "Talk? Yeah, sure. I can talk. I can form words and speak. Big words. Lots of words. A plethora of words. I can be like Tolkien and invent a language. Instead of Elvish, I'll call it Newzealish."

He fights the smirk tugging at his lips. "How much have you had to drink?"

I focus on my hand and unfold one finger at time. I wave five digits in his face.

He shakes his head, leans into the wall, and crosses his arms. His smirk vanishes, a steely expression hardening. "I'm leaving. Heading out tonight."

Leaving? *Tonight?* He can't be serious. If anyone is taking off and leaving the other it should be me. *I've* been wronged. *I've* been hurt. Not him. Plus, if he goes it means no sexy stuff, and I really, really want to do sexy stuff with him. Like now.

First, I have to get my brain to coordinate with my mouth and find a way to unleash my kraken. "You're not leaving, Sam. You're not going anywhere until you tell me why you went from perfect to sucky. Why you watched that awful video and did the thing you said you'd never do. I mean, I can admit it's funny in a weird, horrible way. But this is *you*. And you promised." Tears prick my eyes.

Instead of looking apologetic, his brows pinch together, confused.

Blood rushes in my ears. "I told you everything. My name. My phobias. My virginity incident. I trusted you. And you..." I bite my lip, my anger leaving with my next breath. "You laughed at me."

He doesn't beg forgiveness. He doesn't promise to be my slave until the end of time. He says, "What the hell are you talking about?"

I open my mouth, close it, then open it again. "The Public Speaking Video. This morning. At the computers. *You. Laughed. At. Me.*" No way is he going to pretend this didn't happen and make me feel like I'm in the wrong.

He squints at me, rubbing the back of his neck. "I didn't watch any video. I didn't laugh at..." He lowers his eyes, his brows pulling tighter. "Those dudes beside me."

I shake my head, bewildered. "Beside you? Aren't you even going to apologize?"

"*Apologize?*" His tone makes me wince, his voice getting louder. "I didn't do anything wrong. The guy beside me was going on about some chick he saw in the hall and a YouTube video, but I didn't see what they were watching. I didn't do whatever it is you think I did. And it's shit you think that little of me." His kraken just kicked my kraken's butt.

The people at the nearest table stop talking to stare at us. I hunch forward, trying to make myself as small as possible, but I'm pretty sure they can still see me. I wipe my stinging eyes, suddenly very sober. "You didn't Google my name?"

"No, Nina. I was laughing at some crap on Facebook, waiting for you so we could research schools."

I stare at the floor, trying to remember everything that happened this morning. I washed up, ran into that tall guy, put my stuff away, then the awful sounds from my video drifted down the hall. Along with Sam's deep laugh. But…Sam wasn't the only one on the computers. My belly churns. The guy from the hallway—the one who said I looked familiar—was beside him with some friends. *Oh, God.* "Sam." I look up, tears building again. "I'm sorry. Just…the timing of it. Telling you my name last night and everything." I reach for his hand, but the stiffness in his stance stops me.

"Whatever. It's done." He kicks off the wall and steps toward the door. "Anyway, I'm taking off. Thought you'd want to know." His gaze drifts down my body. A flash of something twists his face but disappears quickly.

"Look, I'm sorry. Really sorry. It was a misunderstanding. Can't we go to the hostel and talk…or, you know, *not* talk. Just make up." When he doesn't respond, my chin trembles. "What about Florida and our plans?"

Standing tall and stoic, not flinching in the slightest, he says,

"I made one imagined wrong move, and you were ready to throw those plans in the trash. It's been fun, Nina. I've had a great time with you, but I'm done. This thing we have, it isn't what I thought it was. Better to cut our ties now."

He locks his jaw tight, pausing for the length of time it takes for my heart to shatter. Then he turns his back and walks away.

"But I love you," falls from my lips in a whisper.

I doubt he hears it above the rowdy bar. I doubt he hears the sob that rises up my throat. I doubt he even cares.

No longer able to watch him, I hurry to the bathroom and lock myself inside. I lean against the door, sharp breaths spiking through me. *Sam's leaving. Tonight. We're over.* Earlier, this was what I wanted. So angry at what I thought he'd done, I threw our relationship in his face. Did it crush him like this? Did he feel like he was dying, too? My hands tremble, it hurts to breathe, and swallowing is an effort. I don't even know how we got here. We had a fight. Couples fight. It was a misunderstanding. We should be having wild, crazy, romance-novel make-up sex. Instead, he broke up with me.

Needing to speak with Leigh, I yank my phone from my purse. I look down, blinking back tears, and a message greets me. My hands shake more. *Please be Sam.* But it's Mom, *finally.* It took her long enough to reply. My empty power bar glows red as I read her message, my momentary relief at seeing her name spiraling into dread.

Nina, call me when you get this. Anytime. Day or night. It's important.

I read it once. Then again. Then a few more times.

Something's very wrong.

I go to dial home, but my cell dies after the first ring. *Shoot.* I swivel off the door, my too-tight skirt dragging along the rough wood, and a nail catches the thin fabric. If Sam didn't leave me, if Mom didn't incite DEFCON 1 panic, I would stop and gingerly remove the nail lodged in my skirt. But Sam did, and I'm near hysterical, so I jerk away. My body moves as predicted; my skirt, however, does not. It seems fate has decided I've gone too long incident-free, and I need to be reminded I'll never rid myself of the ability to achieve greatness in ridicule.

My skirt tears. In half. *Oh, God.*

The stretchy material practically disintegrates, leaving me in a sheer tank top, black bra, and black thong underwear. A fist thumps on the door, and the handle wiggles. I should move. I should breathe. I should do something. All I do is stare at the tattered fabric on the floor. If my phone were working, I could call Leigh for help. If I weren't paralyzed with shame, I could find a way to clutch the material and exit the bathroom with some decency. I can't even come up with Choice C.

The knob wiggles again.

I lean back against the door and slide down its length, my shredded skirt protecting my butt from the nasty floor littered with crumpled paper towels. Tucking my knees to my chest, I wrap my arms around them. The tears fall. They stream. I try to tune out Mom's text and Sam's words, but it's all too much. I glance at the nail beside my head and sigh. I may have survived paragliding, but I'm still me.

Maybe the loner locked in her bedroom is the girl I'm supposed to be. Traveling to the other side of the world hasn't made me any less of a freak. All it's done is given me a taste of normal, which amplifies my crazy. I wish I were at home with Mom and my books and my computer. *Mom.*

Through my next sob, I flash to last night, to Leigh, Bruno, Callum, and Brianne laughing. *With* me. I wipe my eyes. They saw exactly who I am, freak flag and all, and they didn't care, didn't judge. They didn't mock me. If I walk out of this bathroom half naked, I'm pretty sure they'll be as cool. My other option is to stay in this grimy prison, wasting away while I wallow in self-pity. The sound of passing gas floats through the wall from the bathroom beside mine, and I stand up. Streaking through a bar full of guys is preferable to listening to *that* concert. And I need to call home.

Stretching the black fabric awkwardly around my hips, I turn the knob, shove the door, and face my humiliation with my head held high.

Twenty-one

SAM

I'm almost out of gas. The needle hovers on empty, the red light on the dash glaring at me for thirty minutes now. I drove two hours after leaving the bar, slept for four at the side of the road, and it's been another four of eating pavement since then, but I can't stop. If I take my foot off the gas, I'll come undone. Unravel. Every mile I put between Nina and me, it gets harder to keep it together.

Leigh's not helping, either. Her first text came about an hour on the road.

You're a selfish asshole.

Her second one was classic Leigh.

If I ever see you again, I will carve out your spleen with a spoon.

The next few message had me pressing harder on the gas.

Get back here. Your spleen will have to wait.

I'm not fucking around, Sam. Get your ass here. Now.
Nina's a mess. She needs you.

All I do is drive faster. I keep replaying the moment Nina looked at me, defiant, telling me she wasn't sure she wanted to move to the States. It cut. Deep. And we've only known each other a couple of months. Add a few decades filled with memories, laughs, kids, fights, anniversaries, and birthdays, and losing her wouldn't just hurt, it would destroy me. I may not have known why she was pissed with me, but I knew I had to get away.

With each press of my foot on the gas, though, it gets harder to fight the urge to turn around. Her tear-filled "But I love you," as I left her, broken, in that bar drowns out the bad nineties on the radio, and Leigh's "*Nina's a mess*" twists the knife deeper. The sob Nina tried to swallow as I walked away haunts me. She apologized and I spat in her face. *Asshole.* I grit my teeth as I mumble my mantra, "*This. Is. For. The. Best.*" It loops through my mind as I try to block how good it felt to be with her this morning, her hips moving with mine, her nails gripping my back. I repeat it over and over as my car slows. Fucking crawls. Practically wheezes. I have just enough time to pull over to the side of this winding road, my hunk-of-junk ride officially out of gas. I drop my forehead onto the steering wheel.

This is for the best.

I'm not sure how long I stay like that. My phone is on the passenger seat, still vibrating incessantly, but answering it would mean moving. An unpleasant option. My head feels about a thousand pounds, my heart even heavier, but the thing won't shut up. With a groan, I shove myself upright and grab my cell. Leigh, *again*.

Her most recent message is like a shot of Red Bull in my veins.

Get the fuck back here. This isn't a joke. Nina's mom has breast cancer.

My reaction is instant. Fumbling with my seat belt, I get it off and shove my door open. My racing heart powers me out of the car, and I jog—I run—the sharp pain in my ankle not even close to the crushing weight on my chest. I need to hitch to a gas station.

I need to get to Nina.

I keep looking over my shoulder, desperate for a car to come sailing around the corner. If I get filled up and on the road in the next hour, I can get back by three or four. With each heavy footfall, grief claws at my throat. Unbridled anguish in all its glory. It's an all too familiar feeling.

After the accident, I'd lay awake for hours, alone in the hospital, consumed by sadness and regret. When the dust settled and I accepted Mom was gone, I replayed every decision, sure one different choice would mean she'd still be alive. Each possibility tormented me. I wouldn't talk to anyone. I'd stare at the sterile hospital ceiling and ignore all visitors. Until the day James went Schwarzenegger on me. The dude slapped me across the cheek and pounded my chest until we were both a sobbing mess. The counseling helped after that. I developed my new life motto to live in the now and speak my mind. Embrace each day. And here I am, running away from Nina because I love her too much. Like *that* shit wouldn't chase me senseless.

Screw my fear of losing her and ending up like my dad. Life's too damn short. And no way am I going to abandon her like

Lacey discarded me. Nina needs me to man up and help her get through this. I need to man up so I can live with myself. Live the best life I can. Crunching gravel has me flipping around and throwing my thumb to the side. The Honda slows, thank God, and pulls off to the side.

I lean on the lowered window, breathing fast. I nod to the older man behind the wheel. "Just need a lift to the nearest gas station."

He unlocks the door. "Hop on in. It's not far."

Not far, my ass. Each second away from Nina is an eternity.

It's after five by the time I pull up to the hostel in Christchurch. The traffic during the day is a hell of a lot worse than before sunrise. I'm about to pull out my phone to text Leigh I'm here, but I spot her and Paige talking outside the front door. The second she sees me, she says something to Paige and stalks over to my car.

If I had to sculpt one of those creepy wax statues to capture Leigh, it would mirror the aggressive pose she strikes: arms crossed, cheekbones sharp, an angry scowl on her face. I get out, uncurl my body, and stretch my legs, then face the Dragon Lady to take the beating I deserve.

She huffs out a breath. "First, I can't believe you hopped in your piece-of-shit car and left Nina. I'd kick your ass to the curb, but I don't want to get fined for littering. Second, if you pull that crap again, I'd sleep with one eye open. I'm skilled with markers, a razor, and super glue."

I hang my head, waiting for the tirade to pick up in pace and nastiness. When all I get is crickets, I peek up with one eye. "That's it?"

If looks could kill…

"No, jackass, that's not it. But time is of the essence, and my other insults are too long. Here's the deal. I think I know why you took off, but Nina needs you more than you need to pretend you don't love her. It's hard for everyone to risk their hearts. You're not special. But it's the difference between good and great, average and awesome. Nina's your awesome. She's upset about her mom, but she's equally upset over losing you. God knows why, but it is what it is…and I can't cure cancer. So remove your tampon and find your spine. She's resting in the room you guys had. Don't make me regret texting you."

The silence stretches until I'm sure she's done, then I grab her shoulders and kiss her cheek. "Thanks. I owe you one." She scrunches her face as I push past her.

I need to get to my girl and beg for forgiveness. I can't waste another second trying to hide from the truth. For selfish reasons, I hurt Nina. Self-preservation seemed more important than living life to the fullest, and she got caught in the crossfire.

This ends now.

I don't knock on the door. I push it open and step inside, closing it quietly behind me. She's curled up on the covers, balled-up Kleenex in a pile by her hand. She seems to be sleeping. My side of the bed is neatly tucked; my drawers still open and empty from when I packed. *I'm a total dick.*

Sensing me, she stirs and blinks her eyes open. "Sam?"

I nod, too afraid to speak.

"What…? Why…?" She pushes up onto her knees, loose strands of red hair falling in her face.

I step forward, but stop myself from joining her on the bed

and crushing her to my chest. "Leigh texted me about your mom. I'm sick about it. Can't imagine what your family's going through. What you're going through. And I want you to know I'm here and that…" Glancing down, I rub my foot back and forth along the carpet. *Man up, asshole.* I lock eyes with her. "I'm sorry. So sorry. About your mom and about us, too. I'm an idiot. I was scared. Not that it's an excuse. But you, Nina, fucking *you*. It's too intense sometimes, the way I feel. Losing you one day seemed a hell of lot more terrifying than walking away now. But I was wrong. I get it now. You're worth a thousand heartbreaks. If you'll let me, I'll make it up to you. Anything you need. Just…please say you forgive me."

Her eyes well up, but with her mom and everything, I can't tell if they're happy or sad tears. The longer she chews her lip and stares at me, the deeper I shove my hands into my pockets. Then she says, "How come she's sick?" and she reaches for me.

My chest caves at the sorrow in her voice, but that's all I need to hear to close the distance between us. I'm on the bed in seconds, needing to ease some of her pain. The instant I wrap my arms around her, she dissolves. I hold her closer. "I'm here, baby. It sucks. I know how bad it sucks. But I'm here." She fists the back of my shirt, her shoulders shaking as she lets me absorb her sadness. I'll shoulder it for her best I can.

* * *

I've barely slept over the past thirty-six hours. Nina is curled up beside me in bed, her swollen eyes finally shut, her breathing steady. Mine gets ragged. I've held it together for her, tried to be strong, but the weight of it all has me cracking. When my tears come, I suck back air to stop from shaking. I don't want to wake her. Don't want her to see me like this.

It still hasn't sunk in. *Breast cancer.* Two horrific words that have turned our lives and plans upside down. Before I freaked and bailed on Nina, we had it all figured out with school and jobs and Florida. One second we're good, then it implodes. Time is fickle like that—on your side one moment, against you the next.

After she forgave me, my first thought was selfish: I can't go home without her. How could life betray me like this? Again? Who the fuck did I piss off? Then my mind went back to losing my mother, dredging up all sorts of crap I'd rather let lie. The whole while, Nina's been a wreck. The tears, the questions, the what-ifs. I've lived those fears, drowned in them. It kills me to see her following the same path.

I'm sick about her mother. Through Nina's endless stories, I feel like I know the woman even though we've never met. But my tears right now, the ones falling on Nina's hair as I hug her tight, those tears are for us. I can't leave my dad. Not now. He's been up and down because I left. One moment he's taking care of himself, cooking, shopping, and calling my sister to check on her. Then he's back in bed, trying to find a reason to get out. He was better when I was home, better with me around. When I took off on this trip, I knew he might get worse. I also knew I was floundering and needed to get away.

So this is my punishment for putting myself first.

My sister is off at college, and I made her promise to stay in school. My uncle has a new job, more demands, and can't be around as much. That leaves me to make sure my dad makes it through. It also puts Nina and me between a rock and the Mount Everest of hard places.

I know people do long-distance relationships, but I also know most of them don't work. Too many milestones that can't be shared. Too many nights alone. Too many distractions. It's not me I'm worried about. I'd wait a lifetime for Nina. I know that now. Once we're apart, though, I'm not sure she'll be okay with me and my legs if someone whole comes along. And if her mom doesn't pull through…

A band tightens around my ribs.

Nina stirs, her long lashes blinking against my neck. "Sam?"

"Mmhmm." I give my head a shake.

"I feel guilty."

I slide down so we're face-to-face, our foreheads practically touching. "That's ridiculous. Guilty about what?"

She sniffles and runs her fingertips over the scar on my chin. "I'm upset about my mom. Really worried. I'm sad for her, for my dad, my family. And me. But I'm lying here, and all I can think about is us. I just…" The words get swallowed by a sob.

I grab her wrist and press her palm over my heart. So much for me not bawling in front of her. Wetness coats my cheek. "We'll get through this." I blow out a breath and blink the sting from my eyes. "We're the fucked-up guy and disaster-magnet girl ready to take on the world, remember? We'll Skype. We'll text. We'll send fucking letters in the mail. This doesn't end here. Not by a long shot. Look at me and promise. Promise me this doesn't end."

She nods, more tears falling. "Yes. *God*, I promise. This doesn't end. We don't end. We can't. But we need a plan. I need to know

I'll see you again, even if we change it or the worst happens. I need to have something to hold on to."

She's right. We need an endgame. An objective. I have to treat this like college football: playoffs, tied in the fourth, one second left, a failed field goal the only thing between me and a mad dash toward the end zone. Like my coach says, "You fail at a hundred percent of the goals you don't set."

"One year," I say. "How about a year? To the date. Your mom said she thinks she'll need six months of chemo after the surgery. And people beat breast cancer all the time. Figure in the recovery, and one year is doable. She'll be as good as new, and we can pick up where we left off." I kiss her as another tear slips out, the liquid running over our lips.

But those damn ifs pile up. *If* her mom's not okay…*if* the worst happens…*if* my dad's never okay enough for me to live somewhere else. I pull back, bitterness and sadness all I taste. *Goals. Endgame.* Focus on the positive. "We'll squeeze in some weekend trips, too. I'll visit you. You'll visit me." I say a silent prayer to my mom to help make this right, to heal her mother and bring this girl back to me. "Will you wait for me, Nina? For a year?"

She nods. "Yes. Forever. Yes, yes. But…" She pauses, and I can't catch my breath.

But? Nothing good ever follows *but*.

I'd rather eat glass than hear her say *but*.

A lifetime passes before she speaks. "But I don't think we can see each other during that time. No visits. No weekends. This, right now, what I'm feeling—I can't do this again and again. It hurts too much. I'll have my mom and her stuff to deal with. I'm not sure I can take it if my heart breaks with each good-bye."

One whole year without a touch or a kiss. One whole year without her naked body under mine. My emotions settle in my chest again. The tightening, the deep ache. As much as the idea pains me, I know what she's getting at. If I have to feel this every time we separate, it could drag me down until I'm not much better off than my father. I need to be there for him, Nina needs to be there for her mother. If we want to make it out the other side, we need to do this. "Okay. No visits. But I'm not caving on the Skyping. And there will be sexting. Lots of sexting."

Her chin trembles, and her lips find mine. "Yes, yes," she says against my mouth. "Lots."

Then we're pressing so tight I'm worried she'll break. Or maybe I will.

* * *

Nina's flight leaves in six hours, mine in eight. As much as I want to lie in bed all day, imprinting myself on her, there's something I need to make right before we leave our room. While Nina finishes packing, I slip into the bathroom, gather the bag I hid under the sink, then step out and watch her profile. The curve of her cheek. The pout of her lips. Of all New Zealand's mind-blowing scenery—mountains, fjords, beaches, glaciers—this is the view I'll miss most.

One fucking year.

"Hey," I say, and she turns, expectant. Still in my boxers and T-shirt, I cross the room and sit legs folded on the bed, placing the plastic bag beside me. "Come sit for a sec."

She studies the bag, then takes a seat facing me, tucking her skirt under her crossed legs. Suddenly, her eyes well up. "What is it, Sam? What's wrong?"

The last thing I want is to be the one making her cry. I shrug. "It's about my name. I've decided to take Leigh's advice and change it to Samantha." Considering I've spent part of the last thirty-six hours bawling like a chick, it would be fitting.

She tips her head back and laughs, soothing and sweet.

One. Fucking. Year.

"Come on," she says, "What's up?"

Her hands are on my bare ankles, our knees touching. Reaching forward, I run my fingers over the necklace I gave her—the Maori Koru design that represents peace, tranquility, personal growth, and positive change. I pull an identical necklace from my bag. "I thought I'd get the same one. I want to be reminded of you every day for the next year."

Again, her eyes well.

Again, my chest constricts.

Quickly, I add, "It was either this or tattooing a pinup of you on my arm."

She rolls her eyes and, *thankfully*, smiles. "My mom has a tattoo. A grouping of mushrooms on her hip—of the magic variety. For my sixteenth birthday, she asked if I wanted to get one of my favorite teddy bear." Her skin blanches. "Not that I have a teddy bear. Or dolls. Or anything like that. My room's very grown-up. Very adult. Sexy, even. And there are no Harry Potter posters or paraphernalia anywhere. At all." She drops her head. "Oh, God."

I laugh. Damn, do I love this girl. "I need pictures, Canada. A full panoramic view of this very sexy, adult room of yours with the stuffed animals, posters, and figurines you don't have. I expect it sent immediately when you get home."

But there it is again. Home. Apart. Away.

She ties my necklace in place, her hands feathering over my skin.

Time for part two.

Without a word, I extricate a small bottle of vodka and two shot glasses from my bag and hold the glasses out to her.

She wrinkles her brow. "What are you up to?"

I wink, not giving anything away. Frowning, she takes the glasses, holding tight while I fill them up. Once the bottle's down, I take mine. "I thought we'd play a quick round of Never Have I Ever."

"Sam…" she says on a soft exhale, then nothing but a dreamy look crosses her face. She leans closer.

I lean in, too, shot glass in hand. Although I'm pretty sure how this will play out, I can't calm my bouncing foot or my racing heart. Here goes everything. "Never have I ever…fallen in love with a guy in New Zealand."

Her hand wavers, vodka spilling over her fingers and onto my leg. The smile that follows has me wishing we could spend the rest of the day in bed. She slams her shot back and scrunches her nose, coughing while she fans her face.

Fucking A.

She touches the smooth bone secured around my neck. "Never have I ever…fallen in love with a girl in New Zealand."

I don't hesitate. I do what I should've done the night before I took off, exactly what my heart desires. I give her all of me, no holds barred. She's had me for weeks, anyway. My head goes back, heat burns my throat. Then I kiss her for every minute I wasted. "No regrets, Nina. I'm all yours," I say, our lips still touching. Pulling back, I study her, wanting to memorize every detail. The casual ponytail, that beauty mark. After hours of crying, her green eyes look more emerald, her skin flushed. She's fucking perfect, and she's willing to wait for me. I lean down for another kiss, every touch more important than the last. Every brush catalogued for the days when I need to remember the feel of her. Reluctantly, I release her. "I'm all yours," I say again.

Her gaze flicks down to the bulge one kiss from her inspires, and a breathy moan passes her lips. If we had time, I'd push her back and go down on her until she's cursing and chanting my name.

If we had the time.

I've done this before, no sex or girls for what feels like forever. Still, now that I've had Nina and know how she works me up like no one else, it feels a lot harder. I'll have to get her talking dirty on the phone. The thought sends more blood pumping south. "Come on, let's finish up. Leigh's probably waiting for you." I give her a chaste kiss. Anything more and we'd miss our flights.

* * *

The rest is a blur. If my trip with Nina felt like seven years in travel time, these last hours are a heartbeat. I keep freezing midsentence to stare at her, hoping I can slow the minutes. They press on. Too fast.

Back at the hostel we say our good-byes to Callum, Bruno, and Brianne, the three of them heading south to the dramatic cliffs of Milford Sound. Leigh's farewell takes longer. Paige took off to give her and Nina some privacy. I step back, too, which sucks. My goal today is to have my hands on Nina for every last second we're together, but Leigh's death glare sends me a few feet away. I cross my arms and bounce my leg, my arms itching to get around my girl. I can't hear what they're whispering about, but they hug for like ten minutes.

Leigh struts toward me and plants her hands on her hips. "Sam."

"Leigh."

"It's been real. Fun, actually. You're not the douche I thought you were. But if you hurt Nina again, if you fuck around on her, I will fly to Florida and perform an unassisted spinal tap. Through your ear."

The Dragon Lady lives on. "If I fuck around on her, I'll do the procedure myself. And yeah, meeting you has been…interesting. Look me up if you're ever in Florida on a non–mutilate-Sam visit. And take care of the car. I've grown fond of her." I toss her the keys and she scowls at me.

I sold her my rusted travel car, but instead of money, I traded it for something more valuable. Aside from touching Nina at all times, my other goal today has been to keep her tears at bay. When I saw the karaoke machine at the hostel, I knew the best way to do just that. I made Leigh sing "Age of Aquarius." There's nothing like watching a furious chick spit out lyrics while doing an uncoordinated version of Nina's routine. Paige laughed her ass off, but it was Nina's giggling that made Leigh's humiliation even better.

Leigh pockets the keys, her dark eyes turning black. "There

will be revenge." She goes to hang with Nina as we wait for our cab.

It arrives. We get in. The airport appears. Lines move. People rush. Tickets are given. *Fucking fickle time.* Before I know it, we're through security, the two of us fidgeting with the straps of our small carry-on packs.

"So," she says.

"So." Heat builds behind my eyes. No words are adequate. We're standing across from each other, frowning, sniffling, neither of us closing the gap. This whole time she's been locked to my side, but now that the good-bye is official, awkwardness amplifies between us.

She reaches for my hips, her fingers curling into my jeans. "I'm sorry, Sam." Her gaze stays focused on my waist.

"About what? That your mom's sick?"

She sighs. "No. It's just, if I didn't feel the need to be there, to look after my family, then—"

"Nina, stop. If you ditched your family now, at a time like this, we probably wouldn't make it. The girl I fell in love with on this trip is loyal and caring. *That* girl's worth waiting for. That girl's worth moving heaven and earth for. Enough of this 'sorry' bullshit."

"Okay. Sorry." She purses her lips and does that funny frowning thing, likely giving herself a mental beating for apologizing. Again.

I even love that ugly-ass face she makes.

I lift her chin, needing to see her eyes. "We'll get through this. I love you. Your mom will be fine. We'll be fine. *We'll get through this.*" I say it in my head a few more times, desperate to believe it.

The saddest smile I've ever seen mars her beautiful face. "Yeah," she says, but the doubt there, the worry, has me searching for the perfect line to make her understand. To make sure she knows how I feel.

She *has* to wait for me. This *has* to work.

Terrified, I mirror her "Yeah," because my throat's too tight to say much else.

We kiss again, but it's not fueled with passion. It's not the kiss of two people promising themselves to each other. It's a brushing of lips, distant almost. It's worse than swallowing nails. Then she's on the moving walkway, gliding away. From me. *Fuck.* She keeps her gaze ahead, doesn't look back. I'm guessing she doesn't want to fall apart. She's trying to keep it together. But I can't let her go like this.

"Nina," I call.

Her ponytail whips around, and the lady behind her moves before they collide.

"Wait. Just wait!" I'm doing my half-hop, half-run beside the moving walkway while Nina says, "I'm sorry," and, "Excuse me," to each person she nudges as she tries to walk the wrong way toward me.

When I reach her, I lean over the railing, grab her neck, and kiss her for forever. For each day we'll be apart. For each night I'll miss her. I keep time with the gliding walkway, oblivious to the stares and murmurs of passersby until a pile of luggage blocks my way. She slips from my fingers.

I swallow hard and holler, "I love you, Nina!"

A grin rounds out her tearstained cheeks. She leans over the handrail. "It's Pininfarina, and I love you, too, One-syllable Sam."

Hearing her own that awesome name has me swelling with pride, but One-syllable Sam? I almost call after her to find out what that means, but she looks ready to crawl into her carry-on bag, her trademark blush flushing her face. Then she's off the platform and walking away, her ponytail swaying, my chest constricting. I'm not sure how I'm going to make it through the next year. This pressure against my ribs isn't the type of ache that eases with time. Nina's craziness is my lifeline, her insanity a shot of adrenalin to my heart. She's funny and clumsy and sexy and sweet. She turns me sideways in the best way.

Being apart will be tortuous. Unbearable. But I can do this, right? We can make it, right? The erratic pounding of my heart and the sinking feeling in my gut has me turning and walking away, unable to watch her any longer. With each step, my optimism joins my heart. In a freefall.

One fucking year.

One Year Later

PININFARINA

I smooth my skirt for the tenth time, shifting from foot to foot. Am I early? Did I mess up the time? Where is he?

My tai chi classes are supposed to help with my nervousness, but my heart still feels ready to make a jailbreak. Although I conquered a slew of my phobias with Sam, the shaky, jumpy, neurotic tendencies that send my brain into overdrive haven't lessened. Pininfarina Gabri is still in full effect. These days, though, I go with the flow.

My first day working at Daisy's Bakery this winter was a typical *me* day. I dropped a bag of flour, burned a batch of brownies, and I made a tray of crème brulée with salt instead of sugar. If Daisy didn't feel so bad for me, I would've been fired on the spot.

That night, all I wanted was to disappear in Sam's strong arms and broad chest, get lost in his warmth. Instead, we Skyped and

I laughed about it. We both fell asleep with our heads on our pillows, our laptops open. There have been a lot of nights like that. And calls. And letters. God, I love his letters. Then there's the phone sex. It took a lot of convincing on his part to get me to partake. When I did, I unleashed a wild side I didn't know existed. The stuff I'd say, the dirty words. Sam has advised me that the state of his priapism is becoming dangerous. He might need medical attention. He might implode. He says it's all my fault, and I love it.

I scan the quiet park. No Hot Guy to be seen. With the way I'm digging my heels in the grass, I'm surprised I haven't tunneled to China. It's been one year since I've seen him, and the anticipation is sucking the oxygen from my lungs, breathing now an effort, my hands shaking at my sides.

I'm a big hot nervous mess. And he's still not here.

Sam didn't want to pick me up at the airport. He said he couldn't see me for the first time with all those people around unless I was okay with him tackling me to the ground and recreating our tent experience. Being all cryptic, he told me to take a taxi to this park and meet him at the old oak tree by the pond.

So I'm here. Waiting. Freaking out.

Then my phone buzzes.

I sift through my purse, frantic, and the thing falls to the ground. As a nearby squirrel natters at me, I pluck my phone from the grass and chirp back at the angry rodent until he scurries up the expansive tree, its thick foliage shading my skin from the Florida sun.

I tap the screen, and one word appears:

Hi.

I whip my head up and study the area more closely. A family of ducks swims across the pond while a woman and two kids play on the far side. There's a couple farther off lying in the grass, their legs intertwined as they read. Circling my back is nothing but thick bush. Birds whistle, crickets chirp, but not another living soul is visible in this peaceful park.

My heart picks up its pace as I text back.

Hi.

I wait. And wait. Until:

Sam: You look beautiful. You're almost hard to look at.

My eyes snap up, searching the park again.

Me: Where are you?

Sam: Close enough.

Me: I beg to differ. Please get over here.

Sam: I need to watch you for a bit.

Me: The sentiment's nice, but I need to see you. Like now.

Sam: Patience, Canada.

Frickin' Hot Guy. I've been patient for a year. One whole year. My body is buzzing to feel his, to wrap around his until we're tangled together. What part of him thinks now is a good time to play with me?

Me: Patience has been tried and tested. It's proving rather difficult.

Sam: I'm nervous.

Me: To see me? You don't do nervous. I do nervous.

Sam: Do you like the park?

The change in topic irks me. He's stalling and I don't know why.

Me: I'd like it better if I were in your arms.

Sam: This is where I write your letters. It's where we scattered my mom's ashes.

My rapid breaths slow. Suddenly, everything about this serene place changes. I see him sitting under the large oak, scribbling on the blue stationery he sends me. I see him staring off into the pond, his heart full, as he remembers his mother.

I see a piece of him.

Me: It's amazing. Like you.

Sam: I wanted to meet you here, because I wanted you to meet her. She's why I went on that trip. She's why we met. And I think she's why you're here now. She would have loved you.

My throat gets tight.

Me: I wish I'd met her. But I feel her here.

I may not have lost my mother, but I came close. If the worst had happened to Mom, I'd be like his dad, drowning in grief. But Sam is strong. Because of him, his father is in therapy and getting better each day. Because of him, I got through the hardest year of my life. I thought I knew hardship. Thought the ridicule I endured was as bad as life could get. Now I know different. I'd live through an eternity of embarrassment if it meant keeping Mom healthy.

I snort despite my heavy thoughts, remembering the e-mail she sent Sam.

Me: Did you get my mom's pics?

Sam: Fucking amazing. But don't you think it's odd my girlfriend's mother is sending me topless photos? Doesn't that cross a line or something?

Me: My mom doesn't have lines. You know that.

To celebrate her official remission, Mom came home last week with two wings tattooed over the scars from her double mastectomy. The shading and colors are mind-blowing, the feathers covering much of her upper chest. It's breathtaking. Vibrant. Full of life. It represents her. No breast reconstruction for my mom. She's proud to be a survivor and wants the world to know it. So proud, she tried to drive me to the airport topless, claiming that without boobs she's no different than a guy, ranting about inequality and women's rights. When I threatened to take a cab, she got dressed reluctantly.

Me: Why are you still hiding?

Sam: I told you, I'm nervous.

Me: Why?

A silent phone answers me.

Me: If you can see me, you'll see I'm making my angry-old-lady face. I'd suggest answering. Radio silence isn't an attractive quality. Actually, there's that cute guy walking his dog by the rosebushes. Maybe he'd like to talk to me.

Sam: One step, Canada, and I hide your knives on your first day of school.

Now he's playing with fire. He knows how excited I am to go to culinary school, to fill in the gaps of my self-taught knowledge. Come January, I'll throw on my monogrammed chef jacket (my first Christmas gift from Mom that didn't involve tie-dye. It says *Pininfarina* in large black cursive), I'll wear my chef hat (Leigh's gift with the words *Eat my pie* stitched inside), and I'll be carrying my brand-new chef knives (Sam's gift—the one I was allowed to show my folks). No way am I going to school without those knives.

Again, I turn a full circle, looking everywhere for him.

Me: You hide my knives and I sleep in the spare room. With the door locked.

Sam: I will kick the door down ninja-style.

I tip my head back, laughing.

Me: Okay, tough guy. But seriously, why won't you show yourself?

A full minute passes before he responds. A full sixty seconds of my nerves getting the better of me, a thousand possibilities crowding my mind.

I wish Leigh were here. Every time I lost it this year, every time I was sure Sam would change his mind and decide I wasn't worth the wait, I'd call her and spew a lengthy rant. I'm not sure if she listened or simply said, "Yeah," and "Mmhmm," at the right times, often following with, "Man-candy loves you. Stop being such a freak." Either way, I wouldn't have made it without those calls.

I've been there for her, too. When she and Paige broke up, I hashed it out with her until the sun came up. And when she sees her mom, that unpleasant woman who's always trying to convince Leigh her sexual preference is a "phase," I send her one of my family lip-synching videos. Her favorite is "Baby Got Back." She's been through a lot this year, but she never backs down from owning who she is, family support or not, and she's built a community of friends in California. The one thing that concerns me is her career choice. If I walked into an office to find Leigh as my therapist, I'd bolt Road Runner fast.

I fear for all future patients.

Unfortunately, she's not here to calm me down while Sam takes his sweet time replying to me. Then my phone buzzes.

Sam: It's been a year. There's buildup with that. I'm worried you won't feel the same.

This boy must be out of his mind. The past year has been difficult on so many levels. My mom. My job at the bakery, which was fun, exciting, hard, and grueling. Not being with Sam, which was tortuous. Still, we've talked tons and been there for each other when it counts; it's hard to believe he's questioning my feelings. I touch the bone pendant around my neck before replying.

Me: I don't.

Radio silence.

Then, You don't feel the same about me?

Me: No.

Deafening silence.

Sam: Breathing has become difficult. Paramedics may be needed. Maybe mouth-to-mouth. Explain yourself.

I've thought a lot about us and the choices we've made, specifically my choice to not see each other this past year. I know it was for the best. I needed to be there for my mom, needed my focus on her when she'd wake up noxious after chemo. Or get the chills. Or get angry. My dad could've handled it on his own, but I *wanted* to be there. Still, the place in my heart that Sam occupies has grown. Exponentially. I've changed. We've changed. If faced with another family trauma, my choices will change, too.

Me: Simple. I'm more in love with you than I was a year ago. No matter what happens with our families, we have to be together when we deal with it. I won't be apart from you again.

It's scary to say it, to put it out there. But it's true. I stare, unblinking at the screen, until: Can I get that in writing?

Me: You just did, smart guy. Now PLEASE GET OVER HERE.

Sam: I still like watching you. You wore my favorite skirt.

Now he's being difficult. For the fun of it.

I'm no longer nervous. There are a plethora of colorful words that better describe my current mood. Incensed. Vexed. Wrathful. *Lascivious*. I doubt he wants to deal with my oversexed self, hyped up to the point I'm more starved than when Mom put me on that stupid juice diet to cleanse the toxins from my body.

I want my man. I want him now. And I know how to get him.

Me: Baby, I'm so turned on, I might have to lie down in the grass and use my hands to ease the ache.

The bush to my left comes to life, the crashing, rustling, and breaking twigs a sure sign I've fished my wish. One-syllable Sam comes stumbling out of the leaves and stops a foot away. His chest rises. Mine stills. The air barely stirs. His gaze travels over every inch of me.

"You're really here," he says.

I bite my lip, suddenly shy. "Someone invited me." I can't blink.

His shoulders are fuller, his eyes brighter, his curls a little messier. But he's my Sam. In front of me. Perfectly messed-up legs and all.

His honeyed eyes flash. "I'm going to attack you now."

I nod, heart thundering. "Yes, please."

He lunges for me, and I'm up and in his arms, being crushed to *that chest*. I drop my purse and phone, my hands trying to grab onto something Sam. Anything Sam. His fingers dig into my ribs. He pulls back to kiss me, and I, of course, inject a dose of ludicrous into this otherwise perfect reunion.

Our noses bump, our teeth clash, and I butt his head. "Shoot,"

I mumble as I twist awkwardly in his arms. Then he's tripping to the ground, still clutching me around my waist, his other hand breaking our fall. He lowers me gently down. Curls. Scar. Shoulders—broad and cut in his white tee. I see nothing else. Nothing but Sam.

Our hearts race in time as he presses closer. "Glad you haven't changed," he says, his nose brushing mine.

I shrug. "Still hurricane Pininfarina."

"Good thing I'm a storm chaser, then." He leans in to kiss me, deep and slow.

And I feel whole again.

I hum against his soft lips. "What if I'm like a category five hurricane?"

"I know exactly who you are, Pininfarina. And I'm all in." He rolls onto his back and tucks me into his side, the thick branches and shimmering leaves dancing above us.

I wrap myself around him and squeeze tight. I know who I am, too, thanks to One-syllable Sam. I'm weird and quirky. A little bit crazy. More accident-prone than a blind three-legged dog. I'm Pininfarina Gabri, disaster-magnet, future chef, and lover of all things Sam. I am me—the good, the bad, and the ridiculous—and now Sam and I get to discover us.

The Public Speaking Incident

I haven't eaten for thirty-six hours. Not a pea. Not a crumb. Not a bite. No nutrition has passed my lips. Light-headed, I lag a step behind Becca as we make our way through the cafeteria. Chatter and laughter echo off the tall ceilings, shoes squeak on the polished floor. A sharp bang pierces my ears, metal clanging against metal, waking me from my daze.

But not from my nightmare.

In one hour, I'll be standing in front of the entire school, poem in hand, to open our Thanksgiving assembly. Hell is more appealing. Or Chinese water torture. Or death by piranha.

I hoist my backpack higher on my shoulders and tap Becca's arm. "I'm not hungry. I'll meet you at our table."

She swings to face me, frowning. "But it's Burrito Thursday."

My saliva gathers, scents of melted cheese and cumin teasing me. Then I picture our auditorium filled with a sea of white, gray, and blue uniforms. Hundreds of eyes trained on yours truly. The mouth-watering smells sour, the pungency suddenly nauseating. I smile weakly. "Maybe I'm coming down with something."

As she heads to the line, I tighten my ponytail and dodge a basketball rolling along the floor. A boy brushes past me, his massive shoulder nearly knocking me on the floor. I offer a quiet, "Sorry." He doesn't even glance my way, but the girl he sits beside, Natasha I think, curls her lip in a snarl.

Although I've attended Strachan Prep since junior kindergarten, being in grade ten means my lunch is now spent with the high school kids—the guys more man than boy, the girls hiking their skirts higher. The cafeteria has become a minefield. One wrong step and I could get dirty-looked to pieces.

I slide into my seat and slip my recently purchased copy of *Mockingjay* from my bag, desperate to escape to another world. One where I don't have to speak to an assembly of my peers. Alone. On stage. With everyone staring at me. *How did I let this happen?* I try to read, but the letters blur, the same grouping of words drifting in and out of focus. My stomach twists. My head throbs. The room spins. I drop the book and press my fingers to my temples.

Breathe. Breathe. Breathe.

When the dizziness subsides, I glance up…and quickly look back down. *Shoot.* I shake my head, sure what I saw was a hunger-induced mirage.

Because there's no chance the eyes trained on me just now, the ones I've daydreamed about so often my science teacher thinks I have ADD, can be focused my way. Not today. Not when I haven't eaten a thing since yesterday morning. Not when I'll soon get on a stage and no doubt embarrass myself.

Convinced my panic attack must have progressed to full-on hallucinations, I glance up again. But, no. No, no, no. A mirage this is not.

It's Drew frickin' Masters.

Looking my way.

Double shoot.

His swoony self—definitely more man than boy—is staring right at me. Dark eyes. Darker hair. Olive skin. Instinctively, I pull my arms to my sides and curl forward, doing my best tortoise impression, minus the shell. But, God, I still feel his eyes on me.

Mom picked me up from school a few weeks ago and caught me drooling over the man himself. Drew may only be a year older than I am, but he's ten castes higher. Firmly entrenched in cooler-than-thou territory. And something happened to him over the summer. His chest broadened, his jaw sharpened. His reedy limbs filled out. It's like he left a boy and came back Captain America. There's a chance my tongue actually hit the ground.

Mom spent the whole car ride home listing my virtues and convincing me that guys like girls to take the initiative. She said I should ask him out. She said I should smile at him.

I can't even look up.

A tray plops down on the table, and Becca squeezes into a chair across from me. It gives me the perfect opportunity to peek again. Her wide frame is my own personal barricade, guarding me from enemy territory. I lean to the left to see past her, and holy heck, he smiles.

At me.

I snap back to my place of cover and whisper, "Oh, my God."

Becca raises her eyebrows. "Oh, my God, what?"

I say a lame, "Oh, my God," again.

Then we have a verbal tango.

Becca: "What?"

Me: "God, God, God."

Becca: "WHAT?"

Me: "Oh. My. God."

She rolls her eyes. "Pininfarina, if you don't tell me what's shrunk your vocabulary to three words, I'm switching tables."

That, however, implies she has somewhere else she could sit, and we both know neither of us would survive two minutes in the trenches. She shovels a forkful of burrito into her mouth and I'm salivating again, the smell of melted cheese too close. Too good. Its savory deliciousness battles against the churning in my belly. Attempting to ignore the perfection that is the Thursday Burrito, I keep my eyes on the pimple by her nose. "Okay...just don't look behind you."

She, of course, looks behind her, then spins back and shrugs. "I don't get it."

"Drew Masters"—I drop my voice so low she leans forward—"he just smiled...at me."

Her blue eyes pop wide. "No."

"Yes."

"No."

"Yes."

"Seriously?"

"God, yes!"

She runs her tongue over her braces. "Did you smile back?"

I snort. "As if. It's Drew frickin' Masters. I probably just had something stuck to my head. Why else would he look at me?" Like I need more stress today.

Instead of taking another bite, she moves the refried beans around her plate. The plate I'd like to shove my face in. "Is he still looking?" she asks.

Chewing on my lip, I inch to the side again. Instead of dreamy eyes and spiky hair, my line of sight falls on the reason I'm starving. The reason my life may implode today.

Mrs. Bramowitz.

I smell her when she's three feet away, her ever-present perfume a pungent mix of mothball, litter box, and fruitcake. Basically, old lady. I spend the better part of most English classes sneezing. As she approaches, I pull up my kneesocks and shift on my seat, dreading whatever bad news she's likely to share. I doubt anything will top last week's excited hand gestures when she exclaimed, "You've been chosen to address the school with your Thanksgiving poem!"

That news mixed with the thick aroma of her perfume almost knocked me out cold.

I'm not sure when my glossophobia—fear of public speaking—kicked in. It could have been in grade two when Suzie Boyd tripped me as I walked up for my planets presentation. Or maybe it was a few years later when Ethan Eckles launched a spitball at my face while I enlightened our class on climate change. The wet paper slid down my cheek like a snail. Whatever the catalyst, the reason for my impending torture stops at the foot of our table.

I sneeze.

Mrs. Bramowitz places her hand on my shoulder. "Are you excited for the assembly, Pininfarina?"

292 Kelly Siskind

Petrified, appalled, and numb are more like it, but I offer a shaky "Sure," all while fighting another violent reaction to her perfume.

"Wonderful. I just wanted to let you know there's a slight change to the format. Instead of opening the assembly, you'll be closing it." She hunches lower, and the glasses chained around her neck almost smack my face. "You'll do great, dear. Don't be nervous."

She can't be serious.

With one more squeeze of my shoulder, she walks away, her thick scent following in a wide wake. Wrinkling my nose, I crane my neck as she passes Drew's table, hoping to catch another glimpse. But he's gone. Along with his smile.

Suddenly, the barely touched burrito on Becca's plate seems like the perfect thing to fill the void left by Drew's departing smile. The need to eat it, or something, overpowers my nerves, this afternoon's performance taking a back seat to the swelling of my fifteen-year-old heart.

Drew frickin' Masters noticed me.

I nod to Becca's plate. "Are you gonna finish that?"

With a sigh, she eyes her midsection and the rolls hanging over her skirt. "No. You can have it. I shouldn't have gotten it anyway. Diet and all." She shoves the burrito my way, and I hoover the thing.

Perfect Thursday Burritos.

* * *

Stupid Thursday Burritos. We're nearly through the one-hour assembly, my impending speech just minutes away, and unnatural things are happening in my belly. Maybe it was the day and a half of fasting, or the awareness that my already low social stock may soon crash. All I know is there's something horrific wrenching and coiling in my abdomen that has me folding forward, desperate for the fetal position.

Becca joins me in a forward slump. "You okay?"

I shake my head. "No. Not okay."

All ability to swallow vanishes as cold sweat pricks my neck. My jaw tingles. Gas expands and builds in my core, an unpleasant silent belch following its escape. Forget the fasting. It was definitely the burrito.

The stupid Thursday Burrito.

To distract myself, I catalogue the domino effect of awful that led me here: Mrs. Bramowitz choosing my poem, me starving myself, Drew frickin' Masters's swoony smile. Me, predictably, eating my feelings—in the form of a rich bean mixture—on an empty stomach. And now I'm going to die in the middle of our Thanksgiving assembly.

"You should go to the office," Becca whispers.

I focus on our matching black loafers, on the hole in her sock she refuses to fix. Her theory: a uniform-wearing girl needs to express her individuality. A sharp internal twist blinds me, and I bite my lip to keep from crying out. Holy crap. If I throw up in front of all these people, in front of Drew three rows ahead of me, I will never leave my house or my room again.

Office…I need to make it to the office.

But my name crackles through the microphone on stage. All five syllables.

Laughs disperse through the room as I fight the urge to curl into a ball on the floor.

"Should I tell them you're not feeling well?" Becca's voice registers as the principal calls my name again.

Fisting my hands, I breathe deeply. If I could handle tasting Mom's curdled crème caramel, surely I can conquer the Thursday Burrito. It will pass. It's just a moment. I probably need to get up and get moving. To avoid my name being called a third time, I stand on wobbly legs and wave at the principal like I'm royalty. The internal stabbing lessens. Slightly. I squeeze down the row, bumping each set of knees as I pass. Once in the aisle, I smooth my pleated skirt and close my eyes, willing the tornado in my stomach to cease. It does. Briefly. Three steps in, I stand taller, hoping my pale skin doesn't look as green as it feels. On the ninth step, I stop.

Something shifts in my gut, something bad, a wave of cramps moving south.

A bubbling that can only lead to one thing.

Holy freaking God.

Suddenly, throwing up is the least of my worries.

I should lunge for the exit, a mad sprint before I erupt. I should pull the fire alarm or call in a bomb threat. I should do anything but continue on my current trajectory. Unfortunately, I stay my course, the movement almost involuntary. Automatic. I clench every muscle down to the tendons in my toes as I make my way to the steps. Then I climb.

One step. Sweat beads under my arms.

Two. My balance wavers.

Three. Four. Five.

I shuffle to the microphone, unsure how I've made it this far. I grab the podium to keep upright. They replaced the old one a month ago, and I grip the clear glass, mortified my knocking knees are visible through the transparent stand. The rows of shirts and ties blend into a massive cloud of blue and white. A voice from behind me, Mrs. Bramowitz maybe, prompts me to speak. All I can do is clench. Clench as if my life depends it, which it pretty much does. Another wave rocks through me. Deeper. Acute. Like if I loosen up in the slightest, if I even breathe, the contents of my stomach will flow down my legs. Glued in place, I barely twitch. My chin trembles as I lock eyes with Drew Masters, who not long ago smiled at me. Who maybe didn't know I was defective. A girl beside him holds up her phone as if videoing my turmoil.

That's the instant Mrs. Bramowitz approaches me from behind. I don't see her. I smell her. My noses twitches the way it does, and the horror of what's about to happen registers. There's no time to cry or blink. Or wish upon a wishing star that I were anyone else but me.

I sneeze. Once. That's all it takes to ruin my life.

See the next page for a preview
of the first book in Kelly Siskind's brand new
contemporary romance series!

Chapter One

SHAY

You can tell a lot about a woman by the type of bra she wears. For instance, the silky black number clutched in my hand as I swing my skis on the chairlift, the one that makes my girls look some kind of wonderful, this one says classy, yet conservative.

"How far is it?" Lily asks, her white-blonde hair almost camouflaged by the wisps of snow collecting on her lilac jacket.

March in Aspen and the snow is heavier than in midwinter, the evergreens lining the runs sagging under pillows of the white stuff. With each blink, the frosted tips of my eyelashes brush my cheeks. "It's closer to the end of the lift. Trust me, you can't miss it."

"You sure this is a good idea? We could come back tomorrow, and you could wear a different bra and carry this one so you don't, you know, have to ski down without…" Her pale gray eyes settle on my black jacket, about midchest. The area housing my braless boobs.

Raven leans forward, her elbows resting on the safety bar, and she nudges Lily's side. "What do you think's gonna happen? You think Shay's bra-mmando boobs will get caught under her skis and send her hurtling down the mountain?"

The snowboarder at the end of our four-pack chairlift snorts to himself while Lily sinks against the back of our seat, reverting to her quiet-as-a-mouse routine. When Raven's around, that's often the safest course of action, especially considering Lily's backbone is lodged somewhere below her tailbone.

I lick the snowflakes from my lips, knowing it's now or never. When we passed the bra-tree on our last ride up the chairlift, its branches weighted down with hundreds of undergarments, I knew what I had to do. It was instinctual. Visceral. My need to shed this bra and all it represents couldn't wait another second. One run and a quick trip to the washroom later, we got in line for this fateful ride. "Thanks for the concern, Lil, but I'm pretty sure my skiing ability won't be affected by my lack of undergarments. The bra-tree *will* be getting another ornament."

"You really want to go through with it, though?" she asks as Snowboarder Dude cranes his neck to check out the black silk gripped in my gloved hand. "I mean, it's *the* bra."

She's right. It's not every day a girl comes across the perfect balance of lift and shape, cleavage and support, no extra skin pushing out the sides or back. Since its purchase, this has been my go-to bra. I wore it the day Richard passed the bar. I bought a new red dress, slinky and clingy in all the right places, but Richard did his usual, "Put on the black one I bought for you last month. The one with the lacy sleeves. I like how it slims your hips." I followed his backhanded compliment with my usual, "Yeah, sure. Okay."

When it came to Richard, my backbone slipped even lower than Lily's.

I tip my skis back and forth, remembering another "slimming" dress he picked out for me—a beaded, black, cutout number—that I wore over this bra to celebrate Richard's new job working for one of the top law firms in Toronto. It was the same day I was offered a promotion. The design firm I'd apprenticed at was closing shop to focus on their Montreal location, and I was asked to come along and help establish them as the frontrunner of Canadian design. That night I wore my *conservative* bra under my *doesn't-make-my-hips-look-huge* dress, agreeing with Richard as he spouted off all the reasons I needed to stay in Toronto to support him and his career.

My spine pretty much disintegrated.

But my favorite event, the moment that inspired this reality, this moment of truth, was the evening I donned *the* bra and a black dress expecting a proposal from Richard. After stumbling across an expensive Tiffany's bill, I just knew. That was it. We were going to take that next step as partners—spouses in support of one another. His promises would be realized, and I'd finally quit my soul-sucking job designing retirement homes and stretch my wings. With his blessing, of course. What I got instead was: I think we've grown apart.

More to the point, his dick had grown toward Deena Wanger.

For five years, I put him first. His wants. His needs. I wasn't even second. A distant third, maybe. I dressed how he wanted, kept our apartment how he liked. The man had me on regular juice cleanses, for Christ's sake. The brazen, confident girl who grew up in a small town got swallowed by the city. And Richard.

Such an appropriate name, really. Even from birth, his parents knew he'd be a Dick.

I huff out a breath, sending a cloud of vapor curling through the cool air. "Oh, I'm sure. This forever-tainted piece of lingerie will adorn that bra-tree. Go-to bra or not, it will be the crowning jewel."

"You can't just chuck that," Snowboard Dude says, his mouth the only thing visible under his massive goggles and helmet. "There are rules."

Raven turns to him, her charcoal eyes likely squinting. "Rules? It's an evergreen tree on a ski slope covered with a pile of colorful bras and tacky necklaces. She can launch it if she wants."

He shakes his head and leans heavier on his elbows. "No way. Tradition is tradition. It's gotta come from the evening's conquest. You bag a chick, take her bra, and sling it on the tree to immortalize the moment. Like I said, tradition. So unless you ladies got busy together last night, or at lunch"—a lazy grin sweeps across his face—"then pocket the bra." If he could see the tattoos inked over Raven's olive skin, he'd maybe look a little less smug. One glance at her in a dark alley, and I'd cross to the other side.

"Let me explain something." She squares her shoulders toward him, head cocked in annoyance. "My girl here just got dumped by a total douche, so we three are hating on men. Since you're the only dude on this chairlift, I'd say your choice is simple. She either hurls her bra on a tree covered in bras, or we channel our angry-girl hormones in your direction. What'll it be?"

That sly grin slips from his face. "Whatever. You wanna spit on tradition, fine by me. But that shit is karmic."

Raven's long black ponytail glides along her jacket as she swings her helmeted head my way. "Forget him. That bra will be taking flight."

I nod in agreement, my helmet bobbing with the movement. I may be hurt and pissed about how things ended with the Dick, but the relief is undeniable. Freeing. Both Raven and Lily made it known they thought I could do better, thought I'd lost a piece of myself to him (like two dress sizes), but I was too scared to step out on my own. Status quo was easier than no quo. I reverted to my prepubescent self, who stuttered and struggled to fit in. But knowing I might have said yes to a proposal because it was easy has anger bubbling up inside of me. I need to toss this bra, forget the Dick, and stop being such a doormat. I just wish I felt sexier in my equipment so I could get my flirt on with a rugged ski dude.

This helmet is the anti-sexy.

"Look, look, look!" Lily bounces beside me, the chairlift swaying in response. "That's it, right?"

As we crest a rise, the pinks and reds and blues of the bra-tree stand out in vibrant contrast to the white-tipped evergreens. A few skiers are attacking the narrow mogul run below us, their skis scraping and gliding between the massive bumps. God, I love that sound. Growing up in a ski town outside of Toronto, the local slopes were in my backyard. Although our hills are glorified mounds, I practically skied from the womb, the blades an extension of my feet. Flying to places like Aspen never gets dull. Never repetitive. Ski trips with their mile-long runs, hot tubs, bars, and shops are my version of the typical girls' beach vacation.

The Dick only booked all-inclusive yawners.

"That's it, all right," I say, my eyes locked on the tree.

Snowboard Dude horks and spits over the side of the chair, likely aiming for the yeti splayed on the snow, skis crossed, butt in the air, a yard sale of his gear smattering the uniform bumps. *Karma, my ass.* I scan the tree up ahead, cataloguing each brassiere I can make out. The hefty beige one looks more like a straightjacket than a bra, the thick material folded over a lower branch. It screams dull, trite, supportive, and dead boring. Above it, a flirty number in bright purple and swirling lace dangles, its owner definitely more sassy than mundane. Swallowing thickly, I glance at the black bra I once loved, hating what an easy read it is.

Classy. Conservative. Proper. Poised.

The perfect accessory to pressed suits and silk ties. The chosen undergarment to accent my slimming black dresses. *The Dick.*

At a time in my life when I was struggling to adapt to the city, overwhelmed and friendless and out of my depth, Richard swooped in with his easy charm and charisma. He was larger than life. He took me out, bought me things, and introduced me to his friends. Lily and Raven were away, all of us busy with our own studies, and I latched on to him, needy and desperate to belong. To not feel so alone. To not be the insecure, stuttering child I thought I'd banished. Worried he'd move on and I'd have to start over, I molded myself into his perfect girl. I became *that* chick.

Of course I'd rather suck kale through a straw than eat solid food.

Job promotion? Who needs it? I didn't want a real life anyway.

Bring on the vanilla sex. Experimentation and excitement are overrated.

Every so often, though, I'd toss one of my hidden cookies into his smoothies…carbs and all.

"You better get ready," Raven says.

We're one chair back, and I raise my arm, readying myself to slingshot the bra, my past, and all things Richard into oblivion. As I do, a red lacy thing catches my eye. This piece of feminine lingerie is the perfect combination of sultry and flirtatious, the elegantly patterned fabric dipping low in the center, punctuated with a red bow. My heart quickens. *That* is the girl I was, once upon a time. The girl that got smothered by the Dick. That bra screams spontaneous and confident, a little wild and a lot of fun. It's the one I'm buying the second we get to town.

"Come on, Shay. If you wait any longer, you're going to miss it." Lily nudges me.

I clench my jaw, determination setting in.

I draw my arm back, whip my wrist, and let the fabric go. It sails through the air in an elegant arc, my 34Cs taking flight, before being caught up in a gust of wind and tumbling down, down, down and landing smack on some guy's head. Amidst his *what the fucks*, the girls and I giggle as Snowboard Dude scoffs with a snarky, "Karma."

It may not have hit the tree, but that bra is out of my life. Along with the Dick.

We push off the chairlift at the top, and I can't keep my eyes from flitting around. *I'm not wearing a bra.* The secret is enthralling, wanton. A shiver of excitement runs down my spine, and a need for recklessness consumes me. Having been in ski racing programs as a kid, I can handle the expert terrain better than Lily and Raven. Right about now, I could use the adrenaline.

"I say we call it early and have lunch in town. Last run of the day?" Lily asks as she zips the neck of her jacket higher to protect her pale skin. She tucks her blonde strands into the back.

Raven jumps up and down, her skis smacking the hard-packed snow. "Bet your ass it is. There's a hot tub and beer with my name on it."

I eye the large terrain map at the top of the lift. The girls will want to take an intermediate blue run down, but those expert double black diamonds have my name on them. The bra is gone, my spine is back, and the Dick is out of my life. "Why don't you guys take Ruthie's Run? I'd rather take Schiller over to Corkscrew. I'll meet you at the bottom."

Raven pushes off on her poles until we're almost chest to chest, her skis beside mine. She snaps her goggles onto her helmet and looks into my eyes. "Is that the old Shay in there? Has she come out to play?"

A couple guys ski past us, practically colliding as they ogle Raven. Even in her anti-sexy helmet, she draws a crowd. As a teen, I'd catch myself staring at her olive skin, wishing I were sexy and striking with a sheath of shiny black hair. I grew to like my unruly mass of brown curls and wore them down to my waist, thick and untamed. Until I met the Dick, that is. The Dick has a preference for straight hair.

So began the era of the straightener and singeing my hair into submission.

"Yes, bitch, I'm back," I say. "With a vengeance."

I grab her goggles and snap them onto her face, eliciting a gratifying "Fuck" from her. She scowls and adjusts the frames.

I tighten my boot buckles then straighten up and grab my poles, eager to feel the wind blast my face. With each movement my breasts move freely, and I grin wider. "I'll meet you guys at the condo." I'm about to push off when I add, "And we're not going to one of those lame pubs again to hang with a bunch of stoners. Tonight, we're picking up hot ski dudes."

Lily tips her head back and groans. "What am I supposed to do while you two are seducing unsuspecting guys? I doubt Kevin would be too happy about me living it up in Aspen."

"That's easy," Raven says. "Join us. Kevin's a good guy and all, but that relationship of yours is beyond incestuous. Lines need to be drawn when you have naked bath-time pictures together."

Lily tightens her lips until they match her alabaster skin. "We were neighbors, Raven. *Neighbors.* And so what if I've known him forever. He gets me."

When Raven yawns in Lily's face, I skate past them and call, "Don't take forever. We're shopping for bras before we head out."

With that, I'm off, snow crunching, gusts of cool air snapping at my cheeks. There's nothing as freeing as carving across the hill, edging into large swooping turns as my skis dig deeper and my thighs burn. Nothing exists but the movement. The speed. The effortless up and down. And I'm not wearing a bra.

The first section of moguls is tough. I land hard between the bumps, using my poles and the momentum to propel me into each sharp turn. *Smack. Crunch. Skid.* My blood pumps. My muscles grind. It's my second day skiing, and the altitude and thin air are forcing my lungs to work double-time. The rhythm is unrelenting, exhausting, and by the time I finish the second section, sharp pangs slice through my chest. And the boob sweat is undeniable.

That whole exhilarating, braless-wanton thing is history.

I rest my upper body on my poles as a guy just ahead of me bails on his face. I can't help laughing, and he gives me the finger. The snow has stopped falling, stillness in its place. My heart pounds in my ears. I stare down the hill, regretting my decision to do a marathon's worth of moguls on my last run.

My legs are noodles. My breasts hurt from bouncing. And *God*, the boob sweat.

I maneuver my jacket and press my long underwear top just so, hoping to mop up the uncomfortable wetness. As I shift to the left, I notice a break in the trees. I glance down the till-death-do-us-part run then back at the path. Better to bushwhack through the glades than have my braless and sweaty self rescued by the ski patrol.

Forcing my legs to move, I push forward and squeeze through the opening, dodging the trees as I pick my way toward the next run. There's a steep dip past the last line of branches, the perfect ramp to shoot me onto the groomed trail. A quick breath, a shift of my stance, and I catapult myself forward, gaining momentum. I hit the edge of the run perfectly. My legs relax, the blades on my feet glide, and I'm so relieved not to be pounding the moguls that I let my skis fly. For a moment. Like a second. The length of time it takes for some jerk to blindside me and send me on my ass.

I haven't fallen while skiing since forever. I ski fast and hard but always in control. It's a good thing. Hard-packed snow is about as soft as concrete. My left butt cheek smarts, a bruise no doubt forming, and I immediately regret laughing at that other dude's face-plant earlier. Distant grumbles carry through the frosty air as I gingerly pick myself up and stretch my legs. With all body parts intact, I glance at the idiot a few feet below who skied into me.

My jaw almost hits the snow.

If a hot ski dude is what I'm after, fate just intervened. His helmet is off as he inspects what could be a crack in his goggles, and oh my God, *that hair*. Dirty blond and shoulder-length, tousled in a careless, sexy way that has me picturing my hands dragging through it. Add the stubble, the wide shoulders, and the tight booty that is unmistakable even in his ski pants, and I'm about to land on my ass again.

Richard looked nothing like this guy. His short black hair was always tidy, each strand gelled in place. He was good-looking in a GQ way with his cut cheekbones and Armani style, and Lord knows I found him attractive. When I'd browse his selection of men's magazines in our apartment, though, I didn't linger on the clean-cut images of guys in suits with their button-down shirts and silk ties. I'd pause on the dudes in the jeeps. The ones climbing a mountain, three-day stubble accentuating a strong jaw. Like hot ski dude right in front of me. Maybe it was because those guys were the polar opposite of the Dick, or maybe I don't have a type.

When Mountain Guy stops checking over his gear, he swivels his upper body toward me, that shoulder-length hair doing some sort of model thing as he rakes a hand through the layered strands. "Next time you merge onto a run, you should look uphill so you don't run someone down. And you owe me a pair of goggles. These are trashed."

Come again? The throbbing pain on my butt returns, along with a searing anger that has me shaking. He *may* be kind of right, but his tone and righteousness snaps my spine straight. I'm tired of taking crap. Tired of pussyfooting around guys because they think they run the world. Normally, I'd be all *I'm sorry* and *It won't happen again*, but I tossed that bra and that girl off a chairlift. "You can't be serious. You totally blindsided me. Skied right into me. I'm not buying you squat."

He stretches his neck, the shorter strands of hair by his chin falling across his face. He slings his small pack off his shoulders, unzipping it and shoving the damaged goggles inside. Then he straightens and flicks *that hair*. "The skier coming down has right of way. It isn't rocket science. If I were a kid, that shit could've been a lot worse than some cracked goggles. So look the next time you barrel onto a hill." He shoots me a blistering look, like the dude owns the freaking mountain. Like I've never skied before. Then he mutters, "Idiot."

Come to think of it, I do have a type. I'm pretty sure it's Ass. Hole.

"Get over it." I jab my gloved middle finger in the air, fist my poles and push off, skiing past his cute butt and model hair as the word *bitch* follows behind me.

I don't glance back. I ski hard, taking wide, sweeping turns, picking up as much speed as I can, leaving the Asshole and my anger behind, because *wow* was that liberating. My skis are barely on the snow, the wind whipping something fierce, my breasts unrestrained. This must be what crack feels like. Or eating the largest bowl of Lucky Charms. Marshmallow-only Lucky Charms. Now I just want to let loose and swear a bunch and speak my mind. And buy Lucky Charms.

And that red bra.

About the Author

A small-town girl at heart, **Kelly Siskind** moved from the city to open a cheese shop with her husband in northern Ontario. When she's not neck-deep in cheese or out hiking, you can find her, notepad in hand, scribbling down one of the many plot bunnies bouncing around in her head.

She laughs at her own jokes and has been known to eat her feelings—Gummy bears heal all. She's also an incurable romantic, devouring romance novels into the wee hours of the morning.

Learn more at:

KellySiskind.com

Twitter @KellySiskind

Facebook.com/AuthorKellySiskind

CPSIA information can be obtained
at www.ICGtesting.com
Printed in the USA
FFOW04n0622210316
22482FF

9 781455 565207